Tales from
DEADWOOD

The Troopers

Mike Jameson

BERKLEY BOOKS, NEW YORK

THE BERKLEY PUBLISHING GROUP
Published by the Penguin Group
Penguin Group (USA) Inc.
375 Hudson Street, New York, New York 10014, USA
Penguin Group (Canada), 90 Eglinton Avenue East, Suite 700, Toronto, Ontario M4P 2Y3, Canada
(a division of Pearson Penguin Canada Inc.)
Penguin Books Ltd., 80 Strand, London WC2R 0RL, England
Penguin Group Ireland, 25 St. Stephen's Green, Dublin 2, Ireland (a division of Penguin Books Ltd.)
Penguin Group (Australia), 250 Camberwell Road, Camberwell, Victoria 3124, Australia
(a division of Pearson Australia Group Pty. Ltd.)
Penguin Books India Pvt. Ltd., 11 Community Centre, Panchsheel Park, New Delhi—110 017, India
Penguin Group (NZ), 67 Apollo Drive, Rosedale, North Shore 0632, New Zealand
(a division of Pearson New Zealand Ltd.)
Penguin Books (South Africa) (Pty.) Ltd., 24 Sturdee Avenue, Rosebank, Johannesburg 2196,
South Africa

Penguin Books Ltd., Registered Offices: 80 Strand, London WC2R 0RL, England

This is a work of fiction. Names, characters, places, and incidents either are the product of the author's imagination or are used fictitiously, and any resemblance to actual persons, living or dead, business establishments, events, or locales is entirely coincidental.

TALES FROM DEADWOOD: THE TROOPERS

A Berkley Book / published by arrangement with the author

PRINTING HISTORY
Berkley edition / March 2009

Copyright © 2009 by Penguin Group (USA) Inc.
Cover illustration by Bruce Emmett.
Cover Design by Steven Ferlauto.
Interior Text Design by Kristin Del Rosario.

ISBN: 978-0-425-22672-8

BERKLEY®
Berkley Books are published by The Berkley Publishing Group,
a division of Penguin Group (USA) Inc.,
375 Hudson Street, New York, New York 10014.
BERKLEY® is a registered trademark of Penguin Group (USA) Inc.
The "B" design is a trademark of Penguin Group (USA) Inc.

PRINTED IN THE UNITED STATES OF AMERICA

10 9 8 7 6 5 4 3 2 1

Prologue

⌒⌒

Montana Territory, along Rosebud Creek,
June 17, 1876

As he listened to the wild *ki-yip*s of the savages and tried not to choke on the clouds of dust and powder smoke that clogged his throat, Major Stephen Ransome thought that if he never saw another Indian in his life, it would still be too fucking soon.

Of course, Ransome reminded himself, if not for some of the Indians around him—the Crow and Shoshone scouts fighting on the side of the United States Army—he might well be dead, feathered with arrows or skewered by the lance of some painted, yelling barbarian . . . such as the one who charged at him now on a spry little spotted pony. The Sioux warrior shrieked out his hatred and leveled his lance at Ransome while the major attempted to reload his Colt Single Action Army revolver in time to save his life.

Fear made his fingers fumble momentarily with the last cartridge, but finally he shoved it home and snapped the cylinder shut. Just in time, too, because the Indian was almost on him. Ransome jerked the gun up, pointed it, and pulled the trigger, yelling, "Take that, you son of a bitch!" as the weapon roared.

Ransome had always been a good shot, and that remained true even under these trying circumstances. The .45-caliber slug caught the Sioux high in the chest, right under his throat. Blood spurted from the wound as the impact rocked the warrior back. He didn't fall, though. He clamped his knees on his pony's flanks, and as his war cry died away into a blood-choked gurgle, he still aimed the lance at Ransome.

"Die, damn you!" the major yelled as he cocked and fired the Colt as fast as he could. Three more slugs crashed into the Indian's body and finally drove him off his horse. The buckskin-clad warrior thudded to the ground in a limp sprawl.

Ransome jerked his mount around and tried to see what was happening. The action was spread out all along the banks of the creek. General Crook's forces had been taking a morning rest in a natural amphitheater beside the stream when shots began to ring out somewhere nearby. Moments later, a couple of Crow scouts, one of them seriously wounded, galloped back into the temporary camp shouting, "Sioux! Sioux!"

"Get up there and see what this is all about, Major," Crook had ordered Ransome. The major was one of Crook's staff officers, valuable because he spoke a smattering of the Crow tongue. His father, the Reverend Charles Ransome, had been a missionary to the Plains Indians, and young Stephen had learned how to speak several of their languages before his mother took him back East.

The Reverend Ransome had gone west to convert the heathens. His son had returned to the West to kill them, as part of the three-pronged summer campaign against the Sioux. General Crook's column had moved north from Fort Fetterman while Colonel John Gibbon led a column eastward from Fort Ellis and General Alfred Terry's column headed west from Fort Abraham Lincoln. All three columns would converge on the Sioux hunting grounds between the Yellowstone and Powder rivers.

Until today, Crook had not encountered any hostiles, but that had changed in a hurry.

The Shoshone scouts under Chief Washakie had been approximately five hundred yards out in front of the rest of the column when at least a thousand of Crazy Horse's Sioux attacked. Washakie had hated the Sioux for years, and fighting a defensive action wasn't in his nature anyway. So, despite being heavily outnumbered, he had launched a counterattack, which had gotten under way just as Ransome and a small detachment of cavalry arrived to check on the situation. Ransome and his troopers had been swept up in the action, and now he found himself fighting for his life in the midst of a crazed swirl of men and horses, gun smoke and dust.

This wasn't Ransome's first Indian fight. He had been with Crook in Arizona and had taken part in the general's clashes with the Apaches there, the battles that had earned General George C. Crook the reputation of being the best Indian fighter in the whole army. But despite that experience, Ransome still felt fear burning through his veins. He had never gotten used to having death stare him in the face, and he supposed he never would.

As the dust cleared for a moment, Ransome spotted three of the men under his command stretched out behind a low hummock of earth, firing at the Indians from that position. He hadn't given the order to dismount. His men were supposed to be on their horses, taking the fight to the savages. Anger welled up inside Ransome as he sent his horse toward the three troopers.

"Mount up!" he shouted as he came up behind them. "Mount up, damn it!"

They turned to look at him. He recognized them—three privates named Brundage, Hollis, and Lamont—and wasn't surprised to see them together. They were friends and spent most of their time in one another's company. They were troublemakers, as well, too fond of boozing and brawling for Ransome's taste, even though he knew the men had to let off steam somehow.

"Get on your horses and engage the enemy!" he ordered them, just as a shrill cry sounded behind him. He wheeled his mount in time to see a young warrior on horseback emerge from a nearby cloud of dust. Without thinking, Ransome jerked his pistol up and fired. The Indian doubled over as the bullet ripped into his belly. He caught hold of his pony's mane to keep himself from falling.

Only then, as the pony came to a trembling halt and the wounded man lifted his face to stare at Ransome, did the major realize he had just shot one of the Crow scouts, a young man called Spotted Dog. As Ransome watched in horror, the scout's pain-distended eyes rolled up in their sockets and he toppled off his pony.

"My God!" Ransome muttered. Why did all the blasted savages have to look so much alike?

He glanced over his shoulder, unsure whether the three troopers he had just been upbraiding had seen what he'd done. The air was so thick with smoke and dust they might not have noticed who Spotted Dog really was. They wore blank expressions, so Ransome couldn't really tell.

"Mount up," he ordered again in a thick voice. Then he heeled his horse into motion. He didn't look back at either the dead scout or the three troopers.

So he didn't see when one of the men raised a carbine and pointed it at his back.

CLYDE Brundage knocked the barrel of Dewey Lamont's Springfield carbine upward just as Lamont pulled the trigger. The shot went high and wild over the battlefield. The tall, sandy-haired officer didn't seem to notice as he rode away. He probably thought the shot had been directed at one of the hostiles.

"Damn it, Clyde!" Lamont said. "I would'a plugged that shit-faced major! He had it comin'. He's been ridin' us the whole campaign."

"I know that." A grin creased Brundage's lean, dark face. "But think about what we just saw."

"He shot one of our redskins," Matt Hollis put in. "Killed him, too, looked like."

"That's right," Brundage said. "Major Ransome killed one of our own scouts. I reckon knowin' about a thing like that might come in handy, somewhere on down the road."

Lamont and Hollis began to grin, too, as they realized what Brundage meant. They had something they could hold over Major Ransome's head now . . . and they were just the kind of men to take advantage of that, if they could.

Brundage got to his feet and said over his shoulder, "Come on." Carrying his carbine, he trotted toward their horses, which he and his friends had left tied to a bush not far off. The cavalry mounts trembled from the noise and the smells of blood and gun smoke, but they didn't bolt. They were too well trained for that.

Lamont and Hollis scrambled after Brundage. "I thought we said it'd be safer squattin' behind that hump," the burly, ginger-bearded Lamont called.

"Major Ransome gave us a direct order," Brundage replied. "Reckon we've got to follow it. Besides, I want to make sure he lives through this skirmish."

"Because he can't do us any good if he's dead," Hollis said. "I get it."

Brundage jerked his head in a nod. "That's right." He jerked his horse's reins loose from the bush and swung up into the McClellan saddle. "Ransome may not know it, but he's got himself three guardian angels."

He grinned at the irony of that as he rode off in the direction Ransome had gone, followed by Hollis and Lamont. The three of them were about as far from angels, guardian or otherwise, as you could get. Fallen angels, maybe, thought Brundage.

The terrain along Rosebud Creek formed a natural trap. Ridges and bluffs bordered the stream, and there was no telling how many Indians might be hiding behind those heights. Surely plenty to wipe out the luckless troopers who had followed Crook into this mess. Brundage knew that the general had quite a reputation as an Indian fighter, but as far as he could see, luck had played a big part in that success.

Brundage just hoped that Crook's luck hadn't run out today, because if it had, that'd mean the rest of the poor bastards with him would probably die, too.

Spotting Ransome up ahead, Brundage banged his boot heels against his horse's flanks and hurried after the major. He realized that Ransome was heading toward the rear, likely to make a report to General Crook. When a couple of yipping Sioux went after him, Brundage waved for his companions to follow him and galloped ahead. As he guided his horse with his knees, he brought his carbine to his shoulder and tried to draw a bead on one of the savages. He might not be able to do a lot of things, Brundage reflected, but killin' redskins from horseback was one of the things he was good at. The carbine bucked against his shoulder, rewarding Brundage with the sight of a Sioux warrior throwing up his hands and pitching sideways off his pony.

Hollis and Lamont downed the other hostile with their shots. Ransome, the clueless bastard, didn't even seem to be aware of how close he had come to death. That was all right, thought Brundage. Just one more thing to put the major in their debt.

And when the time came, they would make him pay off that debt.

A few minutes later, Ransome found Crook and reported the situation to him. The general, as was his habit, wore a civilian suit, including a broad-brimmed, flat-crowned hat, instead of an army uniform. The outfit made him look more like one of the newspaper reporters traveling with the column rather than its commander, but you couldn't argue with the man's record.

"We'll move up to support our scouts," Crook ordered. "Washakie was just here, telling me how pleased he is that the Sioux have come against us today so that he can kill them."

"Yes, sir," Ransome replied, not knowing what else to say to that. He didn't care about the old hatreds between the tribes. Some fools back East liked to write articles for the illustrated weeklies and make speeches about how the Indians were peaceful by nature and lived in harmony with the land and each other, which in Ransome's experience was the biggest pile of bullshit he had ever heard. Indians liked nothing better than killing each other, and anyone who believed otherwise was just deluding himself.

Crook issued the orders for the entire column to move up and join the battle. The outnumbered scouts had given a good account of themselves, not only holding their position against the superior force but actually driving the Sioux back and forcing them to retreat. However, by the time the soldiers reached the area of the battlefield where most of the action was concentrated, more of the painted, feather-wearing savages had appeared, pouring down from the hills and ridges as Crazy Horse attacked yet again.

The morning continued in that fashion, charge and countercharge, until midday, when General Crook made the strategic decision to split his forces. He sent some of his cavalry farther up the Rosebud because he was convinced the Sioux had a village somewhere nearby and that to win the battle, he would have to destroy that village.

It seemed like a risky plan to Ransome. Against all odds, Crook's forces had remained in control of the battlefield, but only because of the efforts of the Shoshone chief Washakie and his Crow counterparts. Splitting the column now would just weaken it and perhaps embolden the Sioux to increase their attacks. The general hadn't asked his opinion, though, Ransome reminded himself.

"Take some men and go with Captain Mills as my liaison, Major," Crook ordered.

Ransome snapped a salute, said, "Yes, sir," and looked around for a few troopers to take with him.

Brundage, Lamont, and Hollis sat on their horses

nearby, and when Ransome saw them, he realized they had been dogging his trail ever since he'd found them taking shelter behind that hummock. "Blast it, what are you three doing here?" he demanded.

"Just lookin' out for you, Major," Brundage said. "With all these kill-crazy heathen around, we didn't want nothin' to happen to you."

"I'll be fine," Ransome snapped. "Since you're here, though, I suppose you can come with me."

"Where are we goin', Major?" Hollis asked.

"Up the canyon of the Rosebud. General Crook thinks there's a Sioux village up there, and we're to destroy it, as well as draw off Crazy Horse's forces from the rest of the column."

Ransome wasn't sure why he felt like he had to explain the strategy to a trio of privates, especially no-account ones like these three who, if they hadn't been in the army, would probably be locked up in jail somewhere. The worry still nagged at him, too, that they had seen what happened to Spotted Dog.

Maybe it was a good thing they seemed bent on following him around, Ransome decided. That way he could keep an eye on them and make sure they didn't start talking to anyone about what they might have seen.

Ransome conveyed General Crook's orders to Captain Anson Mills, who gathered his cavalry companies and split off from the main column, circling around the battle to proceed up the canyon formed by the stream. Ransome and the three troopers rode with him. The group hadn't gone very far when the shooting behind them suddenly increased in frequency and intensity.

Ransome looked back and cursed. From the sound of it, the Indians had noticed the cavalry companies pulling out and hit the remaining troops even harder. This could be a recipe for disaster unless General Crook took quick action.

The general must have realized that, too, because only a few minutes later a galloper caught up to Captain Mills with an order to turn back and rejoin the column.

Ransome had reined in next to Mills, who glanced over at him and said, "The general has ordered us to return, Major, but he didn't say by what route. I think we should circle again and try to hit those red devils from behind."

Ransome nodded. "I agree, Captain. We'll take them by surprise that way."

Mills shouted the orders, and the troopers wheeled their mounts and galloped back along the stream for a ways before peeling off to race over the prairie. Ransome rode near the front of the force with Mills. His heart pounded in his chest as the confrontation drew nearer and nearer. He could see the Indians now, phantom warriors flitting in and out of dust and shadow, but there was nothing phantom about their rifles and arrows and lances. Those weapons were real and deadly.

For some reason, though, the Sioux didn't appear to see the cavalry coming. Mills drew his saber and waved it overhead. The blade glittered in the sunlight. Ransome slid his own saber from its sheath. The fight would be close, bloody work, so he shoved his fear far to the back of his mind and tried to clear his thoughts of everything except the objective: to kill as many of the savages as possible.

The cavalry charge crashed into the Sioux from behind. For a few moments, chaos reigned around Major Ransome as he hacked and slashed with the saber. Many of the warriors had stripped to the waist for battle, and he saw crimson spurt from flesh as his blade ripped into the ones he could reach. His mind grew dull. Nothing existed except the world right around him, which was filled with dust and screams and blood.

Caught by the pincers movement that General Crook hadn't planned at all, the Sioux broke and ran, fleeing up the valley. Ransome lowered his bloody saber and watched them go. The soldiers milled around, uncertain what to do next, and disorganization prevented the order to pursue from being given.

Just as well, thought Ransome. Crook's force was still outnumbered, and only luck and the valiant efforts of the

Crow and Shoshone scouts had kept the enemy from wiping them out. The valley, which had been so pretty when they first rode up, now bore the marks of battle. The hooves of hundreds of horses had trampled the grass and wildflowers into the dust. Wounded men lay here and there, groaning in pain. Other figures lay quiet and motionless in the unmistakable stillness of death. As Ransome looked around, he drew a cloth from his saddlebags and used it to clean his saber. Wiping the blood away gave him a chance to calm his rattled nerves.

"Quite a fight, eh, Major?"

The question made Ransome look around. Brundage—who had spoken—and Lamont and Hollis sat their horses next to him. Powder smoke had grimed their faces, and blood trickled from a cut on Lamont's cheek into his bushy growth of beard.

"My God!" Ransome burst out. "Why are you three always there every time I turn around?"

"We just don't want anything happenin' to you, Major," Brundage said with an ugly grin. "In the thick o' the fightin' like that, a fella could get hurt awful easy. Why, a fella on his own side might even get carried away and shoot him, if you can imagine that!"

Ransome's eyes widened in shock. No doubt about it now. The way the three of them were grinning, he knew they had seen him shoot Spotted Dog. The question remained: What would they do with that knowledge?

No matter what the answer, Major Stephen Ransome was certain of one thing.

He was royally fucked.

Chapter One

Deadwood, Dakota Territory, September 16, 1876

THE pitiful caterwauling from the alley drew Dan Ryan's attention as he passed the Grand Central Hotel on Deadwood's Main Street. It sounded like somebody was sick or dying back there. Dan paused and frowned, started to go on, and then stopped again. People got sick all the time in Deadwood. They died even more often, sometimes from illness but more often from a gun, a knife, or a bludgeon. Hardly a day went by without a robbery victim turning up in an alley somewhere in town, either dead or the next thing to it. Whoever was back in this alley, whatever had happened to them, Dan told himself, it was none of his business.

So, naturally, he went back there anyway to see what the hell was going on.

Stocky, graying, on the verge of middle age, Dan had retired from the army as a sergeant to take up prospecting for gold, an attempt to make his fortune before he was too old to enjoy it. So far that hadn't worked out too well. He had found some color in his claim up Deadwood Creek, but not much. His dream of being rich remained hazy, like something peered at from a great distance. Sometimes he thought he never should have left the army. He had functioned well in its orderly confines, and he still had a sense of duty.

That sense of duty was probably what led him to venture down the shadowy alley. The narrow space stunk of garbage and shit. As the wailing grew more pathetic, Dan rested his right hand on the butt of his holstered revolver. This could be a trap. A gang of cutthroats might be waiting back there, with the cries designed to lure some Good Samaritan so they could lift his purse after they walloped him on the head or stuck a knife between his ribs.

Dan's eyes adjusted to the dimness between the buildings and picked out a single forlorn figure lying huddled against the wall of the hotel. The person's shoulders shook with sobs. A reek comprised of nearly equal parts of whiskey, vomit, and unwashed flesh rose up and assaulted Dan's senses. He recognized the distinctive stench and knew then who was lying in the alley.

"Oh, my poor Bill!" Calamity Jane moaned. "My poor sweet B-Bill! Lyin' m-moulderin' in the g-ground! I'll never feel that big ol' pecker o' his in me again!"

Dan sighed. Calam was drunk again. That had been a common enough occurrence even before Jack McCall shot Bill Hickok in the back of the head more than a month earlier, but Calamity hadn't been sober a day since then. As far as Dan knew, the great tragic love affair between Miss Martha Jane Cannary, better known as Calamity Jane, and Mr. James Butler "Wild Bill" Hickok had been completely one-sided and mostly in Calamity's mind, but that didn't make her grieving any less real.

Dan reached down to take hold of the woman's arm. "Come on, Calamity," he said. "Better get up now. You wouldn't want to drown in that mud."

The floor of the alley wasn't just mud. Copious amounts of both human and animal wastes were mixed in with it, making the smell wafting from Calamity Jane that much worse. Dan tried to breathe through his mouth as she pulled away from his grip and said, "Lemme 'lone! What'm I supposed to do now without Wild Bill around to fuck me?"

Dan didn't figure Hickok had ever laid a finger on Calamity, let alone gotten a poke from her. The late Prince of Pistoleers had been much too fastidious an hombre for that. But from what Dan had seen, Hickok had taken pity on Calamity and kidded her along. She had looked up to him with a mixture of hero worship and lust and convinced herself they were lovers. In her perpetually inebriated state, that fantasy had become reality.

"I reckon you'll just have to find somebody else," Dan told her now as he struggled to lift her to her feet. Calamity packed considerable meat on her bones, and it was all deadweight right now.

"Ain't nobody else'll ever be as good as Wild Bill was," she moaned. "Ain't nobody else'll ever be as pretty."

"He was a handsome man, I'll allow. But he's gone, Calamity. It's been more than a month. I'll bet old Wild Bill would have wanted you to get on with your life and not spend the rest of it cryin' over him."

Calamity finally made it to her feet. She leaned against the wall and rubbed the back of a muck-encrusted hand across her nose as she sniffled. The resulting smear didn't improve her looks any, which weren't too striking to start with.

"You . . . you really think so?"

"Well . . . I didn't know Wild Bill all that well, of course . . . but I think that's what he would've told you."

Calamity let loose with a sour belch that made Dan wince. "You know," she said, "I think you m-might be right." She squinted at him. "Who the hell are you, anyway?"

"Dan Ryan. We've met a few times."

"I don't really . . ." Calamity lifted a hand to her forehead and rubbed it as she frowned, smearing more dirt and shit on her face. "It's so hard t' remember anything these days . . . I reckon I remember you, but I ain't sure . . ." She shook her head and winced at the painful explosions that the movement must have set off inside her skull. "It don't really matter. You want to fuck me, Dan Ryan?"

The question caught him flat-footed, and all he could do was stare at the lumpy, filthy, buckskin-clad figure that had absolutely nothing feminine about it. And yet, obviously a woman's heart beat in the mostly flat chest of Calamity Jane. Dan felt a sympathetic twinge as he heard the poignant longing Calamity put even into that crude question.

But he would've had to be a whole hell of a lot more sympathetic to take her up on the offer.

"I'm sorry, Calam," he said, trying to sound like he meant it. "I'm afraid my, uh, heart belongs to another lady."

That much was true, at least, even though Dan couldn't act on the strong feelings he had for Lou Marchbanks, the cook at this very same Grand Central Hotel beside which they stood. Lou had been born a slave, and even though she had feelings for Dan, too, she had made it clear to him that nothing was ever going to happen between them.

"White men been beddin' nigger wenches for as long as they been bringin' us over here from Africa," she had told him, "but they don't sit down to dinner with 'em or take 'em to dances, and they sure don't marry 'em. So you best find yourself somebody else, Dan, 'cause it ain't gonna be me."

He had resolved himself to living without Lou, but he hadn't yet accepted the idea of trying to find somebody else. For one thing, other than whores, there weren't that many women in Deadwood yet. And with the lack of luck he had had on his claim, Dan wasn't sure he was even going to stay. He might just move on.

Calamity Jane said, "Aw, ain't that s-sweet!" and tried to pat him on the shoulder but missed. "It ain't your heart I want, though. It's what you got down here."

She moved with surprising speed for somebody so drunk and grabbed his crotch, causing Dan's eyes to bug out a little as she started squeezing and rubbing. He wasn't sure what he was going to do next—pull his gun and clout her over the head, maybe, since it might take that to discourage her—but luckily he didn't have to make that decision. A big commotion broke out on Main Street, distracting Calamity Jane and allowing him to slip out of her grasp before she did any serious damage.

Dan heard a lot of people yelling but couldn't make out the words. He said to Calamity Jane, "Why don't we go see what that's all about?"

"Well . . . I reckon we could, if'n you're sure you don't wanna cavort with me first," she allowed.

"Maybe another time," Dan said, hoping the Good Lord would forgive him for lying. He had no intention of cavorting with Calamity Jane—ever.

They slogged through the muck of the alley toward the street, and as they approached the front of the hotel, Dan began to make sense of the shouting. "Soldiers!" one man yelled as he ran past in the street. "Soldiers comin'!"

Dan felt his pulse quicken. For several days rumors had been flying up and down the gulches about the presence of cavalry in the area. Everybody knew that the army had set out on a campaign against the Sioux several months earlier—and everybody knew as well that the campaign had been disastrous. General Crook had fought the Indians to a stalemate at Rosebud Creek, and then just a few days later Crazy Horse and his allies had caught Colonel George Custer and the Seventh Cavalry on a hilltop overlooking the Little Bighorn River and wiped them out to the last man. Since then, Crook and General Terry had done a lot of chasing around after the savages but precious little actual fighting.

Despite that, the settlers in Deadwood and the surrounding mining camps would be glad to see the soldiers. They had lived in fear of the Sioux ever since coming to the Black Hills. Even though Deadwood had grown into a good-sized town over this summer of '76, the possibility that the Indians might attack it always lurked in the back of the inhabitants' minds.

Dan and Calamity stepped out onto the boardwalk in front of the Grand Central in time to see a man galloping down the street as he waved his hat above his head. "Hurrah for the cavalry! Hurrah for the cavalry!" he shouted, and people who flocked out of the buildings to see what was going on quickly took up the cry.

Calamity seemed to have sobered a little. She clutched the sleeve of Dan's shirt and said, "I done some scoutin' and some bull-whackin' for Gen'ral Crook. Be good to see the ol' sumbitch again." She looked over at Dan. "You was in the army, wasn't you?"

He nodded. "That's right. Sergeant in the cavalry."

"Under Crook?"

"Nope. George Custer. I was with him a couple of years ago when he first came up here to the Black Hills."

Calamity let out a low whistle. "Good thing you got out when you did, elsewise you would'a lost your hair with the rest o' them boys."

With a solemn expression on his face, Dan nodded. "I know. I've thought about that a lot this summer."

Life in and around Deadwood had been too full of other things—the killings of Wild Bill Hickok and Preacher Smith, as well as the everyday murders and robberies and claim jumpings—for him to brood too much about what had happened to Custer and the other boys from the Seventh. Dan had personally known nearly every officer and noncom who had died on those windswept Montana hills, though, and he would never forget them.

To get his mind off that now, he asked, "How do you know it's Crook who's coming?"

"Couple o' his officers rode in here a few days ago beggin' for provisions to be sent up to the troopers. Charley Utter put together a little supply train for 'em."

Dan shook his head. "I didn't know that. Been workin' up at my claim until today."

"You know the best thing about the cavalry comin' to Deadwood?" Calamity asked.

"No, what's that?"

She gave a hearty laugh as she hauled off and smacked him between the shoulder blades. "Them soldier boys is always horny! Ol' Calamity is gonna have herself a time, yessireebob!"

Dan couldn't help but laugh, too. If those troopers now approaching Deadwood knew what they were really letting themselves in for, they might just turn around and go back to looking for Crazy Horse some more.

Chapter Two

⁕

THE past three months had been some of the most miserable—no, *the* most miserable—of Major Stephen Ransome's life. Not only had he been forced to endure the miseries of pursuing the Indians on short rations and in terrible weather, but he'd also had to put up with those three troopers who knew his secret.

And all too often the memory of the look on Spotted Dog's face just before the young scout died had haunted him, too.

Most of the time, though, Ransome had been too wet, too hungry, and too exhausted to dwell on what had happened to Spotted Dog. After the battle at Rosebud Creek, General Crook had been convinced that catching up to the Sioux would be simple. With speed being of the essence, Crook had ordered that all of the column's wagons, tents, and extra supplies be left behind as they pursued Crazy Horse. As soon as the soldiers had dealt severely with the Indians, they could return for what they had abandoned.

Unfortunately, things hadn't worked out that way. The Sioux had proven to be extremely elusive as they slipped away from Crook's column. The general continued the pursuit anyway and became even more dogged about it when word reached him of Colonel Custer's fate. A cold shiver had gone through most of the men in the column when they heard about that dreadful massacre. If a few things had happened differently, it could have just as easily been them dying to the last man at the hands of those bloodthirsty savages, and they all knew it. Rosebud Creek might have wound up as infamous as the Little Bighorn was bound to be.

General Crook had thought it would take only days to catch the Sioux. Those days became weeks, and the weeks stretched out into months. Crook and his command stayed on the trail anyway, never returning for the wagons and supplies they had left behind, as June became July and then August.

The weather turned unseasonably cold and wet as they moved east into Dakota Territory, still following rumors of Crazy Horse's Indian army. Rain pounded down for days on end, turning the ground into a sea of thick mud that clung to horses' hooves and made the going abominably slow. Without the tents they had abandoned, the men couldn't even get any relief from the downpours at night. They slept in the mud, and some of the men began calling this futile pursuit the Mud March.

Others dubbed it the Horse Meat March, because the lack of supplies meant that anytime a horse or a mule collapsed from exhaustion and couldn't get back up again, it was quickly slaughtered and cooked to stave off starvation. Ransome thought that no matter how long he lived, he would never get the awful taste of horse meat out of his mouth. He even wondered about the fate of some of the infantry soldiers who had wandered off the trail and "disappeared," but as with what had happened to Spotted Dog, he tried not to think about that.

At a place called Slim Buttes, the column had stumbled onto a Sioux war party, as much by accident as by design, but the ensuing battle, if you could even call it that, didn't last long or amount to much. The Indians had galloped around, whooping and hollering and shooting, and the half-starved, bone-weary troopers had returned their fire for a few minutes before the Sioux dashed away. That ended the battle, because nobody on the cavalry side had the strength or energy to go after them.

At last, General Crook had given up and turned south toward the mining camps in the Black Hills. Emissaries rode ahead looking for help, and a wagon train bearing food and other supplies sent from the largest of the settlements, Deadwood, intercepted the column on September 13. For the next couple of days, Crook had allowed his men to rest and recuperate and fill their famished bellies with something besides horse meat, berries, and wild onions. Because of that, as the column came within sight of the boomtown nestled between steep, thickly wooded ridges where the gulches of two creeks merged, the men weren't in quite as bad a shape as they might have been otherwise, but they were still filthy and haggard from the ordeal they had endured over the past three months.

Ransome heard music and cheering as he rode in with General Crook and the other staff officers at the head of the column, but weariness prevented him from lifting his head right away. When he did, he saw throngs of people in the broad street, crowding in from both sides so that only a lane remained through which the riders could make their way. General Crook had taken the lead, of course, and as he proceeded down the street, he doffed his wide-brimmed straw hat and waved it over his head as he bestowed beaming smiles upon the populace.

Hail the conquering hero, Ransome thought bitterly. These cheering fools had no idea that Crook had almost gotten his command wiped out, or that he had taken them on a wild-goose chase that had killed dozens of horses and not a few men without accomplishing a damn thing. They were just glad to see the army because the presence of the soldiers made them feel safer.

Ransome put the number of people who had turned out to welcome them in the hundreds, maybe even upwards of a thousand. And not only the street was crowded, but also the windows of every building the troopers passed. Especially the second-floor windows, Ransome noted, many of which were occupied by women who smiled and waved lace handkerchiefs at the blue-clad soldiers.

Inevitably, most of those women were prostitutes, and as the head of the column moved past a large building sporting a sign proclaiming it to be the Gem Theater, several of the women in the second-floor windows suddenly pulled their gowns down to reveal their breasts. An amply endowed redhead cupped both of her fleshy globes, shook them at the passing soldiers, and shouted in a loud, coarse voice, "Come suck on these titties whenever you're ready, boys! They'll be waitin' for you!"

Ransome looked away and thought about his wife, Louisa, the mother of their three children. She certainly wouldn't appreciate him staring at some painted harlot's bare bosom. As usual, thinking about Louisa made it easier for Ransome to control his base urges. He didn't need to visit whores because he had a perfectly good woman at home and would be seeing her again sooner or later.

Despite his intentions, though, a spot of color suddenly drew his eye, and he glanced up at the second floor of the Gem in time to see one of the women closing the curtain and turning away from the window where she had been watching. She wore a bright red dress and had long, straight fair hair that hung down her back. Ransome caught only a glimpse of her profile, but that was enough to tell that she was quite attractive. Without meaning to, he thought about what it would feel like to run his fingers through that long blond hair and how it would look spread out on a pillow around what was undoubtedly a lovely face. . . .

He swallowed and then shifted a little in the saddle, trying to make himself more comfortable. That presented a challenge, since his organ had grown quite stiff without any warning. Ransome closed his eyes for a second and shoved the image of the blond whore out of his mind. He thought about his wife again and relaxed after a moment. That had taken care of his erection.

But it would probably be an excellent idea, he told himself, if he steered clear of the Gem Theater while the cavalry was here in Deadwood.

There hadn't been time to set up a reviewing stand and drape it with bunting or anything like that, but a delegation of the leading citizens in town waited up ahead, in front of the Grand Central Hotel. As General Crook reined in and lifted a hand in a signal for the rest of the column to halt, these men strode forward, all smiles and cheap suits. The one in the lead took off his bowler hat and held it over his heart as he said, "General Crook, sir, my name is E. B. Farnum, and as the duly-elected mayor of Deadwood and on behalf of all the citizens of this settlement, we bid you and your valiant soldiers the heartiest of welcomes!"

Crook smiled down at him. "And on behalf of myself and my men, Mayor Farnum, we thank you for your welcome," the general said. "After the privations we have all suffered during our tireless pursuit of the hostiles, I assure you that entering this fine community of yours is more than a little akin to entering the Elysian Fields themselves!"

"Your sentiments are much appreciated, General."

"As were the provisions you and your fellow citizens so thoughtfully provided for us!"

"Indeed," Farnum went on. He cleared his throat and then continued with a glance toward the long line of men in filthy, mud-stained uniforms, men whose faces were also coated with grime. "In noting the condition of your gallant officers and men, I feel compelled to point out that Deadwood is home to several excellent public bathhouses, as well as a number of mercantiles where clean duds can be obtained. I feel that I can also state with a degree of certainty that the local merchants would be well-disposed toward making more than equitable arrangements for any purchases you or your men might wish to make."

It took considerable effort to spew more hot air than a general, Ransome thought, but this mining camp mayor might be just the gent who was capable of it.

Crook wasn't going down without a fight, though. "As always, sir, I never fail to be impressed with the hospitality and sheer generosity of the denizens of our great American frontier!" Holding his hat above his head again, Crook turned to smile at the crowd, which rewarded him with another loud series of huzzahs. When the cheering died down, the general went on. "There's also the matter of a suitable bivouac for the enlisted men and proper quarters for my officers and staff, as well as the gentlemen of the press who accompanied us on our campaign. Allow me to introduce Mr. Joseph Wasson of the *New York Tribune*, Mr. John F. Finerty of the *Chicago Times*, Mr. R. B. Davenport of the *New York Herald*, Mr. Robert Strahorn of the *Chicago Tribune*, and Mr. T. B. MacMillan of the *Chicago Inter Ocean*."

The journalists, who were as worn down as anybody else in the column, barely nodded to Mayor Farnum and the other local leaders, one of whom stepped forward and said, "I'm A. W. Merrick, editor and publisher of the *Black Hills Pioneer*. Welcome to Deadwood, gents, and if you require any assistance in preparing and filing your dispatches, I stand ready to offer my humble services."

Farnum let the local newspaperman get that self-serving suggestion out, then moved in front of him again. "Naturally, General, you and your staff and these gentlemen of the press will be domiciled here in the finest accommodations Deadwood has to offer, the Grand Central Hotel. We have two other excellent hotels, the Centennial and the IXL, that would be glad to offer rooms at reduced rates to the men of your command, and there are numerous other places where rooms can be rented. Not to mention the great open spaces, of which there are aplenty around here. I would urge that your men exercise a certain amount of caution in traipsing about the countryside, however, since mining claims have been filed on much of the property and the men working those claims can be a mite, ah, touchy about interlopers."

"I shall ensure that everyone under my command is aware of the situation, Mayor," Crook responded with a solemn nod, "and they'll be staying close to the settlement anyway, as long as we're here."

"Which, I assure you, everyone in Deadwood hopes will be a good long time!" Farnum said with a smile. "For too long, General, these fine people have lived in fear of the depredations carried out by the Sioux and other savages. Over one hundred citizens of this region have lost their lives to the Indians since Deadwood was established. Why, last month the redskins even killed our preacher as he walked to a neighboring community to spread the Gospel!"

"Shocking! You may assure your constituents, Mayor, that they may sleep soundly now, thanks to the United States Cavalry!"

Ransome swayed a little in his saddle as he wondered how long the general and the mayor were going to trade bullshit like this. While all the pontificating went on between the two blowhards, the rest of the column sat there so tired they had to struggle to keep from falling off their horses. Finally, though, Crook and Farnum finished their impromptu speechifying, and the order to fall out passed back along the line. Ransome swung down from his mount and handed the reins to a trooper. Hostlers gathered the officers' horses and took them down the street to a livery stable with a large corral out back.

As Ransome followed Crook into the hotel, he glanced over his shoulder to look around for his three shadows, but for once Brundage, Lamont, and Hollis were nowhere in sight. They had probably headed for one of Deadwood's myriad saloons and whorehouses as soon as their company commander dismissed them, he thought. With any luck they would stay there for a while, lost in lust and debauchery. With even more luck, they might get their throats cut in an alley by thieves, and then he wouldn't have to worry about them anymore.

Thinking about Deadwood's whorehouses made an image flicker unbidden through his mind as he went into the hotel . . . an image of a young, aristocratic-looking blond woman in a red dress turning away from a window, letting a lace curtain slip from her pale, slender fingers and fall closed.

He sighed. Louisa, he told himself. Louisa.

But this time it didn't work. The memory of that fleeting glance stayed with him, torturing him with the thought of her enticing beauty.

Sweet torture.

Chapter Three

A stocky, broad-shouldered, dark-complected man stood just inside the entrance of the Gem Theater's barroom, gazing out over the batwings at the long line of soldiers stretching down Main Street. His teeth clamped on the unlit cigar between them, and he said around it, "Look at 'em, Dan. Profit on the hoof. Every one of those fucking soldier boys is champing at the bit to come in here and spend his last nickel on whiskey, pussy, or cards."

The burly, aproned bartender who stood beside him shook his head and said, "I dunno, Al. The gov'ment don't pay those troopers worth shit."

"Maybe not," said Al Swearengen, the owner of the Gem, "but when there's enough of it, even shit adds up." He took the cigar out of his mouth and grinned. "You hear that popinjay Farnum talking about how Indians killed the preacher?"

Dan Dority, chief bartender and Swearengen's right-hand man, rubbed his thick jaw and said, "Yeah, I heard. Folks've pretty much accepted that story, just like you said they would, Al."

Swearengen nodded. He was one of the few people who knew the truth about the fate that had befallen the mysterious Preacher Smith, but if the citizens of Deadwood wanted to think Indians were to blame for the sky pilot's death, that suited him just fine.

The grin disappeared from Swearengen's face as he turned away from the batwings. Nobody stood at the bar drinking, and the poker tables and the faro layout were empty. All the customers had crowded up to the windows to gawk at the soldiers. Even some of the men who'd been upstairs with the whores had left off their fucking and had come down to find out what all the commotion was, tucking in their shirts and buttoning up their trousers as they descended the stairs.

As the owner of the Gem, such inactivity annoyed the hell out of Swearengen. The only way to make money was to keep the whiskey flowing, the cards flying, and the pussy pumping. He raised his voice and announced to the room at large, "This ain't a fuckin' museum. You want to stand around gawking, go somewhere else!"

He had a reputation as a man with a bad temper. He also had the best saloon and whorehouse in Deadwood, especially since someone had . . . eliminated . . . some of the competition. Nobody wanted to cross him, and anyway, the show appeared to be over as the soldiers were dismissed and began to disperse around the town. The men inside the Gem returned to the bar, the poker tables, and the whores.

That was more like it, thought Swearengen as he watched Dan Dority plucking coins from the bar and dropping them in the cashbox. At the end of the bar, tall, skinny Johnny Burnes sat on a high stool with a scattergun held across his knees, just in case anybody got any damn fool ideas about trying to rob the place. As the buzz of conversation and raucous laughter rose in volume, Swearengen nodded in satisfaction and headed for the stairs. The Gem was back to normal.

Well, almost, he amended. There was still that gal upstairs. . . .

Al Swearengen had a strict rule. He didn't put any whores to work until he'd tried 'em out himself. The blonde had turned up in Deadwood about a week earlier. Swearengen didn't know for sure how she'd gotten there. The stagecoaches didn't run to Deadwood yet, although rumors abounded that stage service would start up soon, and no wagon trains had come in around the time the woman showed up. It was like one minute she wasn't there, and the next minute she was.

Dority had looked nervous as a cat when he came into Swearengen's office on the second floor and said, "Uh, Al, there's a gal downstairs who wants to see you."

Swearengen hadn't been too interested. "Some slut who wants to work here?" he'd asked without looking up from the ciphering he was doing in a ledger book.

"Well . . . she says she wants to talk to you about makin' an arrangement, she called it." Dority scratched at his head. "But I wouldn't call her a slut. There's just somethin' about her . . ."

Like all Irishmen, Dority had a sentimental streak that cropped up from time to time. Swearengen hadn't put much stock in what he said about the woman being different. In his experience, a woman was a woman, and all women were whores, when you got right down to it. So he'd just grunted and said, "All right, bring her up here. I reckon I can talk to her."

His smirk made it clear that he intended to do more than talk before he'd even consider allowing the woman to work at the Gem.

But then Arabella came in, with Dority bowing and scraping behind her like she was some sort of fucking queen or something, and damned if Swearengen didn't understand what the bartender meant. This woman *was* different.

For one thing, she was genuinely pretty, which ninety-nine out of a hundred soiled doves weren't. She didn't wear a lot of paint on her face because she didn't need it. Her hair was like corn silk under the dark blue hat she wore that matched her traveling outfit. The body under that dress was slender but womanly. And the eyes that looked over Swearengen's desk at him . . . Lord, he had never seen such a lovely shade of blue.

She held out a hand to him and said, "My name is Arabella, Mr. Swearengen. I'm told that you have the most popular entertainment establishment in Deadwood."

Swearengen had stood up and taken her hand, but even as he did so, he steeled himself. It took more than a pretty face, nice hair, and bluer-than-blue eyes to make him forget who he was. His voice held a hard edge as he said, "If by that you mean the biggest and best saloon and whorehouse, then, yeah, I do."

She gave him a cool smile. "That is exactly what I mean, Mr. Swearengen."

She had moved her hand and made a little noise, and Swearengen realized about then that he still had hold of her hand. He let go of her, muttered, "Sorry," something he almost never did, and waved toward the chair in front of the desk. "Won't you sit down, Miss . . . ?"

"I told you, my name is Arabella," she said as she lowered herself daintily into the chair. "That's all you need to know."

"You don't have a last name?" Swearengen asked with a frown.

"I don't care to share it. Does that matter?"

He sat down himself and scowled Dority out of the room. The bastard would stand there making calf's eyes at her unless Swearengen shooed him out. Once the bartender was gone, Swearengen said, "Your last name probably doesn't mean shit to me, but I suppose it really depends on what you want from me."

"Maybe *you* might want something from *me*."

He had grinned again then, glad that his judgment had been confirmed. Sooner or later things always got down to this point. At least this gal didn't believe in wasting time.

"Now you're talking," he told her. "There's a bed in the next room—"

He stopped short when he saw those blue eyes of hers suddenly turn bluish gray, the color of ice. They were as cold as ice, too, and so was her voice as she said, "That's not what I meant at all."

He leaned back in his chair and shook his head. "I don't put any whores to work for me without fuckin' 'em first."

"Well, you see, there's your mistake. I'm not a whore, and I have no intention of fucking you."

Hearing the word come out of her pristine mouth just aroused Swearengen even more. A growl rumbled in his chest. He said, "What are you doing here then? If you're looking for a job as a dealer, you'll have to try somewhere else. I don't have any female dealers." He laughed. "It's not ladylike."

Arabella shook her head. "I'm not a gambler. I told your man I wanted to make an arrangement with you, and that arrangement does indeed involve sex. That's the only thing you seem to have assumed correctly about me, Mr. Swearengen."

He had almost lost his temper then. She was talking down to him, and he didn't like that. He opened a wooden box on the desk and jerked out a cigar. He bit off the end and then put the stogie between his teeth, leaving it unlit. "Why don't you just spit it out?" he asked in a harsh voice, then laughed. "I reckon plenty of men have probably said *that* to you before."

Still unfazed, she said, "There's no need to be coarse. I'm not a common prostitute, Mr. Swearengen, not one of your disease-ridden soiled doves. I'm a courtesan who has been with lovers all over Europe."

"Thought you sounded like a foreigner," Swearengen snapped. "Listen, I know what you're talking about, and a high-class whore is still a whore. You bed men in this place, you do it by my rules."

Arabella had shaken her head and said simply, "No."

Swearengen stared at her. "What do you mean, 'no'?"

"I mean I don't work that way. My proposal is that you

furnish me with a room here, and I sleep with who I want, when I want, and charge what I want."

"And what the hell do I get out of that?"

"Thirty percent of whatever I make."

Swearengen rolled the cigar from one side of his mouth to the other. What she proposed ran counter to everything he believed in. He was the boss around here and always had been. Yet he found himself somewhat intrigued by the idea anyway. Once word got around that he had this incredibly beautiful woman staying at the Gem, and that not just anybody could buy her favors, a lot of men in Deadwood would want her that much more. They might be willing to pay a pretty penny for the privilege of having her.

His eyes had narrowed, and he said, "You're not a two-dollar fuck, are you?"

"Mr. Swearengen," Arabella said, "I'm not even a ten-dollar fuck."

His bushy eyebrows rose. "What do you intend to charge?"

"Twenty dollars," she said calmly.

He took the cigar out of his mouth and laughed. "Forget it! Nobody's going to pay twenty dollars for pussy. Not even yours, lady." He squinted at her again. "Maybe for a go at all three holes, if a fella was particularly flush . . ."

"Twenty dollars," she repeated, her voice firm. "It *is* worth the price, and enough men *will* pay it for you to find the arrangement quite profitable."

Swearengen spread his hands. "I got no way of knowing what it's worth, now, do I?"

She got to her feet. "You're an incorrigible man," she said, "and I should have known better than to try to deal with you. I'll go over to the Bella Union, or better yet, find a place of my own—"

"Hold on, hold on." Swearengen had set the cigar aside, placed his hands flat on the desk, and pushed himself out of the chair. His goal was to have less competition in Deadwood, not more, and he sure as hell didn't want some classy bit of fluff like this going into business against him. "I never said we couldn't work something out. Thirty percent isn't enough, though. I want a fifty-fifty split."

She shook her head. "I suppose I could live with giving you thirty-five percent."

"Well, I couldn't. Sixty-forty, final offer."

She had thought it over then, but only for a moment before nodding. "Sixty-forty it is," she said. "And *no* special privileges for you or any of your employees."

"I'll tell the boys to steer clear of you," Swearengen had promised. He'd been careful, though, not to pledge anything regarding his own behavior. For something this prime, he might be willing to be patient for a while. . . .

But not for too long. Sooner or later he'd have her squealing under him, he had vowed, and when he was done that way he'd flip her over and make her squeal even more.

As he climbed the stairs now, that thought replayed itself in his mind and caused a thin smile to appear on his lips. So far he hadn't made much progress with the mysterious Arabella, but it had only been a week. During that time she'd had only two customers, both of them prominent Deadwood businessmen who wouldn't have been caught dead screwing one of his regular whores. The word was starting to get around, though. . . . Arabella strolled through the barroom at least once every evening, looking cool and beautiful, not talking to anyone, not accepting any of the offers to buy her a drink that came from the filthy, buckskin-clad miners and freighters, just smiling faintly to herself as if she knew secrets that had never been revealed to anyone else.

Of course everybody wanted to fuck her, thought Swearengen. Who wouldn't?

When he reached the second floor he walked down to the room at the end, the one he'd had cleaned up and fixed up specially for her. He knocked on the door. He heard her footsteps on the other side of the panel, but she didn't open it.

"Who is it?"

"Al," he said. He could be friendly when he wanted to.

The door opened, but only a few inches, just wide enough for him to see that she wore a beautiful red dress. "What can I do for you, Mr. Swearengen?"

"I guess you saw the soldiers come in to town."

"It would have been difficult to miss their arrival. There was everything but a brass band."

"Yeah, well, I'm glad they're here, and you should be, too."

"I've never been particularly frightened of Indians."

"I'm not talking about the redskins," Swearengen said. "I'm talking about those soldier boys. You should be able to find some new customers among them."

"Privates in the army don't make the sort of money to be able to afford me," she said.

"Maybe not, but the officers do. If you want, I'll steer as many of them as I can your way."

"Officers," she repeated. "That's an interesting idea. I haven't been with a general since I was in Paris."

Swearengen shook his head. "I wouldn't hold out much hope where Crook's concerned, if I was you. He's too interested in making speeches for the reporters and posing for the rotogravure. But a column of that size will have at least a couple of colonels with it, and a passel of majors and captains."

"I'll keep that in mind."

"You do that," he told her with a nod. "Seems to me you're not really producing enough income yet to make our deal worthwhile. I don't like gettin' the short end of the stick."

"Neither do I, Mr. Swearengen," she said as she began to ease the door shut. "Neither do I."

He was halfway back down the hall to his office before he stopped short, frowned, and said aloud, "What the *fuck* did she mean by that?"

Chapter Four

STEPHEN Ransome thought that perhaps he might still be human after all. A hot bath, a shave, and some clean clothing made an amazing difference in the way a man felt. He turned to the right, then to the left, as he looked at himself in the pier glass set up in the haberdasher's shop. The brown tweed coat and trousers he wore over a white shirt and matching vest lacked the stylish flair of a suit he could have gotten back in Boston, of course, but the outfit was still a vast improvement over a cavalry uniform that had been splattered with mud and horse shit and drenched with rain for weeks on end.

He straightened his cravat and nodded to the shop's proprietor. "This will do fine. You'll see to it that my uniform is cleaned and pressed?"

"Yes, sir, Major, I'll send it down to the laundry right away, along with the other officers' uniforms." A steady stream of majors, captains, and lieutenants had come in looking for fresh clothes since the column had been dismissed. "Those Chinks do a bang-up job, I'm telling you. When it's taken care of, I'll have your uniform delivered over to the Grand Central. That's where you're stayin', ain't it?"

Ransome nodded. "That's right. General Crook intends to make the hotel his headquarters while he's here in Deadwood, so naturally his staff will stay there, too."

"You don't know just how happy we are to have you fellas in town, Major. The Sioux have raised holy hell in these parts ever since the prospectors came in. They've left the town alone so far, but you can't never tell when those savages'll take it into their heads to raid the place and scalp us all." A peevish tone entered the shopkeeper's voice. "Seems to me the government should'a sent troops in to keep the peace before now."

Ransome couldn't resist pointing out the obvious. "You *do* know that you and all the other citizens of Deadwood are here illegally, don't you? According to the treaties we made with the Sioux, all the Black Hills belong to them. They consider this area sacred ground."

"It's sacred ground, all right, because it's got gold in it. And no offense, Major, but as long as the federal government's got a tax collector here takin' a cut of everybody's money, which they do in General Dawson, seems to me like it owes us some protection from the hostiles."

Ransome couldn't argue with that logic, so he changed the subject instead. "I'm afraid I don't have sufficient cash to pay you the full price of this outfit right now. . . ."

"Oh, that's all right, Major. I'll take your marker for what you owe. General Crook himself told me that there'll be a paymaster's wagon from Fort Laramie showin' up here before too much longer. I'm glad to extend credit to you fine fellas, and at a reasonable rate of interest, too."

Of course there would be interest, thought Ransome. No matter how glad the inhabitants of Deadwood were to see the soldiers, that wouldn't stop them from trying to make every penny they possibly could out of the situation.

"How about this to top it off?" the shopkeeper asked as

he extended a dark brown beaver hat. "It'll look mighty nice with that suit."

Ransome took the hat and settled it on his close-cropped sandy hair, then studied himself in the pier glass again. The hat didn't look bad, although Ransome felt certain the styles in Boston had probably passed it by. He hadn't actually been there in more than a year, he reminded himself, not since his last visit to Louisa and the children while he was on leave, so he supposed he shouldn't pass judgment on the haberdasher's offerings.

"I'll take it," he said. "Add it to my bill."

"I sure will. If you'll wait just a minute, Major, I'll have everything all toted up, and you can give me your marker."

With the transaction concluded, Ransome left the shop a few minutes later. As he caught a glimpse of himself in the window, he was impressed with the way he looked like a gentleman. General Crook had kindly allowed his officers to skip the requirements of appearing in proper uniform for the time being—appropriately enough, Ransome thought, since Crook hardly ever wore his own uniform.

The sun rode low in the western sky above the wooded slopes that surrounded the settlement. Like all the other officers, Ransome was under orders to appear shortly for dinner at the Grand Central Hotel. The leading citizens of Deadwood would be in attendance, too. It was shaping up to be quite an affair, especially for a crude frontier mining camp like this. Ransome could tell that Deadwood's leaders wanted it to be more than a mining camp. They had in mind to make it into a permanent settlement, a real city.

Whether or not they would succeed depended on a lot of things, including the whims of the red gentleman known as Crazy Horse. For now, outlaw town or not, Deadwood was here, craving respectability.

Ransome started to turn toward the Grand Central, but he hesitated as he looked the other way along the street. The Gem Theater was down there, and he thought that he had time for a quick drink before dinner. The possibility of catching another glimpse of the blond woman in the red dress he had seen in the window earlier had nothing to do with his decision to pay a visit to the Gem before adjourning to the hotel for dinner, he told himself.

Crowds still packed Deadwood's Main Street. A celebratory mood gripped the populace. General Crook was supposed to make a speech in front of the hotel after dinner, and people were already gathering for it. Ransome made his way through the throngs on the boardwalks, surrounded by noise and the smell of unwashed flesh. He had almost reached the Gem when a hand fell on his shoulder.

He turned around, suppressing the impulse to reach for the Colt revolver he had tucked inside the waistband of his trousers where his coat hid it. Deadwood had a reputation as a dangerous town, but it seemed unlikely anyone would try to rob him or murder him in the middle of this crowd, when the sun wasn't even down yet.

Private Brundage grinned at him. "Howdy, Major. Haven't seen much of you since we got here."

Brundage's two cronies, Hollis and Lamont, were with him, of course. A flash of annoyance went through Ransome at the sight of their grinning faces. He had hoped that maybe he was rid of them, that they would be so distracted by the decadent pleasures Deadwood had to offer that they would forget all about what they had seen back there on Rosebud Creek.

Yet here the three of them were, as filthy and unwashed as they had been when the column reached the settlement. "You men were supposed to clean up," Ransome snapped.

"We ain't got around to it yet," Brundage replied.

"That goes without saying."

Brundage acted like he didn't hear the comment. "We've been a mite too busy wettin' our whistles after that long, dry ride."

Ransome didn't need to be told that they had been drinking. The stomach-turning odor of cheap rotgut emanated from all three troopers. He said, "Don't let me stop you from what you've been doing—"

"No, sir, we don't want you to think we've forgotten

about you or anything like that. You headin' into the Gem? We ain't been there yet." Brundage licked his lips. "Maybe we'll go along with you and give it a try."

Anger flared inside Ransome. No matter how much cheap whiskey they had already swilled, no matter what they knew about the incident in which Spotted Dog had lost his life, if they thought they were going to waltz into the Gem and have a drink with him, they were sadly mistaken. There were rules about officers fraternizing with enlisted men, and even if there hadn't been, Ransome didn't want to have anything more to do with them.

"You men are off duty and free to go wherever you want," he said with a cold-eyed officer's stare intended to strike fear into their hearts, "but I don't believe I'll be sharing your company this evening."

Brundage grimaced. "Aw, Major, we're just tryin' to be friendly. I mean, after the way we come through the battle of the Rosebud together, with all those Injuns screamin' and dyin' all around us . . ."

That was a not-so-subtle reminder of Spotted Dog, Ransome realized, and suddenly a mixture of guilt, anger, and revulsion overwhelmed him. His left hand shot out and grabbed Brundage's shirt, jerking the weasel-like trooper closer to him. Ransome's right hand reached under his coat and closed around the butt of his revolver.

"Listen to me, Brundage," he said in a low voice. "I'm an officer from one of the best families in Boston. You and your friends are privates and gutter trash to boot. Who do you think everyone is going to believe if you start spreading stories about me?"

Brundage's eyes were wide with surprise, and his mouth opened and closed several times with no sound coming out. Behind him, Lamont and Hollis looked just as shocked by Ransome's actions.

"Besides," Ransome went on, "it was an accident. In all that chaos, no one could be expected to tell one savage from another. *And it was just an Indian.* In the long run, no one cares who shot him or why." He gave Brundage a shove away from him. "So get the idea that we're somehow connected out of your heads. What you saw means nothing, and that's what you three are to me . . . Nothing. Understand?"

Brundage had stumbled a little when Ransome pushed him. He caught his balance against the railing along the edge of the boardwalk and glared at the major. "You got no right to talk to us like that," he muttered. "I don't care if you are an officer."

"Keep it up and I'll have you put in irons," Ransome said. He dug in his pocket with his left hand and pulled out one of his few remaining coins. As he flipped it toward Brundage, he added, "That's enough to buy each of you another drink—and that's the end of it. Come around me again, and unless it has something to do with official military business, you'll regret it, I promise you."

Brundage had deftly plucked the spinning coin out of the air. He rubbed it between his thumb and first two fingers as he glared at Ransome and said, "I reckon you made yourself plain enough, Major. Sorry we bothered you."

Ransome gave them a curt nod of dismissal and turned toward the Gem once again. "One more thing," he said over his shoulder. "Buy that drink somewhere else if you know what's good for you."

Then he stalked on down the boardwalk and disappeared through the batwings without looking back.

"**SHOULD'A** let me shoot the bastard when I wanted to," Lamont rumbled. The troopers had moved over into an alcove that housed the doorway of a closed business, so they were out of the flow of foot traffic on the boardwalk.

"Yeah, maybe you're right," Brundage admitted. He looked at the coin the major had thrown at him like he was some sort of beggar, then, out of habit, bit it to make sure it was real.

"We should've known he'd tell us to go to hell sooner or later," Hollis put in. "It just took him a while to figure out that nobody cares what happened to some stinkin' redskin."

Brundage slipped the coin into his pocket. "Maybe not. I thought the major might care, though. His pa was a preacher, I heard tell."

A rusty laugh came from Lamont. "You figured he'd feel guilty? Shit, they train that right outta officers at West Point. Otherwise they couldn't treat the enlisted men the way they do."

That made Brundage smile a little. "You might just be right about that, Dewey. Ah, well, it was worth a try, I reckon." A thoughtful expression came over his lean face. "We're gonna have to come up with another way to get our hands on some money."

"They say there's a paymaster's wagon on its way. We got wages comin'. . . ."

"I'll believe that when I see it," Brundage said with a shake of his head. "Besides, I'm talkin' about more money than those shitty wages the army owes us. I'm talkin' about real loot."

Lamont's voice tightened as he lowered his voice and said, "You mean enough for us to desert and make ourselves a fresh start somewhere else, like we talked about?"

Brundage nodded. "That's right. Somethin' that'll get us out of these fuckin' uniforms once and for all. In a town this size, with as much money and gold floatin' around as there is, got to be a way for us to latch on to some of it." He jerked his head toward the eastern end of the settlement, where most of the saloons, brothels, and gambling dens were located. "Let's go get that drink and think on it."

Hollis and Lamont agreed, and the three troopers trudged in that direction as dusk began to settle down over Deadwood.

"But I'll tell you one more thing," Brundage added as rage and humiliation burned inside him. "Before we leave this place, that asshole Ransome is gonna be damned sorry he talked to me like that. Yes, sir, damned sorry."

Chapter Five

THE Gem bore scant resemblance to the genteel taverns and barrooms he had patronized occasionally back in Boston, Ransome thought as he looked around. His father, being a minister, didn't hold with drinking, of course, and Louisa, being a good Christian herself, didn't either. But from time to time Ransome liked to go out and socialize a bit while drinking a glass of good port or some fine aged whiskey, and Louisa tolerated that as long as he never came home drunk or stank of spirits around the children.

The smell of liquor certainly filled the air inside the Gem, along with a mingled fragrance of wood smoke, cigar smoke, and other less savory aromas. A multitude of sounds rose around him to go with the smells: the rumble of men's voices, the shriek of women's laughter, the slap of cards on green felt, the clicking of an ivory ball in a spinning roulette wheel. All of it combined in a rather pleasant assault on Ransome's senses as he realized that he was back in civilization . . . well, civilization of a sort anyway.

He found himself in a vast, low-ceilinged room with a

U-shaped bar jutting out from its rear wall. Tables filled the area around the bar. To the right a staircase built in the middle of the room angled back and forth with a landing halfway up to the second floor. Beyond the stairs lay the theater part of the establishment, a large open area with a raised platform at the far end where performers could sing or dance or do whatever it was they did. Chairs stacked against the rear wall could be lined up in rows whenever a show was scheduled. At the moment dancers used the open space to whirl their partners around while a slick-haired gent pounded on a piano and two bearded old-timers sawed away at fiddles they clutched in their gnarled hands. The female dancers wore scanty outfits of stockings and chemises, some of which had slipped down to expose their breasts.

Ransome felt his face growing warm as he watched the bawdy display. He had never seen anything quite so bold back in Boston, but despite that—or perhaps because of it—he couldn't take his eyes off the dancers.

Their number didn't include the blonde he had seen earlier, of course. Even though he had gotten only a brief glimpse of her, he knew that she would be much too refined to take part in such a brazen display.

"Hey, mister! Want a drink?"

Ransome realized the speaker had directed the question at him. He looked toward the bar and saw a brawny bearded man in an apron standing on the other side of the hardwood. Quite a few customers had crowded up to the bar already, but that didn't stop the bartender from trying to drum up more business.

Ransome went over, wedged himself into the crowd of men, and nodded. "Yes, I would," he told the bartender. "The finest whiskey you have."

The man grinned as he picked up a bottle and a glass from the shelf under a long painting of a large, naked woman. "I hope you ain't the picky sort, mister. This is a few steps above panther piss, but it ain't what you'd drink in some fancy place back East."

"It's Major," Ransome told him.

The bartender frowned in confusion. "Huh?"

"It's Major, not mister. Major Stephen Ransome."

The man grinned and nodded. "Oh, I get ya. You're one o' those soldier boys who rode in a while ago." A frown replaced the grin. "But how come you ain't over at the Grand Central? I heard General Crook and all his officers were havin' dinner with the high muckety-mucks from around here."

"That's right. I'm on my way there," Ransome admitted. "I just wanted to stop in for a drink first."

"Oh. Well, we can fix you up." The bartender shoved the glass he had filled across the hardwood. "There you go, Major. Enjoy."

Ransome picked up the glass and tossed back the amber-colored liquid. It seared its way down his throat and instantly kindled a blaze inside his belly. Ransome's fingers tightened on the glass as the whiskey threatened to take his breath away. The reaction lasted only a moment, though, and then the blaze turned into a warm, pleasant glow.

"Not bad," he told the bartender as he put the empty back on the bar.

The man reached for the bottle. "Want another?"

Ransome shook his head and used his palm to cover the top of the empty glass. "I'd better not. As you said, I have that dinner to attend. Maybe another time."

"Sure thing, Major." The bartender put the cork back in the bottle. "That'll be six bits."

"A little steep, isn't it?" Ransome asked with a frown.

"Well, it's the best you'll find in Deadwood."

Ransome doubted that, but he paid the man anyway from his dwindling cache of coins. In order to get full value for his money, he leaned closer and said, "I was, ah, wondering about something. . . ."

A big grin creased the man's face. "No need to wonder, Major! Damn right we got girls who'll go upstairs with you. Any size, shape, age, or color you want. They ain't shy about what they'll do, neither. For the right price you can stick it just about anywhere you damn well—"

"No, no," Ransome stopped him before he could go on. "I was going to ask you about a girl, but not . . . that sort of girl."

"Oh?" The bartender looked genuinely puzzled. "What sort you lookin' for, then?"

Now that he had come this far with his inquiry, Ransome didn't see any point in turning back. "I saw her earlier when we rode in. She was looking out an upstairs window. She had long blond hair and wore a red dress and . . . and was very lovely."

"Oh!" Comprehension dawned on the bartender's face. He lifted a hand and pointed a blunt, sausagelike finger across the room. "You're talkin' about that girl!"

Ransome turned and looked in the direction the bartender indicated. The sight that met his eyes took his breath away even more than the whiskey had.

The blond woman was coming down the stairs from the second floor, and it was as if the somewhat squalid setting around her simply faded away as Ransome looked at her. She might as well have been royalty descending a grand curving staircase in a castle somewhere; she was that stunning. Or a beautiful princess in an illustrated book of fairy tales, Ransome thought as he struggled to take in the sight. The glimpse he had caught of her through the window had done nothing to prepare him for the vision of her true loveliness.

She looked right and left as she came down the stairs, smiling slightly, and those she favored with her gaze fell silent as they stared up at her. Ransome understood the feeling. If he had felt the power of those eyes on him, he would have lost the ability to speak, too.

But she appeared not to have noticed him yet, so he was able to ask the bartender, "Who . . . who is she?"

"That there's Lady Arabella," the man replied proudly. He hastened to add, "She don't call herself that, the lady part, I mean. She just said her name's Arabella. Some of the rest of us . . . well, we just started callin' her that because it seems to fit her, you know."

Ransome understood completely. If ever a woman deserved the title, this one did.

"Is she . . ." He hesitated, as if the mere act of asking the question would sully her somehow.

"A whore? Well . . . there's two ways o' looking at that. She'll take a fella upstairs . . . but it's got to be the right fella, to her way o' thinkin', and the price ain't cheap neither. She's got about as much in common with the other gals who work here as a fine Thoroughbred does with a broke-down ol' plow horse."

The idea that such a lovely creature could be his, even for a limited time, set Ransome's pulse to hammering in his head. He was about to ask the bartender how much it would cost when the realization that such a thing was unthinkable came crashing down on him. He was married, after all. He had taken vows of faithfulness to Louisa. He couldn't stray.

But . . . but . . . Lady Arabella was so beautiful.

And she was looking at him now. Her eyes found him as she reached the bottom of the stairs, and as her gaze sharpened and the smile curved her full, red lips the faintest bit more, she started toward him.

DAN Ryan wasn't sure how or why he seemed to have been appointed Calamity Jane's keeper, but that appeared to be the situation. He'd hiked into Deadwood from his claim, intending to pick up a few supplies and then head back up the gulch, but once he got there he'd decided to have a drink or two, eat a real meal instead of something he threw together in a frying pan over a campfire, and maybe find a warm bed he could share with an even warmer woman.

Just . . . not Calamity Jane. That idea had never entered his thoughts.

She had tagged along with him, though, after all the hoopla over the cavalry's arrival died down, and he didn't have the heart to tell her he'd rather not have her company. Then he'd made the mistake of starting into Mann's No. 10 Saloon for a schooner of beer, and Calam had busted out bawling.

Of course she'd be upset, Dan chided himself. It was right there in the No. 10 that Jack McCall had killed Wild Bill. The table in the back still stood in the same place it had on that fateful day some six weeks earlier. The chair Hickok had been sitting in, the chair where he'd died, was still there, too. Whether Calamity's love affair with Wild Bill had been real or not, she didn't need to see that.

So Dan had taken hold of her arm through the greasy buckskin shirt and said, "Come on, Calam. Let's go on down to the Bella Union. I'll buy you a drink."

She stopped wailing, sniffled a few times, wiped the back of her hand across her nose and smeared the dirt on her face some more, and said, "That's mighty nice o' you . . . What was your name again?"

"Dan Ryan."

"You're all right, Dan." She slung her arm around his shoulders before he could stop her. "You're the finest fella I've met since . . . since Wild Bill. I'll have that drink with you, and then if you want, it'd be my honor to suck your cock."

"You, uh, don't have to do that, Calamity."

"Well, you think about it. Offer's good." She let out a bray of laughter. "Leastways until I pass out, and then, hell, you could do anything you wanted to me!"

Dan didn't say anything, he just led Calamity Jane down the boardwalk toward the Bella Union and thought about how even the simple things in life, like getting a drink and something to eat, sometimes didn't turn out like you expected them to.

They went into the saloon, the second largest in town after the Gem—and some said even nicer than Al Swearengen's place. Billy Nuttall, who was partners with Carl Mann in the No. 10 down the street, owned the Bella

Union and could usually be found here. That was the case tonight. He stood behind the bar, where he lifted a hand in greeting to Dan and wrinkled his nose slightly at the sight of Calamity Jane.

"Dan," Nuttall said with a friendly nod. His tone cooled down considerably as he added, "Calam, I hope you haven't come in here to make trouble tonight."

"Make trouble, hell!" Calamity responded. "I never make trouble. It's always the other fellas who start the ruckuses. I'm about the most peaceable piece o' ass you'll ever see, Billy, and you know it." She slapped a palm down on the bar. "Now gimme a shot o' red-eye!"

Nuttall glanced at Dan, who shrugged and nodded. "All right," the saloon keeper said with obvious reluctance. "But I'm counting on you to look after her, Dan."

"Don't worry, I will."

Calamity snorted. "The way you two go on, you'd think I was some sort o' wild woman or somethin'!"

Nuttall poured the drink for her, then looked at Dan again, lifting his eyebrows inquisitively. "I'll have a schooner of beer," the sergeant-turned-prospector said.

Nuttall drew the beer and slid it across the bar. Dan lifted the schooner and took a healthy swig. The beer was cool and not too bitter—damned good for Deadwood, in other words. He planned to nurse it along for a while so he could stay sober and keep an eye on Calamity Jane, as he had promised.

She had already downed the whiskey Nuttall had poured for her and smacked the empty glass back down on the bar. "'Nother," she demanded. Dan made a weary gesture indicating that Nuttall should comply with the request.

"I hope you know what you're doin', Ryan," the man muttered as he splashed more whiskey into Calamity's glass.

"So do I," Dan agreed with a rueful note in his voice. Lifting the schooner, he turned so that his back leaned against the bar, hooked the heel of one work boot behind the brass rail at the foot of the bar, and looked out across the Bella Union's big main room to see if any of his friends were there tonight.

Instead of friends, though, his gaze fell on three men in stained cavalry blue who sat at a table in the corner. A surprised breath hissed sharply between suddenly clenched teeth as he recognized them. The lean, foxlike, dark-haired trooper was Clyde Brundage. Beside him bulked the stocky, heavy-shouldered, ginger-bearded Dewey Lamont. The third soldier at the table was slightly younger than the other two, with bland, fair-haired good looks, but Dan knew better than to be taken in by appearances; Matt Hollis was just as vicious, greedy, and no-account as the other two. When Dan had first met them, they had been sergeants, like him, but that had changed drastically.

And the *last* time he had seen the three troopers, they had been threatening to kill him if they ever ran into him again.

Chapter Six

CLYDE Brundage couldn't believe it. He'd been sitting here, nursing a beer and his grudge against Major Ransome, when who went and dropped right back in their laps but Sergeant Dan fuckin' Ryan?

He nudged Lamont with an elbow and said, "Look who's at the bar."

Well on his way to getting drunk, Lamont didn't respond right away. After a moment, though, he lifted his shaggy head and rumbled, "What?"

"Look at the bar," Brundage repeated.

Hollis heard him and looked in that direction before Lamont did. "Son of a bitch," Hollis said. "It's that damned Ryan."

"Ryan?" Lamont said, his voice rising as what was going on around him finally penetrated his whiskey-muddled brain. "Where is he? I'll kill him!"

Brundage put a hand on Lamont's shoulder as the burly trooper started to rise from his chair. "Take it easy, Dewey," he snapped. "We don't want to cause a ruckus in here."

"Maybe you don't, but if Ryan's around, I sure as hell

do! That lousy bastard turned us in! I don't care what he said, I know he done it."

"Settle down," Brundage said. "Just look at the bar. Ryan's standin' there with either Calamity Jane or one of the ugliest fellas I ever saw. I can't quite tell from here."

Lamont hitched his chair around a little so that he could see. His scowling face darkened with anger as he finally spotted Dan Ryan, who looked back at the three of them with a frown, obviously recognizing them just as they had recognized him.

"It's him, right enough. I'm gonna go choke the life outta the bastard."

"No, you're not," Brundage told him. "For one thing, Crook would hang you if you killed a civilian like that. He might not even wait for a court-martial. For another, it's been a couple of years since all that trouble. What say we live and let live, boys?"

Hollis and Lamont both stared at him. After a few seconds Hollis said, "Ryan's the one who got us sent to the stockade. He's to blame for us bein' busted back down to privates. I don't know about you, Clyde, but I liked havin' those sergeant's stripes on my sleeve."

"I did, too," Brundage admitted. "It was easier to get away with things that way. But starting a fight with Ryan won't change anything."

"Make me feel a whole heap better to bust his face," Lamont muttered.

"Maybe we can figure out a way to turn this to our advantage," Brundage said. "Smile, boys. Let's be nice for now." He hoisted his mug of beer and made a toasting motion toward Ryan, who watched the three of them with narrowed, suspicious eyes. Hollis and Lamont played along, although it was obvious that Lamont didn't much like the idea.

Ryan didn't respond to the overture, just kept on staring coldly at them instead. The legs of Brundage's chair scraped on the floor as he pushed it back.

"Where are you goin'?" Hollis wanted to know.

"I'm gonna talk to Ryan and find out just what he's doin' in Deadwood."

Lamont said, "I can tell you that by the looks o' the clothes he's wearin'. He's been huntin' for gold."

Brundage thought that guess on Lamont's part was probably right. After getting out of the stockade and transferring from the Seventh Cavalry because ol' Yellowhair Custer didn't want them around anymore, they had heard rumors that Dan Ryan left the army completely. Clearly those rumors had been true, and now they knew why Ryan had left. He wanted to make his fortune just like everybody else, the sanctimonious bastard. He'd been quick enough to throw around words like "honor" and "duty" when he was interfering in somebody *else's* plans. Those long, hellish months in the stockade, Brundage had comforted himself with the thought that one of these days he would run into Dan Ryan again, and then he would settle the score with the man who had betrayed them . . . in blood, if necessary.

Those dark thoughts went through his mind as he stood up. Before he could take a step toward the bar, Hollis stopped him by saying, "You've got something in mind, don't you, Clyde?"

"Maybe," Brundage admitted. The beginnings of an idea anyway.

"I hope it works out better'n that harebrained notion to blackmail Major Ransome," Lamont said. "You said his family had a lot of money and we'd wind up bein' rich because o' what we saw him do, and in the end all he did was tell us to go fuck ourselves."

Brundage felt a surge of anger, but the knowledge that Lamont was right tempered his annoyance. "I ain't forgot about Ransome," he said, "but we'll deal with him later. Right now I'm goin' to talk to Ryan."

It was a matter of priorities. Dan Ryan was here and now. But Brundage had himself a long list of people he intended to kill sooner or later, and Major Stephen Ransome was still on it.

* * *

"GOOD evening," Lady Arabella said as she came to a stop in front of Ransome. The crowd inside the Gem had parted to let her through like the Red Sea rolling back before Moses and the Israelites. Ransome had heard about that miracle many times in his father's sermons, but as far as he was concerned it didn't come close to matching the miracle that was the beauty of the Lady Arabella.

Ransome realized he still had the beaver hat on. He reached up and snatched it off his head, then held it over his heart as he bowed slightly. He had to struggle for a second to find his voice before he was able to say, "Madam, you honor me with your presence. You honor us all."

Something, maybe amusement, twinkled in her eyes. "Well, aren't you the sweet one?" she said in a throaty, musical voice that sent fire coursing along Ransome's veins.

"Not as sweet as your smile, dear lady."

Ransome could have kicked himself for saying something so flowery, but Arabella didn't seem to mind. In fact, she laughed lightly and put a hand on the sleeve of his coat. "Did you just get to Deadwood today? I don't recall seeing you around . . . and I think I would have remembered."

"Yes, I rode in this afternoon with General Crook's column."

Her finely plucked eyebrows rose. "I remember now! I saw you. You wore a uniform. You're one of the soldiers."

"Yes, ma'am. Major Stephen Ransome, at your service."

"You're an officer. I should have known." Her hand still rested lightly on his arm. "Would you like to have a drink with me, Major?"

Embarrassment suddenly warmed Ransome's face. He would have liked nothing more at this moment than to buy a drink for Lady Arabella, but he was almost out of money and even if he emptied his pockets, he wasn't sure if he could come up with enough to pay for the sort of divine nectar she deserved, if the Gem even had such a thing.

He stammered a bit, conscious of her scrutiny on him. The others around them had gone back to their own concerns once Arabella made it clear that her interest lay with Ransome, but he didn't care about them. Arabella was the only one who mattered, and for some reason not disappointing her had taken on a huge importance for him.

She didn't let him suffer for long. She murmured, "I understand," and his heart plummeted all the way to his feet as he thought she was about to turn away and deny him the life-sustaining sunshine of her beauty.

But then she took him completely by surprise as she went on, "Come up to my room. I have a bottle of excellent brandy, but I haven't found anyone in Deadwood worthy of sharing it with . . . until now."

The invitation took Ransome aback so that he gawked like a fool for a moment before he forced a smile onto his face and said, "That would be lovely."

With a graciousness that threatened to take his breath away, she turned and linked her arm with his. They walked toward the staircase, and again the crowd seemed to part magically before them. They were at the landing and turning to complete their ascent to the second floor before two things occurred to Ransome.

He was under orders to attend that dinner at the Grand Central Hotel with General Crook, the other officers, and the community leaders of Deadwood.

And all those men who watched him climb the stairs with Arabella, all the men with jealous frowns on their faces . . . they thought he was taking her upstairs to go to bed with her.

That thought, more than the first one, suddenly froze his muscles. As he paused on the stairs, Arabella asked him, "Is something wrong, Major?"

"I . . . I just remembered something," he managed to say. "General Crook is expecting me at the hotel. He's having dinner with some of Deadwood's leading citizens, and I'm supposed to be there. I just stopped in here for a moment on my way there."

"You don't even have time for a quick jot of brandy with me?"

It cost him quite an effort of will, but he was able to shake his head. "I'm afraid not. I can't tell you how sorry I am—"

"So am I," she broke in, and her voice was cool now, as was the look she gave him. "I really think you would have enjoyed the brandy, Major."

He knew he would have . . . and the brandy wasn't all he would have enjoyed. That's what made it so wrong, so impossible.

Her arm tightened momentarily where it looped through his, and the warm pressure of her touch made skyrockets go off inside him. "If it's a matter of finances," she said, "that's not necessarily a problem. . . ."

"No, I . . . I just have to go . . . to dinner with the general. . . ."

With a slightly sad smile she relinquished her hold on him. Her eyes held a certain look of disbelief, too, and he could well imagine why. Quite possibly no man had ever before turned down an invitation to accompany her upstairs.

"Go on, then," she told him. "I wouldn't stand between an officer and his duty."

"Thank you." He clapped his hat back on, then on an impulse took her hand and lifted it. He pressed his lips to the back of it and murmured, "Perhaps another time."

"Perhaps," she said, but he couldn't tell if she meant it or was just being polite, and the uncertainty tore the heart out of him.

Still, he knew he was doing the right thing. He had his orders, and he had the vows he'd made when he and Louisa were married. Both of those things trumped any base desires he felt at the moment.

Aware that the men in the Gem watched him with disbelief instead of envy now, he clattered down the stairs and headed for the batwinged entrance. He glanced over at the bar and saw the bartender he had spoken to earlier standing there behind the hardwood. The man shook his head and gave Ransome a look of utter disgust that said only an imbecile would pass up such an opportunity.

Ransome agreed completely with that sentiment, but he couldn't do anything about it. He had his duty.

That didn't stop him from pausing at the door and looking back at the staircase. He hoped that Arabella would still be standing there, that she might even lift a hand in a wave of farewell to him. . . .

But she was gone, and as he hurried across the street toward the Grand Central, Ransome felt the pain of an empty space inside him that might never be filled.

Not even the fear he had felt during the battle with the Sioux had been quite so fierce as the fear that he might never see Lady Arabella again.

Chapter Seven

DAN shifted the schooner of beer from his right hand to his left as Brundage approached. Brundage still wore a smile on his face, but Dan didn't trust him for a second. He dropped his right hand down to his side where he wore a holstered revolver. He was no shootist like Bill Hickok, but he could unlimber the Colt fairly quickly and shoot accurately when he had to.

"Howdy, Dan," Brundage said when he came up. "How are you? It's been a long time."

"Almost two years," Dan agreed. "And I'm fine, I reckon. I see you're still friends with Hollis and Lamont."

"Well, sure. We're pards, after all. Just like you and me were . . . once."

Dan wanted to tell Brundage that he never would have been pards with a skunk like him, but Brundage seemed to be making an effort to be friendly. So instead Dan just said, "I didn't know the three of you were still in the army."

"What can I tell you?" Brundage asked with a shrug. "That's about the only thing we know how to do. They busted us back to privates, of course, but when we got out of the stockade they didn't boot us out completely."

"Yeah, well, I'm sorry things turned out the way they did." That much was true, thought Dan. He figured it would have been better for the army if Brundage, Hollis, and Lamont had been dishonorably discharged once they'd served their time in the stockade. He believed in second chances, but not for those three.

Brundage didn't seem to take it that way. He nodded pleasantly and said, "I reckon things always work out for the best in the end. You look like you've made something of yourself. Got yourself a gold claim, do you?"

Dan glanced down at his worn work boots, his threadbare trousers, and the patched and lightweight coat he wore. They were hardly the duds of a successful man. He said, "I've got a claim, but it hasn't produced much color. Every time I think maybe I've found a vein, it peters out. I've been thinking about givin' up on it."

"Well, you're doin' better than us anyway." An ugly edge crept into Brundage's voice. "We're still drawin' privates wages, when we get paid at all, and we've spent the past three months fightin' redskins and sloggin' through the mud after 'em while we half starved."

Dan nodded. "I've heard a little about that. Sounds like you've had a rough patch, all right. Maybe things'll get better."

"Yeah, maybe, but I ain't gonna hold my breath waitin'. Not as long as we're in the army anyway."

"I thought you said that was all you know how to do."

"Well, you never know. Somethin' else better might come along. . . ."

An uneasy feeling crawled along Dan's nerves. Brundage had always been the smartest member of the trio, and he always had some scheme in mind to make him and his friends rich enough to leave the army behind. It was just such a plot that had landed the three of them in trouble and in the stockade at Fort Leavenworth. From the sound of it, Brundage hadn't changed his ways.

The conversation must have finally penetrated Calamity Jane's brain, because she turned away from the bar and stared owlishly at Brundage. "Who're you?" she demanded.

"Clyde Brundage," the trooper introduced himself. "Used to be in the same outfit as Ryan here. Don't you remember me, Calam? You went along with the Seventh Cavalry a few times as a mule-whacker."

"Yeah, I sure enough did." She leaned closer to him, close enough so that her breath made him draw back a little. "You ever fuck me?"

"Matter of fact, I didn't."

"Want to now?"

"Sorry. I can't afford you until the paymaster gets here, Calam."

She waved the hand that held her whiskey glass, and some of the amber liquid sloshed out. "Oh, hell, I'd be glad to take your marker," she said. "Come to that, you don't even have to pay me. I ain't whorin' right now, so whatever we did could just be for fun."

"Let me think about it," Brundage said. He jerked a thumb at the table where he'd been sitting. "You remember Dewey Lamont and Matt Hollis?"

"Nope," Calamity replied forthrightly. "Don't recollect 'em at all. But if you think they'd be interested in a little cavortin' . . ."

"I'll tell them to look you up," Brundage promised. He turned back to Dan. "Want to come over to the table and have a drink with us?"

"Reckon I'd better stay here," Dan said. "Calamity and I are, uh, makin' an evening of it."

"We are?" Calam slung an arm around his shoulders. "Hell, Dan, I didn't know you cared!"

He tried not to grimace as the stench wafting from her filled his nostrils. "Drink up," he told her. He didn't think she could get any drunker than she already was, but he felt a little bad anyway about encouraging her to pour more red-eye down her gullet.

"Reckon I'd better get back to the boys," Brundage said.

"I don't know how long we'll be here in Deadwood, but I imagine we'll see you again, Dan."

Dan gave him a curt nod. Over at the table, Hollis held his face carefully expressionless, but Lamont glowered toward the bar with open dislike on his rugged features. Lamont never had been any good at covering up his emotions, which usually involved either lust or hatred. Dan didn't believe for a second that Brundage's friendly overtures were genuine. The three of them wanted him dead before, and they still did.

"Old friends o' yours?" Calamity Jane asked when Brundage had gone back to rejoin the other two.

"Not hardly," Dan said. "They blame me for them windin' up in the stockade."

Calam belched. "What'd they do?"

Dan hesitated, not really wanting to rehash the whole thing and not sure if it would be a good idea to tell Calamity about it. But in all likelihood she wouldn't remember a thing he said, so he supposed it couldn't hurt.

"They were sergeants, like me," he said to her. "They were in charge of the guard details standin' watch over a big shipment of rifles intended for the Seventh Cavalry. We were at Fort Abraham Lincoln at the time, and the rifles were being kept in a warehouse there while the quartermaster went over them before issuing them to us. Brundage and his friends Hollis and Lamont got it in their heads that they were going to help some outlaws steal those rifles and sell them to the Indians. They would have made a lot of money doing that."

Calamity snorted. "Blood money, if you ask me. The Injuns already got enough rifles without sellin' 'em more."

"That's the truth," Dan agreed with a nod. "I found out what they were up to when I overheard them talking about it one night, and I warned 'em that they'd better forget it. If anything happened to those rifles, I would've turned them in. But I didn't. Somebody else must've found out about their plans and tipped off an officer, because Brundage and Hollis and Lamont were arrested and charged with conspiracy.

They thought I did it, though, and they've hated me ever since. I figure one of them must've gotten drunk and said more than he should have to a soiled dove or a bartender, and whoever that was sold 'em out."

"Could'a happened that way, sure as shit," Calamity agreed with a solemn nod. She poked him in the chest. "I tell you one thing, Dan. You best watch your back whilst them soldier boys are around. One of 'em just might take a notion to shoot you."

That possibility had occurred to Dan, too. As long as General Crook's column was bivouacked at Deadwood, Dan would need eyes in the back of his head.

Of course, that was true of life in general around Deadwood anyway, because you never knew what direction trouble might be coming from next.

THE hubbub of voices from the hotel dining room told Major Stephen Ransome that he hadn't arrived on time. The dinner had already gotten under way. Perhaps he was only a few minutes late, though, he told himself. To be sure, coming in late was better than not showing up at all. General Crook might forgive the former, but he certainly wouldn't the latter.

Ransome moved through the open double doors of the dining room and saw that the party had taken over the whole room, with the tables having been rearranged so that they formed one long, cloth-covered table. General Crook sat at the head, wearing a natty gray tweed suit. The members of his staff, the other officers, and the reporters accompanying the column had seated themselves along the table to his right, while the community leaders and other dignitaries from Deadwood were to the general's left. Ransome spotted a vacant seat among the officers and knew that he was supposed to be sitting there. The men had drinks before them but no food, so he took that to mean the meal hadn't actually gotten started yet. Forcing a smile onto his face, he edged toward the empty chair.

"Ah, there you are, Major." General Crook's raised voice cut through the conversation and silenced it. "I was wondering where you were."

Ransome's face flamed with embarrassment, and he also felt a surge of unaccustomed anger at the general for calling attention to his late arrival. He tried to keep that from showing on his features or in his voice as he replied, "My sincere apologies, General. I'm afraid I lost track of the time."

"Well, you're here now," Crook said, waving Ransome into the chair. "Allow me to introduce you to some of these fine gentlemen we've been getting to know. No doubt you recall Mayor Farnum from the fine welcome he gave us this afternoon."

Ransome nodded. "Of course, sir. Good to see you again, Mayor."

"Seated next to him is General Dawson, the federal government's representative here."

That would be the tax collector the haberdasher had mentioned earlier, thought Ransome.

"And Mr. Wagner, the owner of this fine establishment. Mr. Merrick, editor and publisher of the *Black Hills Pioneer*. Mr. Wood, the local banker. Mr. Langrishe, the owner of the theater across the street, which he has graciously agreed to furnish as a place where we can greet the locals later on this evening. Mr. Bullock and Mr. Star, two of Deadwood's leading merchants. Judge Miller . . ."

Crook went on naming the men from Deadwood, but Ransome lost track of who was who. Not only were there a lot of names to keep up with, but he didn't really care who they were. His mind was still full of thoughts of Lady Arabella. He could have been up in her room with her right now, he told himself, sharing brandy and witty conversation with the most beautiful woman he had ever seen in his life.

And there would have come a moment when she dimmed the lamp and removed her clothes and took his hand to bring him to her bed. He was sure of it. She had indicated plainly enough that she didn't mind if he couldn't afford her usual fee. She had desired him, he thought, as much as he desired her.

Their lovemaking would have been spectacular.

But instead he had turned his back on the opportunity of a lifetime and come here to the hotel, because of his loyalty to his commanding officer and to his marriage vows.

He was the biggest damn idiot in the world, he realized suddenly, and if such an incredible opportunity ever came his way again, he would seize it with both hands.

For now, though, all he could do was settle himself in his seat, sip the wine in the glass before him, force himself to smile, and take part in the conversation that went on around him like a good officer and a good husband and father . . .

When all the while, one thought burned in his brain.

I could have been fucking Arabella right now.

Chapter Eight

D**AN** thought maybe he could get Calamity Jane to sit down at a table in the Bella Union until she fell asleep from all the rotgut she'd consumed. In that case he could have taken her down to the wagon where Charley Utter lived and leave her there in good conscience, knowing that Colorado Charley would look after her. Charley had been Bill Hickok's best friend in Deadwood, and he had sort of adopted the grief-stricken Calamity Jane because of their mutual admiration for Wild Bill. Charley stayed busy with the mail and freight delivery service he had established between Deadwood and Cheyenne, but Dan thought he was in town at the moment.

Things didn't work out that way, though, because Calamity didn't cooperate. After staying at the Bella Union for a while, she decided she wanted to go get a drink somewhere else. "Let's go over to the Gem," she suggested.

Dan shrugged. One saloon was pretty much the same as another, he supposed, although he liked Billy Nuttall more than he did Al Swearengen, the proprietor of the Gem. Swearengen was a dark, violent man who gave the impression of being capable of doing anything to get what he wanted. It wasn't just an impression either, Dan reflected. Swearengen was one of the most ruthless hombres he'd ever seen.

The Gem was almost directly across the street from the Bella Union, but as Dan and Calamity left, the obstacle of several wagons parked in front of the Bella Union forced them to detour down the boardwalk. That took them past the boarded-up door of Miss Laurette's Academy for Young Ladies, an establishment that until a few weeks earlier had been one of Deadwood's most notorious brothels. Right out in front was where a young whore named Carla was gunned down by those claim-jumping Galloway brothers before justice caught up to them.

Laurette Parkhurst, the woman who had run the place, had disappeared not long after that. Most folks, if they thought about it at all, figured that she had taken her money and gone on to greener pastures elsewhere. With her gone, the Academy had closed down, and rumor had it that Billy Nuttall had bought it and planned to knock down the wall between it and the Bella Union so as to expand his own place.

Dan didn't know what had happened to Laurette Parkhurst and didn't care. As far as he was concerned, it was good riddance to her, because she had almost ruined his young friend Bellamy Bridges. For a while there, Bellamy had sunk into a morass of booze and whores and gunplay . . . but he had shaken free of it and gone back home to his family's farm in Illinois. Dan missed him, but he'd been glad to see the kid go. Some people were cut out for life on the frontier, and some just weren't.

And now that the Academy for Young Ladies was gone, the sooner everyone forgot about it, the better.

Dan and Calamity circled around the wagons, and as they started across the street, stepping around mud puddles and piles of horse shit along the way, Calamity said, "I reckon ol' Al Swearengen must've got over bein' mad at me. Last time I was in his place he didn't look like he wanted to kill me no more."

"What did Swearengen have against you?"

"Oh, I helped that whore called Silky Jen get away from him, so's she could run off with the White-Eyed Kid. I reckon Al was sweeter on that whore than he liked to let on, 'cause he was mad as a skinned cat for a while there after she was gone." Calamity let out a laugh. "Al's sweeter on money than anything else, though, so he let me come back in 'long as I had the wherewithal to pay for my drinks."

Dan rubbed a hand over his jaw and nodded. "Yeah, I seem to remember hearing about that Silky Jen business. You took a chance crossing Swearengen."

"Shit, I ain't afraid o' Swearengen! I've fought Injuns and outlaws and ever' other kind o' no-good varmint in my time. None of 'em scare me."

Dan wasn't sure that was a smart attitude to take regarding Al Swearengen. The man was too dangerous to discount the danger of having him as an enemy.

As they stepped up onto the boardwalk in front of the Gem, a man coming along the walk toward the saloon's entrance suddenly called, "Dan? Dan Ryan, is that you?"

The last old acquaintance he'd run into—Clyde Brundage—had made Dan reach for his gun. Out of habit he did the same thing now, but he stopped before his fingers brushed the Colt's walnut grips. He recognized the tall, lanky, buckskin-clad figure coming toward him.

"Cougar Jack! What in blazes are you doin' in Deadwood?"

Dan gripped the leathery hand that the grizzled old-timer thrust out at him. Cougar Jack LeCarde said, "Same as always, scoutin' for the army. I been ridin' with Gen'ral Crook, along with Frank Grouard, Big Bat, Baptiste, and a couple o' other fellas."

"Last I'd heard you were down in Texas chasing after Comanches."

Cougar Jack laughed. "I got tired o' that. Decided to come up here where the Injuns is a mite tamer than them Comanch'." He grew abruptly solemn. "Howsomever, I don't reckon ol' Colonel Custer'd agree with that assessment."

"He got himself in too deep to get out," Dan said, "and that habit of splitting his forces finally caught up to him."

"Yeah. Too bad he had to take a lot o' good men with him across the divide, though."

Dan nodded. "Yeah. Too bad."

He might have said something else, but right then Calamity Jane dug her elbow painfully into his side. "You got friends all over the place, don't you, Dan? Who's this'un?"

Dan inclined his head toward her and said, "You know Calamity Jane, Jack?"

"Can't say as we've ever crossed trails," LeCarde replied. He swept off his floppy-brimmed felt hat, revealing a mostly bald head. "Howdy, Miss Cannary."

"You know my real name?" she asked, sounding surprised.

"Oh, I've heard plenty o' yarns about the famous Calamity Jane. I ain't sure that any of 'em truly done you justice, though."

She tittered like a little girl, and hearing that sound come from such a filth-encrusted creature whose mouth usually spewed obscenities and vulgarities struck Dan as exceedingly odd. But the way Calam and old Cougar Jack seemed to be hitting it off pleased him. Maybe Jack would like to squire her around town for the rest of the evening, he thought.

LeCarde scotched that notion by saying, "I was just about to head in here for a drink. You two want to join me?"

Calamity didn't wait for Dan to answer. She linked arms with both men and practically dragged them toward the door. "Come on, you two rannies. Ever' gal likes to have two men at once ever' now and then, if you know what I mean!"

LeCarde volunteered to buy a bottle while Calamity and Dan found an empty table. Once they were settled, the scout poured the drinks and then picked up his glass and said, "To old friends—and new!"

"I'll drink to that!" Calamity said. She slammed back the

shot of whiskey, added, "Ah!" and thumped the empty glass on the table. As bizarre as it seemed, Dan had started to think that she was getting *less* drunk as the evening went on, no matter how much of the who-hit-John she consumed.

"Dan here run into another ol' friend from the army a while ago," she went on as she reached for the bottle to pour another drink.

"Oh?" LeCarde looked and sounded interested. "Who was that?"

"Clyde Brundage," Dan said, his voice tight.

"Brundage!" The scout's bushy gray eyebrows drew down in a scowl. "You mean nobody's killed the sneakin' son of a bitch yet?"

Dan shook his head. "No, and Matt Hollis and Dewey Lamont were with him. They're all still in the army. You didn't know that, Jack? They came in with Crook's column, too."

"There's close to a thousand men in Crook's command right now," LeCarde said. "And I was usually out on scoutin' missions, too, 'stead of travelin' with the troopers. So I never crossed paths with those polecats. Didn't have no idea they was still around."

"Oh, they're around. Lamont looked like he wanted to kill me, too."

"You best watch your back," LeCarde advised.

"You see?" Calamity said with a grin. "They say great minds think alike. I done told him the same thing, Jack."

LeCarde glared down into his whiskey. "If I'd knowed that I was helpin' to protect those three no-goods, I might not've been quite so diligent 'bout the job. Anybody who'd plot to sell rifles to the redskins . . ." LeCarde shook his head. "Throwin' 'em in the stockade wasn't near enough punishment, if you ask me. They should'a been horse-whipped first, at least. Some tarrin' an' featherin' wouldn't't've hurt 'em none neither."

"Well, it's all in the past now, I guess," Dan said.

"Except for those long memories the varmints got." LeCarde shook his head and downed the rest of his drink.

"I heard you took up prospectin', Dan. You a rich man yet?"

Dan laughed. "Not hardly. In fact, I've been thinkin' that maybe I made a mistake by becoming a gold hunter. I don't think I'm cut out for it."

"Why don't you come on back to somethin' you're good at, then?" LeCarde suggested.

"You mean enlist in the army again?" Dan frowned. "Whether I make it as a prospector or not, I reckon I've had enough of bein' a soldier, Jack."

"That ain't what I meant at all. You ought to sign on with us as a scout. I suspect the gen'ral would be mighty glad to have you."

Dan leaned back in his chair and frowned. It had never occurred to him to take a job as a scout for the army. When he'd mustered out, he had believed that he was done with military life. What LeCarde suggested made sense, though. It would be enough like the life Dan had known before to be familiar, and yet he wouldn't have to follow all the rules and regulations that had sometimes frustrated and annoyed him as a noncom. He had always gotten along well with the other scouts, too.

"I don't know," he said. "I reckon I'll have to think about it."

"Ponder all you want," LeCarde said. "From what I hear, we're gonna be stayin' around Deadwood for a while. The troopers are so starved and wore-out it's gonna be weeks before they're up to any more campaignin'."

Calamity hiccuped and said, "That's damned fine news. I got lots o' old friends in the cavalry, and that'll gimme a chance to renew acquaintances with 'em, if you get my drift."

Before they could say anything else, a cheer went up outside in the street. Calamity lifted her head. "What the hell's goin' on out there?"

"I think the gen'ral was supposed to make a speech," LeCarde said. "Want to go listen?"

"Might as well." Calamity pushed unsteadily to her feet. "Come on, Dan."

Dan didn't much care what General Crook had to say, but he could tell that Calamity wasn't ready to relinquish his companionship just yet. Anyway, if a crowd was gathering, he didn't want her out there by herself. She might trip and fall and get trampled face-first into the mud.

The three of them headed for the door, and they weren't the only ones. The cheering in the street had attracted quite a bit of attention from the Gem's customers. As Dan, Calamity, and Cougar Jack left the saloon, Dan glanced back and saw Al Swearengen standing on the stairs, a scowl on his face as he watched the exodus. Fewer customers meant less money for Swearengen.

Then they were outside and Dan forgot about the saloon owner. He and his two companions followed the flow of people toward the Grand Central Hotel. Several hundred people had already crowded into the street in front of the hotel, and more were arriving every second. Calamity didn't hesitate. She bulled her way through the mob in search of a good place to watch whatever was about to happen. Dan and LeCarde followed her.

About the time they reached the front of the crowd, more cheers sounded. Dan looked up onto the hotel porch and saw that somebody had carried a table outside and set it there, along with a chair. A man climbed up on the chair and from there onto the table. Dan recognized the stern features, the bushy side whiskers, and the jutting, forked beard of General George Crook. As usual, Crook wore a civilian suit instead of a uniform.

Cheers, applause, and whistles filled the air. Someone had lit a small bonfire down the street, and its flickering red glare washed over the hotel porch. A loud boom sounded as one of the celebrating townspeople touched off a charge of powder that he had packed into an anvil. Crook stood there for a long moment, nodding as he let the adulation roll over him, then finally he raised his hands and motioned for quiet. Several more minutes went by before the crowd settled down enough for the general to be heard.

"Fine citizens of Deadwood!" Crook began, his powerful voice raised so that it could be heard plainly anywhere in the street. "Once again I must humbly express my appreciation and gratitude for your most enthusiastic and hospitable welcome! My officers and I are overcome with humility! Thank you, one and all!"

That brought on another round of cheering and clapping. When that had died down, Crook continued. "Mayor Farnum and your other community leaders have treated us to a fine meal in the hotel, and they have asked me to say a few words to you concerning the recent campaign against the hostiles, which has proven to be a smashing success!"

That wasn't quite the way Dan had heard it, but he didn't expect anything less than a glowing public report from a general. As he stood there with Calamity and Cougar Jack, he listened while Crook recounted the events of the clash with Crazy Horse's forces at Rosebud Creek, the long pursuit through Wyoming, Montana, and the Dakota Territory, and the further hostilities at Slim Buttes. Crook cast everything in the most favorable light, of course, but when Dan looked over at LeCarde while the general was making it sound as if the cavalry had almost wiped out the entire Sioux nation, the scout solemnly shook his head.

LeCarde leaned closer to Dan and said in a low voice, "It was just luck the whole command didn't get wiped out at the Rosebud like ol' Custer did on the Little Bighorn. And that fight at Slim Buttes didn't amount to nothin'." He shrugged bony shoulders. "But what do you expect from a gen'ral? He ain't gonna stand up there and tell the truth."

Most of the citizens of Deadwood didn't have any interest in hearing the truth, thought Dan. They just wanted Crook to tell them that they were safe now, and that the army would keep them that way.

General Crook spoke for roughly a half hour as he recounted the events of the summer campaign, then Mayor Farnum said a few words about how happy everybody was to have the cavalry in Deadwood, and finally Judge Joseph Miller got up and waved a paper over his head.

"General Crook," the judge bellowed, "I have here a petition that's been circulating since word of your imminent arrival reached Deadwood, a petition which has been signed by over seven hundred fine citizens residing not only here in the settlement but in Deadwood Gulch and Whitewood Gulch as well! As you are no doubt well aware, the brave souls who have proceeded to the Black Hills to expand the glories and blessings of civilization are some of the finest specimens of humanity that this nation has to offer!"

Well, that oratory stretched the truth a mite, thought Dan as he looked around at the crowd, most of whom were at least half drunk and hadn't had more than a nodding acquaintance with soap and water for a long time.

The judge continued. "Their courage and hard work and boundless enthusiasm for everything that makes this country great should be rewarded with safety and security, but instead they have been forced to live in fear for their very lives! The Indians have murdered more than one hundred of our finest citizens in the past five months, savagely slaughtering them in the prime of their lives! Why, even a man of God has met his untimely end at the bloody hands of the hostiles!"

"Yes, I'm aware of that, Your Honor," Crook said, beginning to sound a little impatient. "What is the goal of this petition you're about to present to me?"

Judge Miller waved the paper over his head again. "This petition most strongly urges the army to establish a military post at some available and convenient point in the northern end of the Black Hills . . ." He paused, spread his arms, and looked around dramatically, making it clear that he meant Deadwood. "So that the rich natural resources of this country may be by the strong arms of the military forces fostered and protected from the ravages of the Sioux and their kindred tribes! It is strongly hoped as well that the presence of your valiant troops will force the murderous bands of redskins who surround the area to sue for peace and nevermore plague our fine citizens with threats of mutilation and death!"

A thunderous response greeted the judge's speech. Even though plenty of different dangers lurked in the Black Hills, everyone regarded the Indians as the worst. The crowd in the street pounded their hands together and shouted their approval of the judge's words at the top of their lungs.

Dan knew good and well that General Crook didn't have the authority to make any sort of commitment to these folks. Any decision regarding the establishment of a fort in the Deadwood area would come from the War Department in Washington. But Crook smiled anyway as he reached out with his left hand to take the petition from Miller and used his right to shake hands with the judge, and then with Mayor Farnum.

Crook turned to the crowd again and held up the petition. "Ladies and gentlemen of Deadwood!" he said as quiet descended. "I thank you for the keen interest you have shown in military affairs, and you have my solemn word that your wishes will be considered! I shall personally present your petition to my superiors and urge them to give it their strongest consideration! In the meantime, however, I believe the most prudent course of action for you to take would be to see to the setting up of citizen militias, so that in times of trouble you can band together and present a united front against your enemies! In this way you can best protect yourselves from any threats that arise!"

"But that's what the army's supposed to do!" a man called out from somewhere in the crowd. Several others shouted agreement with him, and the hubbub threatened to grow until Mayor Farnum stepped to the edge of the boardwalk and shouted, "Hush up now, and let the general talk!"

Crook nodded his thanks to the mayor and then addressed the crowd again. "The gentleman who spoke is absolutely correct! And you can rest assured that the army will always direct its utmost efforts toward the goal of keeping this nation's citizens safe and secure, wherever they may be! To that end, my command will remain bivouacked in Deadwood for the time being!"

That was telling the people what they wanted to hear, thought Dan, without really promising them anything. And judging from the renewed cheering and applause, Crook's words satisfied the crowd. Somebody started sawing on a fiddle, and someone else began singing a patriotic song. The singing spread in a hurry until half the people in the street were bellowing out the tune, mostly off-key.

Not Calamity Jane, though. She tugged on Dan's arm and shouted in his ear, "I done heard enough speechifyin'! Let's go back to the Gem and have another drink!"

That sounded all right to Dan. He nodded, jerked his head at LeCarde to indicate that they were leaving, and then followed Calamity as she stomped through the crowd again. Folks got out of her way, no doubt because of the smell that preceded her.

Dan was starting to get used to it, though . . . and that fact was almost as scary as a bunch of Sioux on the warpath, he reflected wryly.

As they approached the Gem, Dan glanced up and saw a glowing red dot in one of the second-floor windows above the boardwalk. After a moment he realized it was the lit end of a cigar, and as the dot grew redder and brighter, he knew that someone stood there smoking it. Since the window was open, whoever was there had probably been able to hear the general's speech without venturing into the mob of unwashed drunks. Pretty smart, if you asked him.

Then he and Calamity and Cougar Jack stepped up onto the boardwalk, and Dan didn't think anymore about whoever that was in the second-floor window. It was none of his business anyway.

Chapter Nine

AL Swearengen puffed on the cigar and watched the crowd break up in the street after General Crook's speech concluded. A lot of the people who had been listening to the general now headed for the Gem to wet their whistles, and Swearengen thought it was damned well about time they got back to drinking and spending money.

Of course, Crook's speech *had* been interesting . . . or rather, that petition Judge Miller presented to him had caught Swearengen's interest. The idea that the army might build a fort somewhere close to Deadwood hadn't occurred to him before tonight. His initial reaction was mixed. The army's presence meant more of a semblance of law and order in the area, and Swearengen wasn't sure he wanted that. Deadwood, after all, had been founded on a broken treaty with the Sioux and had done fairly well as an outlaw town. On the other hand, it would be good to finally have some protection from the redskins.

And most important, a fort full of soldiers nearby meant that many more customers for the Gem. Most of those bluebellies would find their way here sooner or later to guzzle his whiskey, gamble at his tables, and fuck his whores. That meant more money flowing into his pockets.

Like everything else in life, thought Swearengen, it was a trade-off. The potential profits justified the possible problems.

The question now was . . . what could he do to make sure the army decided to build a post here? He had heard what Crook said about presenting the petition to his superiors and urging them to consider the idea, but Swearengen knew better than to put any stock in what that windbag said. Crook was no different than any other officer, always looking to cover his own ass first and foremost.

A soft knock sounded on the door of his darkened office. He turned away from the window, teeth clenched on the stogie, and asked around it, "Who is it?"

"Arabella."

The melodious voice made Swearengen's eyebrows rise. He stepped to the desk, scratched a lucifer to life, and used it to light the lamp. As he lowered the glass chimney over the wick, he said, "Come in."

She opened the door and stepped into the room. She wore a dark blue dressing gown now instead of the red dress Swearengen had seen her wearing earlier, but she looked just as lovely as she had then. Her hair hung loose, too, instead of being up in its usual elaborate arrangement. That gave her an intimate air Swearengen found very arousing.

"One of the girls said you wanted to see me."

"That's right." Swearengen set the cigar aside in a cut-glass ashtray and then gestured at the dark brown leather chair in front of the desk. "Have a seat."

"I'd just as soon stand, thank you."

Her cool reserve infuriated him. He wanted to step around the desk, grab her by the arms, and give her a good shaking. Then he'd rip that dressing gown wide open so he could see her breasts and plunge his face between them and catch the hard nipples between his teeth . . .

"Suit yourself," he said as he forced that image out of

his mind. He could fuck any woman in the place, he told himself. He didn't need this uppity bitch. But he wasn't going to let her make a fool out of him. "I want to talk to you about this so-called arrangement we made."

"It's working out fine so far, it seems to me."

Swearengen grunted. "Well, it ain't working out fine for me. You're living under my roof, eating my food, drinking my booze, and you're not earnin' your keep. Hell, you look like you're ready to turn in, and the night's still young!"

Arabella shook her head and said, "I won't be working any more tonight."

"Why the hell not? Dan said you had a fish on the hook a while earlier."

"He got away," Arabella said with a cool, humorless laugh.

"Then go find somebody else who's willing to pay top dollar to screw you. There's got to be somebody downstairs with a hard dick and twenty bucks burnin' a hole in his pocket."

She came a step closer to the desk and said, "What would you have me do, Al? Go downstairs, open my gown, and say 'Come ahead, boys, climb on'?"

Swearengen glared at her. "You'd drum up a hell of a lot more business that way!"

She shook her head. "No. I'm sorry. That's not the way I conduct myself. If that's not satisfactory to you, I'll leave." She paused. "And for the record, I haven't drunk any of your liquor. I have my own." Her tone made it clear she thought the swill he served wasn't good enough for her.

Swearengen made a slashing motion with his hand. "I don't care about the damn booze. What happened with the fella you were with earlier? Dan said he started upstairs with you, then turned around and left. What'd you do to scare him off?"

That chilly laugh came from her again. "I didn't scare him off. He changed his mind. He's one of General Crook's officers and said that he had to attend the dinner being given for the general at the Grand Central Hotel tonight."

"He turned you down to go eat with a bunch of stuffed shirts?" Swearengen shook his head. "I'm startin' to think we made a bad deal."

"He'll be back," Arabella said, her voice firm with complete confidence. "And as a member of General Crook's staff, he'll be a good man to know."

Swearengen frowned in thought. She had a point there. If the man served on Crook's staff, that meant he had the general's ear. He might be able to influence the decision-making process when it came to that proposed fort, or at the very least provide inside information about what was going on.

But only if he returned to the Gem and Arabella could wrap him around her little finger, as she seemed certain she could do.

"What's this fella's name?" he asked.

"Major Stephen Ransome."

"Well, what makes you so fuckin' sure that Major Stephen Ransome is gonna come back?"

Arabella smiled. "I saw the look in his eyes. He was scared. He probably has a wife back East somewhere, some pale little nothing who'll only let him touch her once a year or so, if that often, and he doesn't like the idea of being unfaithful to her. But he wanted me. He'll be back."

Swearengen picked up the cigar and pointed it at her. "See to it. I want Ransome so hot for you that he'll do anything you tell him."

She gave him a shrewd look and said, "Something tells me this isn't just about how much money the major will have to pay for my favors."

"Just get him back here, get him in your bed, and keep him coming back," Swearengen said. "Whatever it takes."

RANSOME tossed and turned in his bed in the room he'd been given in the Grand Central Hotel. The bed was comfortable enough. His trouble sleeping came from another source. How could he relax and doze off when thoughts of Arabella filled his feverish brain?

Although comfortably furnished with a decent bed, a washstand, a small wardrobe, a chair, and a woven rug on the floor, the hotel room possessed one oddity: The walls that partitioned it off from the rooms on either side stopped a good foot short of the ceiling. Because of that, everyone staying in these rooms could hear the talking, coughing, farting, and shifting around in bed that went on in the other rooms. That kept Ransome from reaching down to his groin and relieving the insistent hardness that throbbed there. The thought that someone might hear him doing that mortified him.

He gritted his teeth to keep a groan of despair from welling out. A listener might think that he was abusing himself. And of course in a way he was, because the confusing mixture of thoughts in his head was nothing if not mental abuse.

All through dinner he had struggled with the memory of Arabella's beauty and grace. Afterward, during General Crook's speech to the citizens of Deadwood, she had still been much on his mind. Once the speech was over, the general and his staff had adjourned to Jack Langrishe's theater across the street, where Crook had spent a good hour shaking hands with the citizens and listening politely as they expressed their fear of the Indians and their hope that the army would build a fort nearby to protect the settlement. Finally, the troupe of entertainers featured at the theater had put on a variety show, which had been very well received by the officers.

Ransome hadn't paid much attention to the singing and dancing and dramatic orations, though. He'd been too preoccupied by what had happened earlier in the evening.

His decision to leave the Gem without going upstairs with Arabella had caused mixed emotions. On the one hand, he felt that he had done the morally correct thing by not betraying his marriage vows. On the other hand, when, if ever, would he get another chance to experience the joys of lovemaking with a creature as exquisite as Lady Arabella? And there was no denying that his wife, Louisa, no matter how much he loved her, was something of a cold fish.

As he lay there in the hotel room, he remembered the last time he had tried to make love with Louisa, how she had turned away from him in their bed and lay there stiffly, ignoring his caresses and entreaties until in a fit of anger and frustration he had gotten up and gone to sleep in one of the spare rooms in their Boston home. She had fended off his advances with a variety of excuses all during his leave, until finally it was nearly over and they had one last opportunity to indulge in the pleasures of the flesh.

That night Louisa had offered no excuses. Her chilly attitude made it plain enough that she simply no longer desired him. At moments such as that, he had to wonder if she had ever felt any real passion for him. She had always had a certain reserve about her, as if she were unwilling to give herself fully to him and share in the great passion he felt for her.

A shudder went through Ransome. He wanted Louisa even now, despite everything, despite the feelings that Arabella had aroused in him. If he truly thought that there was any real hope of a revival of his wife's desire for him . . .

But he could think of no evidence to support such a hope, based on the times they had been together in recent years . . . and his mind kept returning to the fact that he might never again have the chance to be with someone like Arabella, with her soft, silky fair hair, her beautiful heart-shaped face, her exquisitely curved body . . . Then, too, there was the fact that while she was no ordinary saloon whore, she no doubt possessed a wealth of experience when it came to the amatory arts. From time to time he had unusual . . . urges . . . that he had never dared even express to Louisa, let alone ask that she permit him to indulge them. In all likelihood, things like that wouldn't shock Arabella, whether she agreed to them or not. Ransome ground his fists against his temples as he thought about Arabella kneeling before him on elbows and knees with her creamy, perfectly rounded buttocks thrust into the air, the puckered aperture between them awaiting his gentle but filling thrusts. . . .

The hell with it, thought Ransome as he reached down and grasped his erect member, pumping it as slowly and quietly as he could. He hoped that no one in the neighboring rooms would hear him and know what he was doing, but at this moment, with that wanton, obscene image of Arabella filling his mind, he was beyond really caring.

"I have to have some relief," he whispered to himself. "Whatever it takes."

BRUNDAGE, Hollis, and Lamont wound up in a tiny, hole-in-the-wall saloon called Kilroy's. The place had only two tables. The three troopers occupied one of them while a pair of drunken prospectors snored at the other. The bald, fat, slovenly man behind the bar mopped the planks with a dirty rag and ignored his customers. Brundage and his companions had a bucket of beer on the table between them and dipped tin cups in it from time to time.

Lamont downed the beer he had in his cup, belched, and grunted. "I say we bushwhack that son of a bitch Ryan. Anything more'n a bullet in the back'd be too good for that motherfucker."

"Do that and you'll have the law down on you, as well as Crook," Brundage warned.

"Not if they don't know who done it!" Lamont dipped up some more beer. "Anyway, they ain't got no real law here in Deadwood. There's a town marshal, but ever'body says he's a no-account. They ain't got around to havin' an election for sheriff yet. Now, if Wild Bill was still alive and wearin' a star, like he did in Abilene, it'd be different. Him, I'd worry about."

Hollis put in, "Hell, Hickok was half blind when he got himself killed, from what I hear. He was old and careless, that's for damned sure, elsewise he wouldn't have let that fella get behind him like that."

"You two are wasting your breath," Brundage told them. "Hickok's dead, so he don't have anything to do with this. What we have to figure out is what we're gonna do about Ryan."

"And Ransome," Lamont reminded him.

"I ain't forgot about Ransome," Brundage said. "We may have to let it go, what he did, though."

Lamont scowled. "I don't like the sound o' that."

"I don't much care for it either, but I think it's more important that we get our hands on enough money to rattle our hocks and shake the dust of this place—and the army—off our boots."

"How we gonna do that?"

Brundage lifted his cup and drank. "I've been thinkin' about that," he said as he lowered the cup and smiled. "Dan Ryan's gonna help us."

"Ryan?" Lamont snorted in disgust. "He's already helped us once, right into the fuckin' stockade. What makes you think he'd lift a finger to help us do anything?"

"He won't have any choice." Brundage leaned forward and lowered his voice. The other two hitched their chairs closer to hear him. "You remember a soldier named Jessup? Ezra Jessup?"

Lamont's scowl darkened, as if trying to remember made his brain hurt. Hollis recalled the name, though. "Crazy little pissant?" he said. "Always on the prod, and would argue with a noncom or even an officer, even though he was just an enlisted man?"

"That's him," Brundage said with a nod.

"I sorta recollect him now," Lamont rumbled.

"What about him?" Hollis asked. "Somethin' happened to him while we were posted at Fort Lincoln, didn't it? He got killed in a robbery in town or somethin' like that?"

"That's what everybody thought. His body was found in an alley across the river in Bismarck, with his neck broke and his pockets empty. The local law found out he'd been drinkin' mighty heavy in one of the saloons earlier that night and figured somebody followed him out and jumped him."

Hollis shook his head. "I don't see what Jessup's got to do with Ryan."

"That's what I'm tryin' to explain to you. I never told you fellas about this—"

"Why not?" Lamont broke in. "We ain't got no secrets from each other."

"I didn't figure it made any difference. Now, just let me finish."

"Yeah, yeah, go ahead," Lamont grumbled.

"I was over in Bismarck the night Jessup was killed," Brundage said. "So was Ryan. Those two had had a dustup earlier in the day when Jessup didn't do something to suit Ryan. Ryan chewed him out in front of the whole company."

Hollis scratched his jaw. "I kinda remember that."

"It made Jessup furious, and he swore he'd get back at Ryan. He drank himself a gutful of courage that night, and when he spotted Ryan he followed him and tried to knife him when Ryan cut through that alley on his way back to the fort."

"Son of a bitch!" Hollis said. "So it was Ryan who really killed him?"

Brundage nodded. "That's right. I saw the whole damn thing. I was hopin' Jessup would gut the bastard like a carp, since we'd already had our own run-in with Ryan. But instead Ryan threw him across the alley and Jessup got his neck broke. Ryan left him there, dead."

"What did you do?"

Brundage sat back in his chair and grinned. "Emptied Jessup's pockets so it'd look like a robbery."

"I don't get it," Lamont said with a shake of his shaggy head. "Why'd you do that?"

"Think about it," Brundage said. "Ryan had something on us, because he knew we were tied in with that plan to steal those rifles. But I had something on him. He'd killed an enlisted man. Unless he went to the law and confessed—something I didn't figure he'd do—I planned to hold that killin' over him and make him leave us alone." Brundage's shoulders rose and fell in a shrug. "But it was the very next day we got arrested, so I never got to use what I knew against Ryan."

Lamont thumped a hamlike fist down on the rickety table. "Shit! You should'a told when Ryan tipped off the brass about our plan. He had it comin' for sellin' us out that way!"

"It wouldn't have changed the case against us," Brundage argued. "It was too late for that. And I thought maybe it'd come in handy sometime in the future." He tapped his temple. "I'm what you call a forward thinker. By keepin' my mouth shut then, we've got somethin' to use against Ryan now and make him do whatever we want."

Hollis didn't look convinced. "This is too much like the business with Ransome, and you saw what happened with that. He told us to go to hell, and likely Ryan will, too. It's just your word against his, Clyde."

"Maybe so, but Ryan's a civilian now. My word might not stand up in a court-martial, but Ryan lives here and he won't want the word gettin' around that he busted the neck of an enlisted man and never reported it. That'd make him look mighty bad. And the army might still want to question him about it." Brundage shrugged again. "Anyway, it can't hurt anythin' to try to get his help."

"His help in what?" Hollis wanted to know.

"The robbery that's gonna make us all rich men." Brundage grinned. "Think about all the money that passes through this settlement. We're gonna cut ourselves in for some of it, enough so we can put the army a long way behind us and make a new start for ourselves somewhere else. Mexico, maybe."

A faraway look came into Lamont's eyes. "Mexico," he said. "I'd like that. I got a taste for that tequila, and I always did like them little greaser gals."

Always practical, Hollis didn't let thoughts of fiery liquor and warm brown flesh distract him. Instead, he asked, "What are we going to rob?"

"I'll have to think on that some more," Brundage admitted. "But it's a good idea, I tell you. We'll wind up rich men."

"But Ryan gets away with what he done to us before," Lamont protested.

Brundage shook his head. "Hell, no. He won't know it until it's too late, but Ryan's gonna take the blame for whatever we do. Don't you worry, he'll get ever'thin' that's comin' to him." He reached for the bucket of beer. "Whatever it takes."

Chapter Ten

DAN woke up alone, as he always did, in his tent the next morning. The night before, he had finally been able to get away from Calamity Jane and Cougar Jack LeCarde as they meandered from saloon to saloon, drinking. Where they had wound up, and whether it had been together or alone, Dan didn't know and didn't want to know. Such things were none of his business.

After splitting off from the other two, he had considered going down to the Badlands, the area adjacent to Deadwood's Chinese quarter where the cribs were located. The girl Ling, who had worked for Laurette Parkhurst, had started calling herself the China Doll and gone into business for herself since the Parkhurst woman's disappearance. She was sweet . . . for a whore . . . but she had been close to Bellamy and eventually Dan had decided that he just wouldn't feel right about going to bed with her. He'd headed back up the gulch to his claim instead.

No one had bothered him, though he'd been ready for trouble, riding with his Colt loose in its holster and a Winchester across the saddle in front of him. By the time he reached the claim, the liquor he'd put away during the evening had started to catch up with him, so as soon as he'd tended to his horse he had stumbled into his tent, rolled up in his soogans without ever lighting a candle, then gone right to sleep.

As awareness stole over him, he cracked an eye open a little and saw sunlight slanting in through the gap between the canvas flaps of the tent's entrance. He groaned. He had slept later than usual. Most mornings he was up before the sun, boiling coffee and rustling some grub for a quick breakfast before taking up pick and shovel and going to work on the steeply slanting wall of the gulch behind the tent. All day long he would chip and gouge at the rock, his eyes searching for the faintest glint of color. He had found numerous nuggets that way in the past three months, but none had been bigger than his thumbnail.

Well, he'd just get a late start on the day's work, he told himself. He could already tell that his head ached. Maybe he'd linger a little longer than usual over his coffee, try to get to feeling better before he started swinging that damned pick.

A rancid smell filtered into his nostrils, and something moved between him and the light.

Dan's eyes snapped open wide. He should have been alone in the tent. For half a second, a couple of terrible possibilities filled his mind. A bear could have gotten into his tent, searching for food, although it was unlikely a bear could have come into camp without spooking his horse. Or Calamity Jane could have followed him out here, still looking for some loving. Dan didn't know which would be more frightening: a hungry grizzly or a horny Calam.

Turned out the intruder was even worse than either of those two. A Sioux warrior loomed above him, face painted for war, knife upraised and ready to plunge down into his heart.

Hung over or not, Dan's instincts took over. With a startled *"Yaaaahhhh!"* he burst out of his soogans and tackled the Indian just as the knife started down toward him. He felt the blade rip through his shirt and scrape along his back, leaving a line of fiery pain behind it as he crashed into the warrior.

But the sharp steel didn't penetrate his body. Instead, the collision between the two men sent the Sioux falling over backward in an out-of-control tumble. Dan and the Indian both sprawled through the tent flaps and onto the rocky ground outside. Dan heard the soft, bubbling music of Deadwood Creek flowing over its pebbled bed a few yards away, and the peaceful sound provided a sharp contrast to the grunts of effort and puffs of breath as the men struggled for their lives.

The Indian had hung on to the knife when Dan tackled him. He slashed at Dan's face with it, and Dan jerked back just in time to avoid the blade. He lunged and got both hands on the wrist of the hand that held the knife. As he tried to wrestle it away, the Sioux balled his other hand into a fist and slammed it against the side of Dan's head.

He was already in bad enough shape from the booze. Getting punched in the head like that made his skull feel like it was about to explode. Sickness roiled in his belly. He held on for dear life, though, and pushed with his knees until he had lifted himself far enough to lower his head and butt the Indian in the face. At the same time, he dug a knee into his opponent's groin. The son of a bitch didn't seem to feel either blow, Dan thought. He just kept fighting.

Dan didn't dare let go to throw a punch of his own. His survival depended on keeping that knife at bay. The Indian tried to claw at Dan's eyes. Dan lowered his head, burying it against the greasy buckskin shirt the Sioux wore. He had smelled the rancid bear grease from the shirt and the man's skin as he woke up.

As he struggled with the Indian, Dan wondered where the rest of the war party could be. Surely this lone warrior hadn't attacked by himself. Dan expected to feel a lance pierce his back or a war club crush his skull at any second. Nothing of that sort happened, though. Dan kneed the

Indian in the balls again. What the hell were they made of, granite?

This wasn't the first Indian fight Dan had been in, of course. But most of the others had been fought at more of a distance, firing a carbine from horseback or the cover of some rocks. Struggling up close like this with a man doing his damnedest to kill you was terrifying. Dan's heart slugged so hard in his chest it threatened to bust out, and his pulse roared like thunder inside his head.

Then his stomach gave up the effort to control itself, and he puked all over the son of a bitch.

The Sioux had fought mostly in silence so far, but now he roared in fury and revulsion and writhed in Dan's grip, arching up off the ground with maddened strength. Dan tumbled to the side, toward the creek, as the Indian threw him off. His fingers slipped off the man's wrist.

Dan came to a stop on his back and clawed at the holster on his hip. His fingers found only emptiness. The revolver had slipped out of leather during the fight. And now the Indian was coming at him again, Dan's vomit dripping from his hate-twisted face, the knife poised to strike downward like the wicked fang of a snake.

A thunderclap roared.

Dan saw the black hole appear suddenly in the Sioux's forehead, saw the man's head jerk backward, and watched the crimson spray explode from the back of his head. The Indian's momentum carried him forward, but the knife slipped from nerveless fingers and thudded harmlessly to the ground. The warrior flopped down half on top of Dan, and as Dan looked over he saw that a fist-sized chunk of the Sioux's skull was missing. The white of shattered bone showed inside the wound, and grayish pink brain matter had been blown out around it, mixing with the blood. This wasn't the first time Dan had seen somebody with their brains blown out, but the awful sight still might have made him throw up if he hadn't already emptied his belly.

Shuddering, Dan pushed the corpse aside and slid out from under it. He rolled over, made it to his hands and knees, and stayed there a second, waiting for the dizziness to pass and shaking his head in an attempt to clear some of the cobwebs from it. When he thought he could stand up without falling down, he pushed himself to his feet. He heard the steady hoofbeats of a horse somewhere nearby and wanted to find his gun in case more trouble was headed for him.

"Take it easy, Dan," a familiar voice called. "It's just me."

Dan stopped searching for the Colt and scrubbed a hand over his face instead. He seemed to be looking through a haze of some sort, but after a moment his vision cleared and he saw Cougar Jack LeCarde riding toward him at a deliberate pace on a rangy buckskin gelding. The scout had a Sharps .50-caliber rifle cradled across the saddle in front of him. A tendril of powder smoke still wisped from the muzzle.

"You killed that Sioux?" Dan asked as Cougar Jack rode up to the camp and reined the buckskin to a halt.

"Seemed like the thing to do at the time," the scout drawled, "seein' as how he was about to stick you with that knife."

Dan glanced down the creek, trying to judge how far away Jack had been. "Must've been a hell of a shot, takin' him in the head like that."

"Was the only way I could make sure to drop him quick enough so that he wouldn't have a chance to stab you anyway," Cougar Jack replied with a shrug. He grinned. "'Course, I run the risk o' missin' him entire that way . . . but I didn't think it was that big a chance."

"And since it was *my* life you were risking . . ."

"That's right. He was far enough away I'd'a had plenty o' time to reload and have another go at him before he could get to me."

Dan chuckled, despite feeling like shit and having a gruesome corpse at his feet. Out here on the frontier, a man couldn't afford to dwell on the bad things. He had to put them aside and move on. Better the Sioux than him.

"You seen any o' his redskinned brethren around?" Cougar Jack asked.

"I didn't even know *he* was around until I woke up and found him in my tent, about to kill me. I reckon if there were any others, though, we would have known about it by now."

Jack swung down from the saddle. "Yeah, they likely would've made their presence known. It ain't all that common for one o' the varmints to be out raidin' alone, but it ain't unheard of neither." He hooked a toe under the dead man's shoulder and rolled him onto his back, then hunkered beside him to take a closer look. "Young fella. Prob'ly out to make a name for hisself by takin' a few scalps. Figured to impress ol' Crazy Horse or one o' the other chiefs."

"Instead, all he got is dead."

"Yep." With a grunt, Cougar Jack straightened. "Damn, these old bones don't wanna unkink like they used to when I was young. I'd give it all up and go find me a rockin' chair on a porch somewhere, if I didn't know that I'd blow my own brains out after a while."

Dan went over to the creek and dropped to his knees on the bank, crushing a couple of wildflowers under his knees. He used both hands to cup some of the icy water and bring it to his mouth. He rinsed and spat several times, until his mouth tasted a little less like a possum had crawled in there and died. Then he leaned over, took a good long drink, and finished by plunging his head into the water for a moment. He came up dripping and shaking, but at least his brain was clearer now.

As he stood up and sleeved some of the moisture from his face, he turned to his visitor and said, "I don't want you to think you're not welcome, Jack—"

"'Specially under the circumstances," the scout said with a meaningful nod toward the Sioux's body.

"Yeah. Anyway, what the hell are you doin' out here?"

"Came to ask you if you'd thought any more about what I suggested last night."

"About signing on as a scout for the army, you mean?"

Jack nodded. "That's right. I talked to Frank Grouard

about it this mornin'. He ramrods the scouts for Gen'ral Crook. He remembers you from when you was a sergeant in the Seventh, and he figures it's a good idea."

"Yeah, I know Frank," Dan said. "He's a good man." He changed the subject by adding, "Why don't I get a fire and some coffee going while you, uh, do something with . . ."

He looked at the corpse.

"Sure. I seen a nice deep ravine back there a ways."

LeCarde took a rope from his saddle, lashed the dead Sioux's feet together, then tied the other end of the rope to his horse. He mounted up and rode off slowly along the gulch, dragging the corpse behind him.

By the time Cougar Jack got back, Dan had found his Colt and gotten coffee boiling and bacon and flapjacks sizzling in a pan. His hangover had faded and he was actually hungry. Nothing like fighting for his life first thing in the morning to clear a man's head, he thought.

The two veteran frontiersmen sat beside the fire. "I already et," Jack said, "but I'll take a cup o' that Arbuckle's."

"You don't look like you feel sick this mornin'," Dan commented. "As much who-hit-John as you put away last night, your head should've exploded."

Jack laughed. "I always did have a holler leg where whiskey is concerned. It don't muddle me none. Good thing, too, or else I might've woke up this mornin' with Miss Cannary snuggled up next to me."

"What happened to her?" Dan felt some genuine fondness for Calamity Jane and hoped she was all right.

"After a while we ran into ol' Colorado Charley Utter, and he took her off my hands. You know Charley?"

Dan nodded. "Yeah. He's been lookin' after Calam since Wild Bill was killed."

"He said he'd take her to his wagon and let her sleep it off. They seemed like pretty good friends. Not like Calamity Jane usually has men friends, mind you. More like she was Charley's little sister or somethin'."

Dan understood, having seen the way Charley could handle Calamity in the past.

"Anyway, how about it?" Jack went on. "You ready to sign on with us?"

Dan grinned wryly and swept a hand at the rugged gulch around them. "What, and leave all this?"

"You think that yeller rock is gonna make you a rich man?" The scout spat. "Lemme tell you how gold huntin' works, Dan, 'case you ain't figured it out already. A few men get lucky and wind up rich as Midas. And I mean damn few. The rest of the poor devils who go to prospectin' either get killed by Injuns, freeze their balls off in a blizzard, or starve to death. You came damn close to the first one this mornin'. Gonna try for the other two?"

"I know what you mean," Dan said, his face solemn now, "but I still have to think about it some more. I've put in several months of work here, and I'm not sure I want to just abandon it."

"Well, don't think too long," Cougar Jack advised him. "You can't never tell how long the army's gonna be here. I know the folks in Deadwood are hopin' there'll be a permanent post, but I wouldn't count on that. Washington's liable to order Crook to go to chasin' Crazy Horse again."

"I'll make up my mind before that happens," Dan promised. "And if it does, some of the people around here are going to be mighty disappointed."

Chapter Eleven

~~

MAJOR Stephen Ransome knocked on the door of General Crook's room in the Grand Central Hotel, and when the general's voice bade him enter, he went in, saluted, and said, "You wanted to see me, sir?"

Crook sat at a table with a tray before him containing the remnants of his breakfast. He returned the salute, then pushed the tray aside, reached for a cup of coffee, and nodded as he lifted it. "That's right, Major. Have you eaten? If not, I can have another tray sent up. That colored woman who works in the kitchen here is as fine a cook as any I've encountered in quite some time."

"No, thank you, sir, I'm fine," Ransome replied. As a matter of fact, he *hadn't* eaten, but he didn't want anything either. Even though he hadn't indulged in all that many spirits the night before, his stomach felt a bit queasy this morning. He'd had some coffee in the dining room, but that was all he wanted.

"Sit down, then." Crook gestured toward one of the other chairs in the room. "I want to talk to you about that petition the judge presented to me last night."

Even though thoughts of Arabella had distracted Ransome, he recalled the incident of which the general spoke. The petition, which hundreds of the local settlers had signed in a short period of time, called on the army to establish a permanent post in the vicinity of Deadwood. Ransome asked, "What would you like me to do, sir?"

Crook frowned. "I find it very doubtful that the War Department will agree to the request put forward by those petitioners. The Sioux are already incensed enough that all these mining camps and boomtowns exist in the Black Hills, which they regard as sacred ground."

Ransome nodded and said, "Yes, sir." The general wasn't telling him anything that he didn't already know. Thinking about the situation provided a welcome distraction, however; otherwise he'd be spending all his time brooding about his troubles with his wife . . . and Arabella.

"The establishment of a permanent military post in this region would be a slap in the face to Crazy Horse, Sitting Bull, and the other chiefs," Crook went on. "Their reaction would likely be to stir up even more violence."

"Begging your pardon, sir," Ransome ventured, "but the Sioux and their allies have already massacred Colonel Custer and the Seventh Cavalry, and they continue their raids throughout Montana and the Dakota Territory. How much *more* angry could they get about a fort?"

"That's one way of looking at it," Crook admitted with a shrug. "However, I still doubt that the War Department will want to do anything that might increase hostilities even further. Sooner or later, there *will* be a negotiated peace between the army and the Indians. We simply can't kill *all* of them, and that's what it would take to settle this clash militarily."

"Another treaty that can be broken, sir?"

Crook's face hardened. "I'm going to pretend that I didn't hear you say that, Major."

"Thank you, sir," Ransome said with a chagrined nod.

Crook cleared his throat and went on. "At any rate, a fort is what the locals want, and I promised that their request would receive full consideration, whether I believe it will ever be acted upon or not. To that end, I want you to take a detail of troopers and investigate the surrounding area to determine the most suitable locations for such a fort."

The order took Ransome by surprise. "You want me to scout the countryside?"

"Exactly, Major."

It would never occur to Ransome to refuse to follow an order from a superior officer, especially the general in command of the entire campaign. But even as he nodded and said, "Of course, sir," a part of his brain realized that this whole thing was nothing but a sham. Crook knew that a fort wouldn't be established here, but he wanted to send Ransome out looking for a good place to put one anyway, simply so the citizens of Deadwood would know about it and think that the army took their wishes seriously.

It seemed like shabby behavior to Ransome, but the decision wasn't his to make. As he got to his feet, he asked, "Was there anything else, sir?"

"No, that's all, Major. You'll provide me with regular reports on your findings?"

"Of course, sir." He paused as a thought came to him. "Permission to recruit one of the locals who knows the area to provide assistance?"

Crook nodded. "That's an excellent idea. I don't have any funds available to pay such a person, however. It will have to be strictly a volunteer effort."

"I'll make that clear, sir." Ransome came to attention and saluted again, then left the room after Crook returned the salute and went back to drinking coffee.

Ransome still wore the civilian suit, but when he got back to his room he found that his uniform had been cleaned and delivered there. The Chinese laundry that had taken charge of the filthy uniforms had done a good job, he saw, leaving only a few small, hardly noticeable stains on the blue cloth. Ransome took off the suit and pulled on the uniform, and instantly he felt better. The assignment General Crook had given him was just what he needed, he told himself. It would get him out of Deadwood for the most part, so that he wouldn't be tempted to go into the Gem and see Arabella again. And having a task to perform, even a somewhat fraudulent one, would make him feel like a soldier again, as did the uniform. Now he could put those moments of weakness behind him and concentrate on his duty.

He clattered down the hotel stairs, crossed the lobby, and stepped out onto the boardwalk. Cool but sunny weather had descended on Deadwood. Winter would come roaring down out of the Canadian northland soon enough, but for now no one could ask for more pleasant conditions. It might actually be nice to go for a ride through the countryside, thought Ransome.

It would be even nicer if he could take Arabella along, perhaps with a picnic basket and a blanket that he would spread on the ground so she could stretch out on it and lift her skirts and open her legs for him . . .

Ransome stopped short and closed his eyes for a second. He had to keep thoughts like that from invading his head.

"You feelin' all right, Major?"

The voice came from behind him. He recognized it and thought, *Shit.*

Brundage.

As Ransome turned around, Brundage came to attention and lifted a stiff hand to the brim of his campaign cap. From the corner of his mouth, he hissed at Hollis and Lamont to indicate that they should follow suit. All three troopers stood there saluting as Ransome frowned at them and finally returned the salutes. "At ease," the major said.

Brundage snapped his arm down and then clasped his hands behind his back. "How are you this mornin', Major? Beggin' your pardon, but you look a mite peak-ed."

"I'm fine," Ransome said. "What are you three doing? Don't you have any duties to perform?"

"Uh, not right now, sir. Most of the boys're takin' it easy

after that long chase we been on, followin' the Sioux. I thought the general wanted us to rest up and get some good food for a change."

"Yes, that's right," Ransome said, frustration and impatience easy to hear in his voice and see on his face. "Go on about your business. I'm busy."

He started to turn away, but Brundage stopped him by saying, "Beggin' your pardon again, Major, but . . . permission to speak freely?"

Ransome sighed. "I suppose. What is it?"

"Well, sir, it's like this. I think the three of us got off on the wrong foot with you, back there at the Rosebud." Brundage had thought long and hard about this, and he'd decided that the best way to mollify any suspicions Ransome might still have would be to pretend to come clean. "It's true we were a mite shocked by what we saw there . . . you know, that, uh, tragic accident . . . but we figured out later you might've thought we were gonna try to hold it over you, and that ain't true. It's the furthest thing from the truth, is what it is."

Ransome frowned and gave a little shake of his head. "What the hell is it you're getting at, Brundage?"

"Just that we know we overstepped our boundaries, Major, and we want to apologize. Ain't that right, boys?"

Hollis and Lamont both nodded. Hollis even looked believable and sounded sincere as he said, "That's right." Lamont just glared and muttered, but that was his usual behavior and Ransome probably wouldn't think anything of it.

In fact, the major looked a little taken aback by the apologies. He said, "I appreciate those sentiments. Now, if that's all . . ."

"We'd sure like to make it up to you for the misunderstandin'," Brundage said.

"That's not necessary—"

"It'd make us feel better." Of course, Brundage reminded himself, there was no reason for an officer to give a damn how a private felt about anything, but Ransome was a weak sister. He liked to keep everybody happy, even the enlisted men. "If there's anything we can do to give you a hand . . ."

Ransome looked like he was thinking it over, and after a couple of seconds he said, "As a matter of fact, General Crook has just given me some new orders and told me to pick a detail of men to accompany me as I carry them out."

Brundage grinned and thumped himself on the chest with a fist. "We're your boys!" he said. "Tell us what to do, Major, and we'll sure do it."

Ransome explained the assignment, and while Brundage didn't much like the idea that they would be out of Deadwood most of the time, there could be advantages to that, too. Out in the wilderness, all sorts of accidents could happen, especially fatal ones.

He and his friends might get a chance to have their revenge on Ransome after all, thought Brundage.

"What I need to do now," Ransome concluded, "is find someone who knows the territory around here and would be willing to volunteer to serve as a scout for us. I'll let you know when we're ready to ride out."

"We'll be around, Major. Thanks for trustin' us."

The troopers saluted again. Ransome returned the salute and then strode off down the street. As the three of them watched him go, Lamont said, "Have you lost your fuckin' mind, Clyde? You said we was gonna get out o' the army, and now you got us a new job, workin' for that bastard Ransome at that!"

"I told you last night, I'm tryin' to think ahead."

Hollis said, "It seems more like your thinking is goin' around in circles, Clyde. First you say we have to forget about Ransome, then you go and volunteer to take on an assignment with him."

"An assignment that'll get us out of town, where nobody's around," Brundage pointed out. "Think about it. What if we was to run into a Sioux war party out there? Ransome might just wind up dead, even though the three of us got away from the Injuns."

Slowly, Hollis began to grin. "I think I see what you're gettin' at. If we say some redskin shot the major in the back, nobody would ever be able to prove otherwise."

Brundage just smiled. Once Ransome was dead, they could proceed with their main plan to make themselves rich and to finally have their revenge on Dan Ryan. Brundage was glad they had come to Deadwood. Things were starting to work out just fine.

AFTER being so hung over when he woke up—and then immediately being forced to fight for his life—Dan didn't really feel like working on his claim that day, so when Cougar Jack suggested that they both ride back into Deadwood, Dan agreed without much hesitation.

"You can talk to Frank," LeCarde said. "Maybe he can help you make up your mind about signin' on as a scout."

"Maybe." Dan had known Frank Grouard for a long time, although months or even years might pass between times that their trails crossed. That was common on the frontier.

The two men kept their eyes open as they rode up the gulch toward the settlement. In all likelihood, the Indian who had crept into Dan's tent to murder him had been acting alone, but he couldn't discount the possibility that a Sioux war party was in the area.

"What did you do with the body?" Dan asked. "If any of his people find it, they'll be mad as hell about him bein' dead."

Cougar Jack shook his head. "They won't find it 'less they dig out the whole side o' that ravine I tumbled down on top of it. All I had to do was start a couple o' rocks slidin', and they took care o' the rest."

"Well, we can hope it turns out that way," Dan said. "The Sioux don't need to be stirred up any more than they already are. Crazy Horse and Sitting Bull and the other old chiefs are going to fight to the death as it is."

"Maybe . . . maybe not. I've smoked a pipe or two with

those fellas. Been in their villages and rode out again with my hair still on my head, what little I got left of it. Even shared buffalo robes with Sioux squaws now and then. I can tell you, those old chiefs ain't fools. They know good an' well that they can run rings around us out on the prairie and even in the mountains. But runnin' rings around us ain't the same thing as *beatin'* us. That they'll never do, and they know it."

"They beat Custer a couple of months ago," Dan pointed out.

Cougar Jack waved a calloused hand in dismissal. "They jumped all over one glory hound who sometimes didn't have the sense God gave a badger! Killed a lot o' good men, too, but you know what? We got more. We got lots more. Crazy Horse is gonna run outta Sioux a hell of a long time 'fore the War Department runs outta soldiers. The Sioux are the best fighters I ever saw, 'cept for the Comanch', but that don't matter when you're outnumbered thousands to one."

What the old scout said made sense, Dan thought. "Are you sayin' that there'll be a real treaty one of these days, one that ends the fighting?"

"I'd bet a hat there will be. The redskins will all come in and give up their arms and go to the reservations. Be a damned shame in a way. Injuns never have been the sort o' noble savages folks back East like to think they are. They're the orneriest bunch I ever saw, and each tribe treats the other tribes as bad or worse than we ever did. But damn it, it was their choice to be that way, and I ain't sure we got the right to tell 'em to be different."

"But you'll help the army hunt them down anyway."

"Oh, hell, yeah. I draw my pay and I do my job. Sometimes I can't help but miss the frontier the way it used to be 'fore we decided to civilize it, though."

Dan supposed he might feel the same way if he had started out as a fur trapper forty years earlier, as Cougar Jack had, and had seen things in what the old-timers called the Shining Times. But he hadn't, and he couldn't change that any more than Jack could change the passing of the old ways.

They reached Deadwood a short time later, and as they rode slowly down Main Street, a tall, sandy-haired cavalry officer hailed Jack and stepped down from the boardwalk to come toward them. Jack reined in, and Dan did likewise. He thought he recalled seeing the major on the porch of the Grand Central Hotel with General Crook the night before, but he wasn't sure about that.

"Mr. LeCarde," the officer greeted them after he had detoured around a few puddles, stumps, and piles of horse shit to reach them. "If you have a moment, I could use some advice."

"Sure thing, Major," Jack said. "By the way, this here is Dan Ryan. Used to be a sergeant in the Seventh Cavalry. Dan, Major Ransome."

"Howdy," Dan said with a nod. "Good to meet you, Major."

"Sergeant," Ransome said. "I take it you're retired."

"Yes, sir." Dan chuckled. "I had some crazy notion that I'd come here to the Black Hills and make my fortune hunting for gold."

"Some people have accomplished that."

"Damn few," Dan said, remembering what Cougar Jack had said earlier.

Ransome turned back to the scout and said, "I'm looking for someone who's familiar with the territory around here to assist in a mission General Crook has given me. Since you seem to be acquainted with someone everywhere we go, when I saw you riding in, it occurred to me that you might know a suitable person here in Deadwood."

Cougar Jack frowned at him. "Hell, no offense, Major, but weren't you *listenin'* just now?" He waved a hand at Dan. "Here's your man, right here!"

"Hold on a minute," Dan said. "I didn't—"

Jack ignored him and went on, "Like I told you, Dan used to be a sergeant, so he knows the army and its ways back'ards and for'ards. And he's been prospectin' in these parts for several months now, so I reckon he knows the territory. What's the chore the gen'ral gave you?"

"I'm to scout out suitable locations for a military post in this area."

Cougar Jack threw his hands in the air. "Well, there you go! Dan's been to most o' the forts west o' the Mississippi, I expect, so he'll know what sort o' place you need. Sounds like a match made in heaven, if you ask me."

"You would seem to be a good choice, Mr. Ryan, if you don't mind neglecting your diggings for a few days," Ransome said.

"Shoot, he was thinkin' about givin' up his claim anyway and joinin' us as a civilian scout," Jack said. "Ain't that right, Dan?"

"I'm considering it," Dan said. "I haven't made up my mind yet."

"This'd give you a chance to think on it."

Ransome nodded and said, "Indeed it would. How about it, Mr. Ryan? Even though I can't offer you any wages, if you volunteer you'd be performing a service for General Crook and the army, as well as doing me a personal favor."

"Well, I reckon if you put it that way . . ." Dan felt a familiar pang and recognized it as something he thought he had put behind him: the call of duty. "I suppose I could take a few days and help you out."

"That's splendid!" Ransome said. "When can you leave?"

Dan shrugged. "Any time you want. I don't have anything on my plate right now."

"That's fine. There are three troopers who will be going with us as an armed escort. I'll find them and let them know we'll be riding out in, say, a quarter of an hour?"

Dan nodded his agreement.

"Meet us down at Clarke's Livery," Ransome went on. "That's where my horse is stabled."

"I'll be there," Dan promised.

"You're welcome to come along, too, if you'd like, Mr. LeCarde."

Cougar Jack scratched his beard-stubbled jaw. "Is that an order, Major?"

"No, not at all, just an invitation."

"Then I reckon I'll pass, if that's all right with you. Been a long time since I visited a town, and I ain't had my fill o' liquor an' women yet."

Dan thought Ransome winced a little at that comment, but he couldn't be sure. He wondered if Ransome might be one of those straitlaced types, an officer who didn't believe in drinking or whoring or even cussing.

You ran into that sort every now and then, even in a place like Deadwood.

Chapter Twelve

RANSOME worried that he'd have to hunt through every squalid dive and sordid crib in the settlement to find Brundage, Hollis, and Lamont, but the three troopers were at the big camp on the edge of the settlement, caring for their horses, when he walked up.

"I'm glad to see that you're tending to your mounts," he told them. "Saddle up and get ready to ride. We're leaving shortly. I've secured the services of a local prospector to help us look around the area."

He didn't mention that Dan Ryan had been a sergeant in the Seventh Cavalry. It didn't seem relevant.

"We'll be ready to go, Major," Brundage said. "One thing, though . . ."

"What is it?"

"What do you think the chances are that we'll run into any hostiles?"

"Given the amount of trouble they've caused around here, I'd say it's possible," Ransome admitted, and he felt a little shiver of fear go through him as he did so.

He didn't possess the sort of audacious bravery that

some cavalry officers did, a bravery that Ransome considered to be foolhardy, in all honesty, but neither did he consider himself a coward. He could fight when he needed to and had demonstrated as much. But only a lunatic wouldn't be wary of an encounter with the Sioux.

"However, from what I've heard," he went on, "they usually attack small groups, often one or two men alone. The local minister was walking by himself to a neighboring camp when he was killed last month. Since there'll be five of us, and we'll be well armed, I think the odds of the savages bothering us are slim."

"I hope you're right, Major. I'd hate to meet up with any o' those bushwhackin' savages."

Ransome gave them a curt nod, then went back to the livery stable where he told one of the hostlers to prepare his horse for riding. There was nothing else left to do except wait for Ryan and the troopers to show up.

His gaze strayed diagonally across the street toward the Gem Theater. Even though it was only midmorning, men went in and out of the place fairly regularly. Ransome supposed that the Gem did a brisk business at all hours of the day and night. Men never tired of drinking, gambling, and fucking. He found the idea of being with a woman in broad daylight appealing. Louisa had never allowed that. She even preferred to blow out all the lamps in their bedroom before she would allow him to touch her.

Once again an image of Arabella sprang into his mind. He saw her lying nude on a fourposter, sunlight slanting in through gauzy window curtains so that it made shifting patterns over her beautiful body as she waited for him to come to her. The curtain billowed slightly from a warm breeze that caressed his face as he walked slowly toward the bed and Arabella smiled and lifted her arms to him. "Stephen," she whispered. "Oh, Stephen . . ."

"Major Ransome?"

A second went by before he realized with stunning force that the sweet, melodious voice he heard was real, not just his imagination. He gasped and snapped his head around to see her standing there just a few feet away, a slightly puzzled smile on her lovely face as she held a parasol that protected her face from the glare of the sun. She wore a flat-crowned straw hat with a pink ribbon on it and a white dress dotted with little flowers. The outfit imparted a freshness and innocence to her that belied what he really knew about the woman.

"Lady Arabella!" he said. His ears grew warm and he hoped that he wouldn't start blushing brightly. If he did, surely she would know what he'd been thinking about just now.

"You don't have to call me that," she told him. "I know some of the men do, but really, Arabella is just fine."

"It seems awfully . . . familiar."

"I don't mind *you* being familiar with me, Major."

The light in her blue eyes threatened to blind him like the light of a thousand suns. No, a thousand galaxies. He said, "If I'm to call you Arabella, then you . . . you should call me Stephen."

"I'd like that . . . Stephen. It's a fine name." She looked past him at the hostler as the man brought up his horse. "Are you about to go riding?"

"I . . . Yes." He thought about how wonderful it would be to go riding with her and asked, "Do you ride?"

"A little. I hope you won't think any less of me, you being a dashing cavalryman and all, but I really prefer a buggy. There's nothing better than a nice buggy ride in the country, perhaps with a picnic. . . ."

Oh, Lord! She had read his mind somehow. Did that mean she knew the other things he had thought?

"Perhaps the two of us could go for a ride sometime," she went on.

"Yes, I . . . I'd like that." He cursed himself for being such a stammering fool around her. No woman had ever affected him like this before. "I . . . I can't right now, though. I have orders from General Crook."

"A military assignment?"

"That's right." He knew that he probably shouldn't share the details with a civilian, but they tumbled out of his mouth anyway. He told her all about how he was supposed to scout the area for suitable locations for a fort, and as he talked he decided that perhaps revealing his assignment to her was a good thing after all. General Crook wanted the citizens of Deadwood to know what he was doing, so they would think that the army took their little petition seriously. So he wasn't *just* a blithering, love-struck idiot, Ransome told himself.

Love? He had known from the first instant he saw her that he wanted Arabella, that she aroused serious feelings of lust in him. But love? That was reserved for his wife, wasn't it?

Maybe. Maybe not.

"I hope the army does put a fort here," she said when he was finished with his explanation. "Maybe you'd be posted there, and I could see you more often."

"That would be . . . wonderful," he said, not caring anymore how he sounded because the feelings he had for her had made him too confused.

"You'll be back this evening?" she asked.

"Oh, I should certainly think so. We won't be going so far outside the settlement that we can't return by evening."

"I'll see you at the Gem, then?"

Now was his chance to tell her that, no, he wouldn't be coming to the Gem anymore. That it wouldn't be wise. That he had a wife and family in Boston, and that he was a good man who didn't frequent saloons and brothels and associate with whores, no matter how beautiful they were.

But then she smiled again, and he heard himself saying words he had never intended to say.

"Yes," he told her. "I'll be there."

SINCE Dan had a few minutes before Major Ransome would be ready to leave, he stopped at the store operated by Seth Bullock and Solomon Star to buy more cartridges for his rifle and revolver, both of which took .45-caliber rounds. The thickly mustached Seth Bullock stood behind the counter and greeted Dan with a solemn smile. Bullock was friendly enough, but he usually had a stern demeanor about him, emphasized by the sober, dark suit he always wore.

Dan asked for a box of .45 cartridges. "Fixing to do some hunting, Dan?" Bullock asked as he took the cardboard box off a shelf.

"You could say that. I'm gonna help one of General Crook's officers look for a good place around here to put a fort."

Bullock's eyebrows rose. "Really? That's good to hear. I signed that petition the judge circulated, you know. Deadwood's getting to be a real town, and we can use the protection of the army."

"When I first came here a few months ago, you never would've thought Deadwood would be anything except a bunch of tents and tar-paper shacks. It's changed a hell of a lot in not much time."

Bullock nodded. "Sol and I have only been here a little more than a month, and I can see plenty of changes just in that long. Including this store, of course. We sold our goods out of a big tent and the backs of our wagons when we started out. Now the town's even got a board of street and health commissioners. I just got elected to it."

"Really?" Dan said. "Congratulations, I guess. I wouldn't want to have the job of trying to set up any sort of town government."

Bullock lowered his voice to a confidential level. "There's talk about having an election for a real sheriff, and some of my friends want to nominate me for the job. I was sheriff of Lewis and Clark County over in Montana a few years ago, and folks around here have sort of been relying on me to keep the peace already."

"Well, you've got my vote, if it comes to that," Dan

assured him. He knew that Bullock was doing a little politicking, but that was all right. A good sheriff had to be a combination of peace officer and politician, and Dan thought Seth Bullock would be well suited for the job.

He paid for the cartridges and left the store, then walked down the street to the Grand Central Hotel. Since he'd be out of town at midday with Major Ransome, he would need something to eat, and he thought he knew where to get it.

Lou Marchbanks answered his knock at the kitchen door in the rear of the hotel. He thought he saw a flash of pleasure in her eyes when she recognized him, but she instantly turned wary. Ever since she had told him that their budding romance was over, they had been mostly avoiding each other. Now she said, "Hello, Dan. What are you doin' here?"

He didn't answer the question right away. Instead, he said, "You're lookin' mighty nice, Lou."

That wasn't empty flattery. Lou Marchbanks was a mighty handsome woman, no matter what color she was. Even now, with a few tendrils of hair escaping from the bun she'd gathered at the back of her head and beads of sweat on her face from the heat of the kitchen where she was already preparing dinner for the hotel's guests, Dan thought she was one of the prettiest women he had ever seen.

"Go on with you, Dan Ryan," she told him. "I don't believe a word outta that Irish mouth o' yours. What do you want?"

"I, uh, I'm gonna be on the trail in the middle of the day today, and I didn't bring anything to eat with me, so I thought—"

"You thought you'd come by here and cadge somethin' from me, is that it?"

He had to grin as he admitted, "Well, yeah."

She frowned at him for a moment, but then a smile began to pluck at the corners of her mouth. "Just so happens I got some biscuits left over from breakfast, and I can slice up some o' the roast I already cooked for today's dinner."

"That sounds wonderful," he told her.

"You wait right there. I'll go fill up a gunnysack for you."

He would have preferred to come inside the kitchen and talk to her some more while she was getting the food ready, but he didn't want to do anything to anger her or make her feel uncomfortable. If she wanted to keep some distance between them, that was fine. Of course, if he took that scouting job with the army, there would be even more distance between them. No telling when—or if—he would get back to Deadwood either.

Maybe he ought to let Lou know that he was thinking about it, he decided. Not that he figured it would make any real difference in the way she felt, but still . . .

When she came back with the sack full of biscuits and roast beef, he thanked her for it and then said, "The fellas who have been doing the scoutin' for General Crook have asked me to join them, Lou."

"You mean to join the army again?"

He shook his head. "No, I'd be working for the army, but I'd still be a civilian."

She thought about it for a moment, and as usual, he couldn't read her expression. Finally she said, "That'd mean when the army leaves Deadwood, you'd have to go with 'em."

"That's right."

If he'd thought—or hoped—that she might tell him not to go, he would have been disappointed. She gave him a slight smile and said, "Then I wish you all the luck in the world, Dan. I been thinkin' about leavin' Deadwood myself."

That news took him by surprise. "Where are you going?"

"The superintendent out at the Father De Smet mine wants me to take over the cookin' for his crew. That's a big outfit, one o' the biggest in the Black Hills, and they'd pay me more'n what Mr. Wagner's payin' me here at the Grand Central."

"Well . . . well, you should take the job, then!" Dan managed to say. This really was a parting of ways for them, he realized. If he went off scouting with the army and Lou went to work for the De Smet mine, it meant the end of what was between them.

But it had already ended, he reminded himself. Right or wrong, the two of them could never be together. The sooner he accepted that, the better. Lou seemed to have already come to that understanding.

Not that he didn't see some regret on her face. Maybe if they'd been in another time, another place, things would have been different. They could be sorry about that, but they couldn't change it.

"You watch out for yourself, you hear?" she told him. "I don't want to hear that no red savage done lifted your hair."

"I'll be careful," he promised. "Good luck with your new job, if you take it."

"Thanks." She held out her hand. "Good-bye, Dan."

He took her hand, feeling the warm strength in the fingers, and wished he could hold on to it forever. "Good-bye," he said, his voice husky.

Then he let go of her, turned away, and left the rear of the hotel as quickly as he could. Lingering wouldn't do either of them a damned bit of good.

Carrying the gunnysack, he retrieved his horse from the hitch rack in front of Bullock & Star where he had left it and headed for the stable at a fast walk. More than a quarter hour had passed, he estimated, and he would probably find Major Ransome and the escort waiting impatiently for him when he got there.

That proved to be the case. Major Ransome and three blue-clad cavalry troopers stood in front of the barn holding their mounts. The horses were in the way so that Dan couldn't see the soldiers very clearly at first, but as he came closer they turned toward him and he felt a shock of recognition go through him.

"Shit!" he exclaimed in surprise as Clyde Brundage, Dewey Lamont, and Matt Hollis all said the same thing.

Chapter Thirteen

AL Swearengen was inside the Gem, standing at the bar talking to Dan Dority, when Arabella came in. The saloon wasn't too busy at this time of the morning, but a few drinkers lounged at the bar, a couple of poker games were going on, and upstairs three gents were getting their ashes hauled.

Swearengen was thinking about doing that himself. He had drunk too much the night before and had a pounding headache. A good fuck probably wouldn't cure what ailed him . . . but it wouldn't hurt anything either.

He grunted in surprise when he saw Arabella daintily push the batwings aside. He hadn't seen her all morning. "Figured you were upstairs asleep," he said as she came over to him carrying a parasol, of all things.

"I've been out working," she said.

"Tryin' to hustle up business on the street? I had you pegged for better than that."

Her eyes glittered with irritation as she said, "I was talking to Major Ransome. Do you know what he's going to be doing today?"

Swearengen motioned for Dority to pour him a drink. If he couldn't get any pussy right now, at least he could have a little hair of the dog. "I don't have any earthly idea," he said in reply to Arabella's question.

"He's taking a detail of troopers and scouting the area for suitable locations for a fort."

Swearengen lifted his eyebrows and looked at her in astonishment. "How the fuck did you manage to arrange that already? I just told you last night to start workin' on Ransome." He grabbed up the shot glass Dority had filled with whiskey and gulped down the liquor.

Arabella laughed softly. "I could tell you that I'm just that good, I suppose. But the truth is that Stephen had already been given the orders by General Crook when I talked to him."

"Stephen, eh?" Swearengen repeated. "Sounds like you're gettin' pretty close to the son of a bitch already. I like that."

"We're going for a buggy ride in the country one of these days," she said with a smile.

"I don't care if you fuck him in a wagon bein' pulled by a twenty-mule team. I don't care if you fuck the mules. Just see that he does everything he can to get that fort established here."

"I think it's safe to say that he'll do his best in that regard. I already dropped several hints that he and I could be together more often if there was a fort nearby and he was posted at it."

Swearengen nodded. "Good. Damned good."

"I suppose that's as close to a thank-you as I'm going to get from you," Arabella said in a cool voice.

"You're workin' for me. I don't thank the people who work for me for doin' what I fuckin' well pay 'em to do."

"That's true," Dority said, then made an apologetic face and moved off along the bar, wiping down the hardwood as Swearengen glared after him.

Swearengen turned back to Arabella. "You look mighty innocent in that outfit, like you're fresh off the farm."

"Maybe I am," she said.

A harsh laugh came from him. "You haven't been on a farm in a long time. Maybe never. More likely you grew up in a whorehouse somewhere. You seem to have taken to it easy enough. If you did grow up on a farm, your pa and your brothers probably had you out behind the barn with your drawers down by the time you were twelve."

If his remarks shocked or insulted her, her face didn't show it. "You're an extremely crude man, aren't you, Al?" she said.

"I say what I think. Hell, I say what everybody else would like to say if they weren't too gutless to open their mouths and spit it out."

"There might be some truth to that," she allowed. "For your information, though, I didn't grow up on a farm *or* in a whorehouse."

"Where did you grow up, then?" Swearengen asked. He wasn't sure why he was even interested, but this snooty bitch had a way of getting under his skin.

"That's my business and none of yours," she answered, which didn't surprise him a bit. If she wouldn't tell him her last name, she wasn't going to tell him where she was from. But in that she was no different than a lot of other people on the frontier, people who adopted new names and backgrounds whenever it was convenient to do so.

She went on. "I just thought you'd be interested to hear that about Major Ransome's new assignment."

"Yeah. Don't let him wiggle off the hook this time, like he did before."

"There's no chance of that," she said. "He promised to be here tonight, and I'll find out everything that he did today. Now, if you'll excuse me . . ."

He didn't say anything or try to stop her as she sashayed over to the stairs and went up to the second floor. He didn't know Dority had come back along the bar until he heard the man sigh wistfully.

"What?" Swearengen snapped.

Dority gazed upward as if he could see through the

boards of the ceiling, or at least wished he could. "She's just so . . . so . . ."

"Yeah, she sure is." Swearengen shoved the empty glass across the bar. "Pour me another drink, damn it!"

RANSOME looked from Dan Ryan to the three troopers and back again. "You men know each other?" Ransome asked.

Ryan responded with a curt nod. "Yeah. From the Seventh Cavalry."

"Oh, yes, that's right. The three of you transferred over from there, didn't you, Brundage?"

"Yeah," Brundage said. "I mean, yes, sir."

"I knew you weren't with General Crook in Arizona. So you all are acquainted with each other." Something about the tension that had suddenly sprung up between the men made a thought occur to Ransome. "There wasn't bad blood between you, was there?"

Lamont spat in the dust of the street. "You could say that."

"But it's all over now, ain't it?" Brundage hastened to add. "We've patched things up, haven't we, Dan?"

Ryan grunted. "If you say so." He didn't sound completely convinced, though.

Ransome felt a surge of irritation and impatience. "Well, if it's going to cause trouble for these men to come along with us, maybe I'd better find someone else to give me a hand, Ryan. Or I can dismiss them and assign some other troopers to be our escort."

The former sergeant shook his head and said, "That's not necessary, Major. Like Brundage said, the trouble's all behind us, I reckon."

"Good. Then let's mount up and move out, shall we? The sooner we complete this mission, the sooner we can get back here."

And the sooner he could see Arabella again, Ransome thought. Now that he had made up his mind to pay at least one more visit to the Gem, he didn't want anything to interfere with that.

Not that he planned to go to bed with her or even go upstairs with her, he told himself as he swung up into the saddle and sent his mount trotting along Main Street. But there was nothing wrong with having a drink and some conversation with her. Despite the fact that she was a prostitute, she seemed intelligent. It would be pleasant just spending some time with her in more innocent pursuits.

"Best head northeast toward the Belle Fourche," Ryan suggested. He rode alongside Ransome with the three troopers following abreast behind them. "The country's more open there. There are so many hills and ridges and gulches right around Deadwood that I don't think you could find enough level ground for a fort. You don't have to go very far toward the river, though, before the terrain flattens out some."

Ransome nodded. "That sounds like an excellent suggestion, Mr. Ryan. Lead the way."

"Is the army *really* gonna build a fort around here?"

"That's not my decision to make. I have my orders to follow, whatever the outcome may be. As a former sergeant, I'm sure you understand."

"Yeah," Ryan said. "Be nice if they did, though. Folks around here have been scared of the Indians ever since they came to the Black Hills."

Then they shouldn't have come here in violation of the treaty, thought Ransome. But he agreed that it would be nice indeed if the army built a fort near here. Even nicer if he was posted there. That way he could see Arabella all the time. . . .

The day passed pleasantly enough as the five men rode over the countryside between Deadwood and the Belle Fourche River. Ransome had brought along a notebook in which he drew crude maps every time they found a place that seemed like it would make a suitable location for a military post, noting all the landmarks Ryan pointed out to him. If General Crook really intended to pursue the matter, he would have some feasible suggestions for the War Department. Of course, things would probably never get that far, but Ransome could take pride in knowing that he had done the job assigned to him and done it well.

He discussed the gold situation in the Black Hills with Ryan, too, since the former sergeant had firsthand experience with prospecting. According to Ryan, a few men had become quite wealthy from their efforts, but most of the individual prospectors had either failed miserably or were barely scratching out a living from their claims.

"I expect what's gonna happen is that the big mining companies will squeeze out all the little fellas," Ryan said. "Instead of prospectin' on their own, men will go to work for the companies as miners. That's already started happenin'. The Father De Smet and the Homestake are big mines, with plenty of men workin' at each of them. The companies that own them can afford to dig deeper tunnels and follow the gold veins wherever they go. One man with a pick and shovel just can't compete against a company mine with all sorts of new equipment."

Ransome nodded, finding the information fascinating. Judging from what Ryan said, the boom in the Black Hills might evolve, but it wasn't going away any time soon.

Whenever they stopped to rest and water their horses, Lamont was sullen and Hollis was bland and guarded, but Brundage seemed to be making an effort to be friendly with Ryan. The former sergeant didn't really warm up to the trooper's overtures, though. Definitely bad blood between Ryan and those three, thought Ransome. He had no idea what had caused it, but he would have been willing to wager that the blame could be laid at the feet of Brundage, Hollis, and Lamont. Ryan seemed rather dull and unimaginative, but solid enough. Ransome suspected that he had been a good sergeant.

They paused at midday to eat. Ransome and the troopers had brought along provisions, and Ryan had food of his own in a sack tied to his saddle. They washed the meal down with cold, clear water from one of the numerous streams in the area and refilled their canteens before pushing on.

Late in the afternoon, the five riders turned back toward Deadwood. They hadn't seen a single Indian during their explorations, but when Ransome commented on that fact, Ryan said, "Just because we didn't see them don't mean they didn't see us."

"I'm aware of how that works, Mr. Ryan. I served with General Crook in Arizona during the Apache campaign. Those savages seem to be well nigh invisible at times."

"Sioux are the same way," Ryan said. "A whole war party can pop up out of a coulee so that it looks like they came right out of the earth itself."

Ransome looked over at him. "Do you think any of them were watching us today?"

"That's impossible to say, Major. But it's been my experience that just when you think there aren't any hostiles anywhere around, that's when you're about to get in a heap of trouble."

"I'll bear that in mind," Ransome said. "Will you be available to ride out with us again tomorrow, Mr. Ryan?"

"I don't see why not." Ryan glanced back without actually looking over his shoulder. Ransome knew he was thinking about the three troopers.

"I can get another detail to escort us," he suggested quietly.

"Do whatever you want," Ryan said with a shrug. "It don't matter none to me."

Despite that, Ransome thought that it *did* matter. He had no objection to picking other soldiers for the detail. He didn't like or trust those three either, even if Brundage *had* tried to mend the fences between them.

When the buildings of Deadwood came into sight, Ransome had to suppress the impulse to gallop ahead. No matter how anxious he was to see Arabella again, he had to make his report to General Crook first. She would be waiting for him at the Gem when he got there, he told himself, and since he had told her that he intended to visit the saloon this evening, surely she wouldn't seek out any other . . . customers . . . to take upstairs with her. It was nice to think that she would be devoting her attention only to him.

As they reached the stable, Ransome reined in and turned to the former sergeant. "I'll see you in the morning, Mr. Ryan. Nine o'clock?"

"That'll do," Ryan said with a nod. He lifted a hand in farewell and turned his horse toward the Bella Union. He probably intended to have a drink before returning to his mining claim for the night. He might even decide to stay in Deadwood, but of course that was none of Ransome's business, as long as the man showed up at the appointed time tomorrow morning.

Ransome turned to Brundage, Lamont, and Hollis. "You men are dismissed," he told them.

"You'll be goin' out again in the mornin', sir?" Brundage asked.

"Yes, but I plan to pick a different escort."

Brundage's face darkened as he frowned. "Didn't we do a good job, Major?"

"I have no complaints about your performance, Private. I simply intend to select some different troopers to accompany me and Mr. Ryan tomorrow." Ransome didn't explain further and was under no obligation to do so. He certainly didn't want to stand around talking to these three while General Crook was waiting for him.

And after he'd made his report to the general . . .
Arabella.

"**What** the hell!" Lamont said. "Is ever' fuckin' thing in the world gonna go wrong? First that son of a bitch Ryan shows up, and now Ransome ain't even gonna let us ride out with him again!"

"It don't matter," Brundage said tight-lipped as they walked toward the camp on the edge of the settlement, leading their horses.

Hollis said, "I thought we were gonna get rid of

Ransome while we were ridin' around out there and claim that the Indians did it."

"Well, we couldn't do that while Ryan was with us, now, could we?" Brundage snapped. "And from the sound of it, Ransome intends for him to come along every time he rides out."

Lamont grunted. "We could just kill Ryan, too, you know. I like the sound o' that."

Brundage shook his head. "Then we couldn't use him to help us get our hands on enough money to start over south of the border. That's more important than gettin' rid of Ransome."

The other two men couldn't argue with that point. Greed was strong in all of them, probably stronger than the hatred they felt for Dan Ryan and Major Ransome.

Hollis still wasn't satisfied, though. He said, "You keep talkin' about all that money we're gonna get, Clyde. Just how do you figure we're gonna put our hands on it?"

Brundage scratched his jaw. "I ain't sure about that yet. I'm still thinkin' on it."

"Well, don't think too long," Hollis said with an ominous tone in his voice. "There's no way of knowin' how long we'll be here. If the general gets orders to move the whole command again, we'll have to either go along or else take off for the tall and uncut right then and there. And I'm not too fond of the idea of desertin' without a good stake to set us up somewhere else."

With a hearty confidence that he didn't really feel, Brundage said, "Don't worry. We'll have our stake. Ryan's gonna help us get it . . . and then he'll be sorry that he ever rode back into the Black Hills."

Chapter Fourteen

CHARLES Wagner, the owner of the Grand Central Hotel, had volunteered the use of his own office for General Crook's headquarters while the general was in Deadwood. Ransome found Crook there late that afternoon.

"At ease, Major," Crook said as he returned Ransome's salute. "How did your explorations go?"

"Quite well, sir." Ransome had torn from his notebook the pages that contained the maps. He took the sheaf of pages from his pocket and placed them on the desk in front of the general. He had made notes under each of the maps. "As you can see, I've located five possible sites between here and the Belle Fourche River where a military post could be established with relative ease. Each of these sites has adequate level ground, a suitable water supply nearby, and sufficient timber in the vicinity to provide lumber. Each is also surrounded by enough open ground so that hostile forces would be unable to approach too closely without being seen. Needless to say, such forces would also be lacking in cover from which to launch an attack."

Crook flipped through the pages and nodded in satisfaction. "This appears to be excellent work, Major."

"Thank you, sir. I intend to carry out another day of scouting, possibly two, and I'm confident that I'll find even more sites that would be suitable."

Crook leaned back in his chair and waved a hand. "Oh, I'm not certain that's necessary, Major. It's unlikely that the War Department will actually want to locate a post in this area. If they do decide to act on the matter, we have these possibilities here to offer them." He tapped the stack of notebook pages with a finger. "If any more exploration is necessary, it can be done then."

Ransome took a deep breath. He had been thinking about this all the way over here to the hotel, and now he said, "If I may speak freely, General . . . ?"

"Of course," Crook said with a slight frown. He nodded toward the brown leather chair on the other side of the desk. "Sit down and tell me what's on your mind, Major."

Ransome sat down, balancing his hat on his knee. "I'm aware that my efforts today were intended as much to mollify our hosts here in Deadwood as they were to accomplish any real military purpose, but as I was riding through the countryside, I realized that it really would be a good idea for a fort to be located here. This gold rush that's going on in the Black Hills isn't going to be over any time soon. It may never be over."

"What makes you think that?"

"I was talking to Sergeant Ryan—"

"Who?" Crook asked. "I don't recall a Sergeant Ryan in my command."

"He's not in your command, sir," Ransome explained. "Actually, he's not even a sergeant anymore. He retired from the Seventh Cavalry and came up here to search for gold. He still conducts himself much like a sergeant, though."

"Retired, eh?" Crook grunted. "Lucky man, I suppose. Might've been with Colonel Custer, otherwise."

"Yes, sir. At any rate, Ryan's the volunteer I got to go

with me and show me the country hereabouts. He tells me that the large mining companies are coming in now, and he thinks that their success inevitably will crowd out the individual prospectors."

Crook nodded solemnly. "That's usually the way it happens. Not that I'm any expert on the mining industry. Go on."

"If the mining companies become well established here, then the mine owners will have considerable incentive to keep their operations safe from the Indians. And men such as that often wield a great deal of influence in Washington."

The general's frown became a scowl as he tugged at his forked beard in irritation. "You don't have to tell me that, Major," he snapped. "Too many civilians already have too much influence in Washington, especially where military matters are concerned. They try to interfere in War Department decisions that affect the soldiers in the field, and that shouldn't be allowed."

"I couldn't agree with you more, sir, but the fact of the matter is, those mining magnates *will* press for protection from the army, and it stands to reason that the best way to provide it would be to establish a fort in the area."

Crook thought about it for a moment before beginning to nod slowly. "You may well be correct, Major. I'll study these maps of yours closely, and you can continue to conduct your explorations for another day or two. I can spare you for that long. Perhaps I really will recommend to the War Department that they put a fort here. But of course, that's no guarantee that they'll agree with the idea."

"No, sir, I understand that," Ransome said. But his hopes rose anyway. If the War Department established a fort near Deadwood, and if he were posted to it, then he could see Arabella whenever he wanted. . . .

And he wanted to see her right now, as a matter of fact, so he continued, "Is there anything else?"

Crook shook his head and said, "No, that's all, Major. Again, excellent work on your part, and good thinking as well. Keep that up and you'll go far."

"Yes, sir," Ransome said as he got to his feet. "Thank you, sir."

Crook returned the major's salute and said, "Dismissed." Ransome left the general's office. He went back down the hall to his own room to wash up and change into the civilian suit before heading for the Gem. He didn't know which outfit Arabella would prefer, but trail dust coated his uniform again and he didn't want to wear it to see her.

Hunger gnawed at his stomach as he clattered down the stairs, reminding him that he hadn't eaten since the skimpy meal at midday, but he didn't want to delay his visit to the Gem long enough to have a meal in the hotel dining room. Some things were just more important than food.

And seeing Arabella again was one of them.

DAN wasn't surprised when Cougar Jack and Calamity Jane hailed him from the boardwalk as he went up Main Street after leaving his horse at the livery stable. "I had a feelin' you two might be waitin' for me," he told them with a grin.

"Damn right," Calam said. "It's our night to howl, and you could do with cuttin' your wolf loose, too, Dan." She didn't seem to be drunk, although the smell of whiskey on her breath told Dan that she had already gotten a start on the night's boozing. She linked her right arm with Dan's left and fell in step beside him.

Cougar Jack flanked him on the other side. "How'd it go with Major Ransome?" the scout asked.

"All right, I guess. He's a mite stiff-necked."

"He's an officer. You got to expect that from him."

"Yeah, I know," Dan said. "Anyway, he really listened when I talked, which is more'n some officers would do. Seemed interested in finding the best place he could in case the War Department really does put a fort out here." He frowned. "Only problem was the escort Major Ransome picked out to go along with us."

"Who was that?"

"Brundage, Hollis, and Lamont."

"Son of a bitch! Those varmints again! Did the major know what happened back at Fort Abraham Lincoln?"

Dan shook his head. "He didn't seem to know a thing about it, but he could tell that those three aren't very fond of me, and vice versa. I didn't go into any details, though, and neither did they. I reckon they don't want to rehash that old business any more than I do. The major offered to dismiss them and find some more troopers to ride with us, but I told him he didn't have to do that."

"They cause any trouble whilst you was out there?" Cougar Jack asked.

"Nope. Just rode along behind us and kept to themselves. We didn't run into any hostiles or any other problems."

Calamity Jane said, "These hombres you're talkin' about . . . they're the motherfuckers who was plannin' to steal them rifles and sell 'em to the Injuns?"

"That's right," Dan said, a little surprised that she even remembered the story. She'd been pretty well in her cups when he told her about it the night before.

"Anybody who'd do that is lower'n a privy rat. I wouldn't trust 'em none if I was you."

"Don't worry," Dan told her. "I don't intend to."

They had come abreast of the Gem by now. Calamity tugged on Dan's arm and said, "Come on. Let's have a drink."

The three of them went inside. The hour was late enough that the saloon was doing a brisk business, with men lined up at the bar. Most of the tables were occupied, and a steady stream of men went up the stairs with the whores who worked here while other men stumbled back down, their pockets lighter and satisfied looks on their faces.

Calamity claimed one of the few empty tables. Its slightly uneven legs caused it to rock a little whenever anybody leaned on it, and the chairs weren't much steadier. Calamity almost kicked over a spittoon accidentally when she sat down. "Shitfire!" she exclaimed. "That would've been a hell of a mess to have to clean up!"

"I'll get a bottle," Dan offered. Jack had bought the drinks the night before, so it was his turn to do the honors. Calamity probably didn't have the price of a bottle, and anyway, Dan wasn't going to let a lady pay for his whiskey—or Calamity Jane either.

He made his way over to the bar and wedged his shoulders through the crowd until he reached the hardwood and caught the eye of Dan Dority. They shared a first name and similar stocky builds, but the resemblance ended there. Dority had long, greasy hair and a beard. Dan suspected that the bartender kept his hair oily for a reason. On numerous occasions he had seen Dority running his fingers through his hair, especially when prospectors were paying for their drinks with pinches of gold dust. Some of those precious flecks stuck to Dority's greasy fingers and then to his hair, where he could wash them out later and pan the color out of the wash water. It was a common trick used by bartenders, storekeepers, assayers, and anybody else who handled gold dust on a regular basis. Al Swearengen had to know what Dority was doing and approve of it, otherwise Dority wouldn't have dared to attempt such a thing. Anybody who tried to steal from Swearengen would be risking his life.

The big iron safe behind the bar provided evidence of that. Johnny Burnes, who perched on the high stool at the end of the bar with his shotgun, not only discouraged brawls that might cause expensive damage, he also guarded the Gem's safe. Dan had heard rumors that the safe contained more gold and other valuables than the one down the street at the bank.

Dan told Dority to give him a bottle and slid a coin across the bar to pay for it. Dority scooped up the coin, handed Dan a bottle from the back bar, and said above the noise in the room, "Ain't got no glasses right now, clean or otherwise. You'll have to drink from the bottle."

Dan shrugged. "I reckon we can manage that."

He carried the whiskey back to the table and thumped the bottle down in the center of it. Calamity grinned and said, "Don't the light shine through it all pretty-like?"

Then she grabbed it, yanked the cork out of the neck

with her teeth, spat it onto the floor, and lifted the bottle to her mouth to take a long swallow. The muscles of her throat worked as the rotgut gurgled in the bottle.

When she finally lowered the bottle and passed it on to Cougar Jack, a good-sized slug of the whiskey was gone. She blew out her breath in satisfaction, then wiped the back of her hand across her mouth. Jack took a smaller drink and handed the bottle to Dan. The warm bite of the whiskey felt good as he swallowed it.

"Well, I'll swan," Cougar Jack said. "Look who just came in."

Dan turned his head to look at the man who had just pushed through the batwings. After spending most of the day with Major Ransome, he recognized the officer right away, even though Ransome wore civilian clothes now instead of his uniform. "Wonder what he's doin' here," Dan mused.

"I got me a hunch it has somethin' to do with the lady yonder," Cougar Jack said as he nodded toward the staircase.

Dan looked in that direction and saw that a stunningly beautiful blond woman had paused at the bottom of the stairs to smile toward the saloon's entrance. Sure enough, Ransome started straight for her, a huge answering smile on his face. He didn't even glance in the direction of the table where Dan, Cougar Jack, and Calamity Jane sat. He had eyes only for the blonde.

"Are we here to drink or to stare at some fuckin' whore?" Calamity asked with a truculent rasp in her voice. If Dan hadn't known better, he would have said that she sounded a mite jealous.

But that was crazy, of course. And Calamity was wrong about one thing, Dan reflected. He didn't know who the blond woman was, but you could tell by looking at her that she wasn't any ordinary whore.

ARABELLA reached out with both hands to grasp his and said fervently, "Stephen, it's so good to see you again," as if it had been ages since they last met, instead of only that morning.

Ransome didn't care. He was only aware of the beauty of her smile. And the warmth of her hands, of course. And the grace with which her body moved in the low-cut, cream-colored gown with the lace-trimmed bodice that called his attention to the enticingly shadowed cleft between her breasts.

Oh, and the way his cock was growing hard . . . He was aware of that, too.

He forced his eyes away from her bosom and took a deep breath as he willed his erection to go away. Determined not to shame himself or embarrass her, he said, "You look as lovely as ever, Arabella. I must confess, you've been on my mind all day."

"Oh, I hope not," she said with a laugh. "I wouldn't want to be held responsible for distracting you from your duties, Major."

Ransome laughed, too. "Don't worry about that," he assured her. "I was able to perform quite capably."

Damn it! Why had he phrased his comment that way?

Thankfully, Arabella didn't seem to take any double meaning from it. She said, "You'll have to tell me all about it . . . but after we've had a drink."

He cast a glance toward the crowded bar and the equally crowded tables. "I'm not sure there's room."

"Not down here, of course. Anyway, you wouldn't want to drink what Al Swearengen serves. I still have that bottle of brandy up in my room, just waiting for someone sophisticated enough to appreciate it."

Sophisticated? He was a New England minister's son and a career army officer. No one had ever accused him of sophistication before.

Which probably explained the glow of pleasure he felt at Arabella's words, he told himself. If she thought that highly of him, well, he didn't want to disappoint her, now, did he?

She let go of his left hand and tugged on his right.

"Come on," she urged. "I have some food, too, if you're hungry."

The idea of sharing an intimate supper with her appealed greatly to him, and that was all it took to make him completely forget about his earlier resolve not to go upstairs with her. Tonight he didn't have dinner with General Crook and the rest of the general's staff to pull him away. He didn't have the excuse of duty. All he had were thoughts of his wife back in Boston. . . .

His pale, frowning wife who wouldn't even let him touch her anymore.

"That sounds wonderful," he said, and he let Arabella lead him up the stairs.

Chapter Fifteen

RANSOME'S heart pounded so loudly that he thought surely Arabella must hear it. It felt as if it might burst out of his chest at any moment. Either that or leap up his throat and choke him. He took another sip of the brandy, hoping that the smooth, potent liquor would soothe his nerves.

Arabella smiled at him from the other side of the table and said, "Tell me about what you did today, Stephen."

He took a deep breath and glanced around the room. For an upstairs room in a combination saloon, gambling den, and brothel in a frontier mining boomtown, it was surprisingly well furnished. Large enough to contain an opulent four-poster without being dominated by it, the room also had a mahogany wardrobe, a dressing table, a washstand, several chairs, and the small table where Ransome and Arabella sat with fine china and brandy snifters between them. A thick woven rug lay on the floor at their feet.

Some, perhaps most of these things had to belong to Arabella. Ransome couldn't imagine a man like Al Swearengen furnishing a room this way. He knew the brandy they were sharing was hers; she had said as much before they ever came upstairs. And the food! Roasted chicken with delicately cooked vegetables . . . Where in heaven's name had she come up with such a meal? Perhaps she had made arrangements with the colored cook over at the Grand Central to provide it. In that case, she must have been quite certain that he would accept her invitation to dine with her.

She knew him too well, he thought, even though they had spent relatively little time together. All she had to do was look at him to know exactly what he was thinking.

And, God help him, there was nothing he could do about that. The emotions inside him were just too strong to control.

He realized that she was waiting for him to respond to her request. He took another sip of the brandy, cleared his throat, and said, "Well, as I explained this morning, General Crook assigned me the task of locating suitable sites for a military post in this area."

"Did you find any?"

"Oh, yes, several." Crook hadn't said anything about keeping his activities secret. On the contrary, the general *wanted* the citizens of Deadwood to know that the army was taking action on their petition. Ransome told her about riding out with Dan Ryan and the three troopers and scouting the area between the settlement and the Belle Fourche River. He started explaining in detail where the sites were that he had selected, but Arabella smiled and shook her head.

"You're wasting your time now, Stephen," she said. "I don't know this area, and I have no head for directions anyway."

"I could draw some maps for you," he offered. "I have an excellent memory for such things and I'm sure I could re-create the ones I turned over to General Crook with a high degree of accuracy."

She started to shake her head in refusal, then apparently changed her mind because she said, "Yes, I'd like to look at them."

Excitement gripped him. He wanted to demonstrate his abilities to her. "If you have any paper, and a pencil . . ."

"Let me see." She stood up and went over to the

dressing table to rummage around in one of its drawers. Even when performing a mundane task like that, she moved with incredible grace and loveliness, thought Ransome. She came back with several sheets of paper and a pencil. Ransome took them, pushed aside the empty dishes from their meal, and began to sketch.

She stood beside him to watch what he was doing instead of going back to the other side of the table. Ransome was aware of her nearness and the effect it had on him, but he tried to concentrate on his cartography. Then she rested a hand on his shoulder in a companionable fashion, and the desire he felt for her grew even stronger. As much to distract himself as anything else, he cleared his throat and began to explain what he was doing, pointing out landmarks on the maps as he drew them in. She murmured, "How fascinating," and leaned over to take a closer look.

That made her left breast press softly against his right shoulder. He felt the warmth of her breath on his ear and cheek. His fingers gripped the pencil so tightly that he feared he would snap it in two.

"What's wrong, Stephen?" Her voice was a tantalizing caress in his ear. "You're trembling."

Without thinking about what he was doing, Ransome set the pencil down and turned in his chair. That brought his eyes level with her breasts where their upper halves swelled above the low-cut gown. He pressed his face between those soft, creamy globes and groaned with the power of the need coursing through him. His lips tasted her flesh, and the heat of her body seared him.

Arabella didn't pull away. She stroked his head, running her fingers through the close-cropped, sandy hair. "Stephen," she whispered, "do you want me?"

He couldn't talk. Too many emotions wracked him, ranging from guilt and shame all the way to passion and excitement. Desire rose so strongly in him that it easily overwhelmed any cautionary feelings that might hold him back. With his face buried in her bosom, he nodded, helpless to do otherwise.

"Then you shall have me," she said. She put a finger under his chin and lifted his head, tipping it back so that he stared up at her in mute wonder. She smiled and said, "Come to bed with me, Stephen."

Just as she had led him upstairs, she took him by the hand now and led him to the four-poster with its thick mattress and lacy comforter. Along the way she blew out the lamp that burned on the table, so that the room was lit only by a candle on the small table beside the bed. Its gentle, flickering yellow warmth made her even more beautiful, if that was possible, thought Ransome. By now his mind wasn't capable of much coherent thought, but he managed that one.

He thought, too, that he shouldn't be doing this. He had sworn a vow of faithfulness, and he had always kept that vow despite the long separations from his wife due to his military duties and the occasional temptations encountered in frontier settlements such as Deadwood.

Never before, though, had he encountered a temptation quite like Arabella. She was stunning, a veritable goddess, and she possessed intelligence to go along with her beauty. Yes, she sometimes sold herself for money. Logically he knew that, but this was different. She hadn't mentioned the subject of payment at all. She wanted to be with him because she liked him and was attracted to him, the same as he felt about her. He was sure of it.

And really, he told himself, Louisa had made this bed for him to lie in with her coldness and her disapproval. If she expected him to remain faithful to her, then by God she should have given him a *reason* to remain faithful!

Anyway, Arabella had already slipped his coat off his shoulders and started unfastening the buttons of his shirt. There would be no turning back now.

He stood there beside the bed and let her strip him down to the waist. Then she moved closer and rested her hands on his chest. She stroked his nipples with her thumbs and smiled up at him. He couldn't resist. He had to kiss her.

The taste of her hot, sweet mouth intoxicated him more

than that bottle of brandy ever could. More than ten bottles of brandy. He couldn't get enough of it, and when her lips parted and her tongue daringly met his, another shudder of passion went through him and shook him all the way to his core.

When she finally broke the kiss, she whispered, "Sit down. I'll take your boots off."

He welcomed the opportunity to sit on the edge of the bed, since his knees had grown so weak and shaky he feared he might fall otherwise. Arabella turned her back toward him and bent over to grasp his right boot, and even though she still wore her gown with at least one petticoat underneath it, the roundness of her rump in this position made him groan again.

By the time she had taken off both his boots, his cock had grown so hard he didn't think he could stand up again. He managed to do so, even though his erection tented the front of his trousers. Arabella smiled and rested her hand on the sensitive bulge for a moment, saying, "You're going to enjoy this, Stephen."

She wasn't telling him anything he didn't already know.

She unfastened his belt, unbuttoned his trousers, and pushed them down along with his underwear so that his organ sprang free at last. Kneeling in front of him as she was, gripping his shaft and running her tongue along the underside of it posed no problem for her. Ransome closed his eyes as that exquisite sensation throbbed through him. Arabella's lips closed around the head and she began to suck gently . . . something else Louisa never would have done for him!

Ransome shoved any other thoughts of his wife and what she would or wouldn't do right out of his head so that he could concentrate on what Arabella *was* doing to him. He had never experienced anything quite so arousing in his entire life. He started to worry that he might attain his release in her mouth, but she expertly applied pressure with her fingers to the base of his cock and suppressed the impulse. Smiling, she stood up and said, "Not yet."

Then she began taking her clothes off.

Ransome sank back down on the edge of the bed to watch in awe as she disrobed. Every inch of smooth, fair skin that she exposed increased his arousal that much more. When she dropped the last stitch of clothing and stood before him, proud in her nudity, he thought that *goddess* wasn't really strong enough a word to describe her. She put Venus to shame with her perfect breasts, her gracefully curving hips and thighs, the neat triangle of fine-spun hair between her legs that was just as blond as the hair on her head. With her bluer-than-blue eyes twinkling, she stepped over to the bed, rested a hand on his chest, and pushed him onto his back. He toppled easily, like a man plummeting into an abyss. . . .

She came into his arms, molding the heated length of her body to his. Their mouths met again as their hands explored and caressed every curve, every hard plane, every recess of their bodies. Ransome had forgotten about General Crook, about the campaign against the Sioux, about the battle at Rosebud Creek and the death of Spotted Dog. He had certainly forgotten about his wife and children back in Boston. Arabella filled his mind so that no room remained for anything except thoughts of making love to her.

That was what he finally did, rolling her onto her back and moving between her wide-spread thighs. They came together naturally, seemingly without any effort from either of them, as he sheathed his hard length inside her. Swept away by his emotions, he drove into her again and again and again . . .

And when they finally shared their culminations in a series of shuddering releases, he knew that he had done the right thing. This was so good it could never be wrong.

He went to sleep, content in that knowledge.

"**WHAT'S** this?" Al Swearengen asked as Arabella slapped down several sheets of paper on his desk. He looked up at her. She wore a thin silk wrapper that clung to her body well enough for him to see her nipples. The sight intrigued him, and he was glad he had told her to come in when she knocked on his office door a few moments earlier.

"Maps drawn by Major Ransome showing prospective locations for a fort between Deadwood and the Belle Fourche River," she explained.

"Is that so?" Swearengen shoved aside the ledger he had been working on and picked up the papers instead. He knew the area well enough to recognize most of the landmarks Ransome had labeled on the maps. "I'd rather these were closer to Deadwood."

"According to the major, the terrain isn't suitable for a post right around the town."

Swearengen shrugged. "Well, these places are only a few miles away. Plenty close enough for the soldiers to ride in when they want a drink or a whore. Hell, most of those troopers would probably walk that far for a fuck." He put the papers down and looked at Arabella again. "Speaking of that, where *is* the major right now?"

"Asleep in my bed." Arabella smiled. "He dozed right off after dinner and . . ."

"Well fed and well fucked, eh? How was he?"

"Very ardent," she said. "I think he felt a little guilty at first, but he got over that in a hurry and forgot all about his little wife, wherever she is back East."

"Yeah, clean-cut types like that always do. They like to think they're better than the rest of us, but they really ain't. They'll lie and steal and cheat just like everybody else when they get the chance. Then they feel all sorry about it and think that makes a damn bit of difference."

"Don't you ever feel any regret, Al?" Arabella asked.

Swearengen put his hands on the desk and shoved himself to his feet. "Regret?" he repeated. "I'll tell you what I regret. I'm sorry I don't have more money than I do. I'm sorry I've let a few people get away with crossing me in the past without my blowing their fucking brains out. And I'm sorry I haven't gotten to feel that hot little pussy of yours around my dick . . . yet."

Her hand came up to the lapels of her wrapper and clutched them a little closer together as she took a step back. He thought that for the first time since he had known her, he might have penetrated that cool facade she always put up, and that thought pleased him. Rattling her was the first step to bedding her. He could have taken her by force and nobody would have dared to say *boo* to him about it, but he realized that for some reason, that wasn't what he wanted. He wanted to shake her up, to get to her, to make *her* want *him*. When that happened, he would gladly fuck her . . . But not before.

Unless he got too horny. Then he might change his mind.

"What are Ransome's plans now?" he asked.

"He's going to continue scouting in the area. General Crook told him that the sites he's already found would be enough, but Stephen wants to locate more. He takes his duty very seriously."

"Well, good for him," Swearengen said, sarcasm dripping from the words. "Now explain to me what it is exactly that *you're* doing to help this process along? Seems to me that Ransome's already doing what we want him to do on his own, without any prodding from you."

"He brought me those maps. He told me everything he's done and everything he plans to do."

Swearengen waved a hand. "That ain't worth the profit I'm givin' up by having you concentrate just on him instead of finding more paying customers. You *are* going to charge Ransome, aren't you?"

"I haven't decided yet."

Swearengen stared at her for a long moment, then abruptly exploded, "For God's sake! Don't go all soft and sweet on the son of a bitch! This is a business!"

"I know that," she snapped. "But if the army puts a fort here and you double your business—and I helped bring that about—then I think I'll have earned my keep, don't you?"

"Just don't let it take too long," Swearengen said. "I ain't the most patient man in the world." He looked her up and down, letting his dark-eyed gaze boldly caress the curves of her body. "I ain't too patient about anything. You'd do well to remember that."

"Trust me, Al," she told him. That chilly barrier was back in place between them. "You've made it impossible for me to forget."

Chapter Sixteen

"**L**OOK at that bastard," Dewey Lamont said with a murderous scowl on his face. "Sittin' there havin' him a fine old time with a gal when we hardly got the price of a drink between us, let alone a piece o' ass!"

Matt Hollis laughed quietly. "That's Calamity Jane with him, Dewey, not a regular gal. I wouldn't be too jealous, if I was you."

"Yeah, well, I still don't like it. Ryan lorded it over us all day, and now we gotta sit here in the same saloon as him. It ain't right."

"Nobody's makin' us stay here," Brundage pointed out. "We can leave any time we want."

Lamont shook his head. "This is the best place in Deadwood. I ain't lettin' Ryan run us out."

The three of them had been sitting at a rear table in the Gem, nursing a bottle that they'd had to pool their money to buy, when Dan Ryan came into the saloon with Calamity Jane and the old scout, Cougar Jack LeCarde. Ryan hadn't even glanced in their direction and seemed to have no idea that they were here. Brundage had told his two companions to just ignore Ryan, but none of them had been able to manage that. All three of them kept casting resentful, hate-filled glances toward him.

Hollis took a nip from the bottle, then said, "At least we don't have to ride out with him and the major tomorrow. Those two sons o' bitches deserve each other. Maybe the redskins really will jump 'em and take their hair."

Lamont grunted. "We ain't gonna be that lucky."

"Damn it," Brundage said, "we still might need Ryan—"

"Why?" Hollis cut in. "Why can't we just pull whatever job it is you got in mind by ourselves, Clyde? We don't need Ryan for shit."

"I told you, he's gonna take the blame."

"I don't think you got any idea what you're talkin' about," Lamont said. "You're just tryin' to act like you're so damned smart, but you don't have no notion o' what we need to do."

Brundage's hands clenched angrily into fists. "I've always done the thinkin' for the three of us," he began.

Hollis said, "Yeah, it was your idea to steal those rifles back at Fort Lincoln, and look how that turned out."

"Maybe it's time Matt and me did some o' the thinkin'," Lamont said.

Brundage felt like telling both of them to go to hell. Instead, he scraped his chair back and stood up. "You go right ahead and do your own thinkin'," he said coldly. "But when you find yourselves up to your necks in shit, don't figure on me pullin' you out."

He turned and walked toward the bar. He didn't have the price of a drink in his pocket, but he thought maybe he could cadge one from the bartender.

"Hey, pard," Brundage said to the bearded man as he bellied up to the hardwood a minute later.

"What'll it be?" the man asked. "Another bottle?"

Brundage didn't answer the question. Instead, he said, "I'll bet you were mighty glad to see the cavalry ride in the other day. As long as we're around, you don't have to worry about the redskins botherin' anybody in Deadwood. No, sirree."

"Yeah, maybe so." The bartender didn't seem impressed. He went on with dogged determination, "What'll it be?"

"I was just thinkin' . . . seein' as how we've risked our lives to make you folks safe and all . . . if you was to want to show your appreciation by standin' a poor, valiant soldier to a drink—"

The bartender held up a hand, calloused palm out. "You might as well stop right there, asshole. Nobody gets a free drink in the Gem, no matter whether he's a soldier or not. General Crook could walk in here and not get a free drink. Phil Sheridan wouldn't get a free drink. Hell, the ghost o' Colonel George fuckin' Custer could saunter in and I'd tell him to pay up or no drink."

Brundage blinked in surprise and whined, "Now, that ain't no way to be."

The bartender's face turned red in anger. He reached across the hardwood and grabbed the front of Brundage's uniform shirt. He jerked the trooper against the bar and pointed with his other hand at the big safe.

"You see that? That safe, and all the gold and silver and greenbacks in it, belong to Al Swearengen. You know how he got all that money? By not lettin' bums like you have no free fuckin' drinks! If you're broke, just get on out!"

The shotgun guard on the stool called, "Got a problem there, Dan?"

The bartender pushed Brundage away and replied disgustedly, "Naw, there ain't no problem here. Just explainin' a few things to this soldier boy."

Brundage tugged his shirt down and brushed it off, trying to salvage as much dignity as he could, which was precious little. With all the noise going on in the saloon, most of the customers hadn't even noticed the slight commotion, but those nearest to Brundage along the bar had. From the corner of his eye, he saw several of them smirking at him. They were nothing but raggedy-ass prospectors and freighters and the like, and yet they felt superior to him. That knowledge burned at him like lye.

"I wouldn't take a drink from you now if you offered me one," he said as he glared at the bartender. With that last word gotten in, weak as it was, he turned away. Everything was going to hell, and there didn't seem to be a thing he could do to stop it.

He had only taken a couple of steps when he stopped and a frown creased his forehead. He glanced back over his shoulder. The Gem was the biggest saloon in Deadwood and did more business than any of the other places. He had thought about robbing the bank down the street, but under the circumstances, that safe behind the bar might have just as much money in it as the one in the bank.

But it was probably better guarded, too, he thought as he cast a glance at the bearded, shotgun-wielding hombre on the stool at the end of the bar. Anybody foolish enough to make a move toward the safe would get blown in half.

Unless somehow that guard was disposed of, or at least drawn away from the bar. . . .

The beginning of an idea glimmered into existence in Brundage's brain. He looked toward the table in the rear of the room, where Hollis and Lamont still passed the bottle back and forth with its rapidly dwindling supply of whiskey. He could talk to them again later, and they wouldn't think he was so dumb then. Right now it was time to make another move.

He headed toward the table where Dan Ryan sat with Calamity Jane and Cougar Jack LeCarde.

DAN had spotted Brundage at the bar a couple of minutes earlier and witnessed the end of the exchange between Brundage and Dority. Brundage didn't have his two shadows with him for a change, but Dan would have been willing to bet that Hollis and Lamont weren't far off.

Not that he cared one way or the other. Spending the

day out on the trail with those three varmints had been bad enough. He sure didn't want to spend any part of his evening with them.

Unfortunately, Brundage had seen him and was now coming toward the table. Dan's jaw tightened. Whatever the trooper had in mind, chances were that it wasn't anything good.

Calamity and Cougar Jack were laughing at a story Calam had told about Bill Cody getting caught with his britches down when a hard gust of wind came along and blew down the outhouse he was using. "What made it even funnier," Calamity choked out between gusts of hilarity, "was that he was beatin' off at the time! He had a bunch o' them fancy Eur-o-pean tourists he was fixin' to guide on a huntin' expedition, and there he was squattin' over a shithole with his dick in his hand!" She whooped and pounded the table.

Cougar Jack wiped away tears of laughter and said, "I like ol' Bill, I truly do, but that's a mighty funny story, Calam. You know, he done some scoutin' with us at the start o' this campaign. Couldn't stay with the column, though, because he said he had one of those shows of his booked at a bunch o' theaters back East, and he had to go trod the footlights or whatever the hell he called it. That Bill . . . he's a character."

Brundage had come over to the table while Calamity and Jack were talking, and now they fell silent as they looked up at him. Dan asked, "What do you want, Brundage?"

The man got one of his usual shit-eating grins on his face as he said, "I thought you might want to buy me a drink, Dan. For old times' sake."

"I don't owe you a drink for old times' sake, or for any other reason," Dan snapped.

"Yeah, well, I was just thinkin' about how well you used to get along with the enlisted men, even when you were a sergeant. Like that night over in Bismarck with Private Jessup, back when we was all stationed at Fort Lincoln."

Dan's breath seemed to freeze in his throat, and he would have sworn that his heart stopped beating in his chest for a full five seconds. Then he forced himself to say, "I don't know what the hell you're talking about."

"Oh, sure you do, Dan. You remember Private Jessup."

Calamity Jane said, "Was this when you was all in the Seventh Cavalry?"

Brundage grinned at her. "That's right, ma'am."

"I don't recollect no Private Jessup in the Seventh. And I ought'a know, since I fucked half the men in that outfit when I was packin' mules for Custer. Tried to, anyway."

"Jessup wasn't there for long. Something happened to him, though I don't rightly recall what it was."

Dan's thoughts spun crazily. He hadn't wasted any time brooding over what had happened to Ezra Jessup, hadn't even thought about the murderous little bastard in months. Jessup had tried to knife him in that alley, had come damned close to sinking six inches of cold steel in his gut, as a matter of fact. Dan hit him only once, a solid blow that knocked Jessup clear across the alley and into the wall of a building. Jessup hadn't gotten up after that, and Dan had gone on back to the fort.

It wasn't until the next day that he found out Jessup was dead of a broken neck.

Dan hadn't reported the fight the night before. He figured Jessup would wake up with a sore head, maybe even a busted jaw. That was punishment enough, to Dan's way of thinking. He didn't want to get the trooper drummed out of the army or sent to prison for attacking a superior. He sure as hell hadn't known when he walked away that Jessup's neck was broken. When he'd heard the news, he had been tempted to go to the commanding officer and explain the whole thing.

But that wouldn't make Jessup any less dead, and it might have caused trouble for Dan. Anyway, the law in Bismarck had written the killing off as a robbery and murder, since Jessup's pockets were empty. Somebody else had come along, found him dead, and done that, Dan thought, because he knew that *he* hadn't stolen anything from Jessup.

So he had put it out of his mind, knowing that what he had done was in self-defense. The only one truly to blame for Jessup's death was Jessup himself.

But now, Clyde Brundage stood there smirking at him, and obviously *he* knew something about what had happened to Jessup. Dan had believed that no one else was around in the alley that night, but maybe Brundage had been there, lurking unseen in the shadows. Brundage had an old score to settle with him, too. What would happen if the trooper started spreading stories about how Dan had killed a young private back in Bismarck? Brundage might even make it sound like Dan had deliberately broken Jessup's neck. There had been trouble between the two of them earlier that same day; a lot of people knew that.

Hell, if Brundage wanted to, he might even claim that Dan had laid for Jessup, instead of the other way around, and had murdered him.

But there was no way he could prove that, Dan reminded himself, because it hadn't happened that way. It would be just Brundage's word against his.

That might be enough to stir up trouble, though, and Dan was in no mood for that. If Brundage wanted a drink, that was a cheap enough price to pay to get rid of him.

Dan slipped a coin out of his pocket and flipped it to the trooper, who caught it deftly. "There," Dan said with as little grace as he could manage. "Go buy yourself a drink."

"Why, I'm much obliged, Dan. Thank you for your kindness." Brundage jerked a thumb toward the bar. "Why don't you come have a drink with me? I reckon your friends can get along without you for a few minutes."

"I'm fine right where I am."

Brundage cocked his head to the side. "Just tryin' to be friendly here, Dan, like I've been tellin' you ever since we ran into each other again. But if you ain't in the mood to be friends . . ."

The son of a bitch was threatening him, Dan realized. If he didn't go along with what Brundage wanted, then Brundage would start telling everybody about Jessup, probably starting with Calamity and Cougar Jack.

He had to scotch this right now, Dan thought. He pushed himself to his feet and said, "All right, I reckon it wouldn't hurt anything to have one drink with you . . . even if I'm payin' for both of us."

"That's the spirit," Brundage said. To Calamity and Jack, he added, "You folks just carry on like you were doin'. I'll have ol' Dan back to you in a few minutes."

He turned toward the bar, and Dan followed. He didn't look around at his two companions, figuring that they would be puzzled as all get-out as to why he was being so obliging to Brundage. Calam and Cougar Jack both knew good and well that he hated the trooper and that the feeling was mutual.

Dan came up alongside Brundage and asked in a low voice, "What the hell do you want, you bastard?"

"That ain't no way to talk to me, Dan." Brundage still wore that grin, but his eyes were as cold and hard as flint as he glanced over at Dan. "You may not know it yet, but I'm your new best friend. I'm gonna make you a rich man, too."

Dan snorted. "Not hardly, to either one of those things."

"Just shut up and listen. Either that, or try explainin' to people how you broke an innocent young trooper's neck and robbed him. Might not be too late to interest the army in that. You were still a soldier when you killed Jessup, Dan. Seems to me that killin' would still fall under military jurisdiction."

Dan's pulse hammered in his head. He had put that whole ugly business behind him, believing it to be as dead and buried as Ezra Jessup himself. Sometimes, though, the past just wouldn't stay in the grave.

"What do you want from me?" he asked quietly.

Brundage's grin turned into a triumphant leer. "Right now, just a drink and a few minutes of your time. And for you to listen while I tell you what we're gonna do. . . ."

Chapter Seventeen

R ANSOME stretched and groaned in delight at the feeling of smooth, crisp sheets against his bare skin. For a moment as he awoke, he didn't think about where he might be. He just reveled in the sensations that surrounded him.

Then a soft, yielding warmth nestled against him, and the events of the night before all came flooding back into his brain.

He had made love with Arabella. Someone with a coarser attitude would say that he had fucked her, but Ransome knew better. That might have been what he intended, but it wasn't what had happened. What passed between them was done out of love. He had no doubt of that whatsoever.

And she still lay there sleeping next to him, even though the gray light of dawn had begun to seep into the room around the lacy edges of the drawn curtains. He had spent the entire night with her, and that knowledge made him glow inside with satisfaction.

He lay on his left side. So did she, with her back to him and her head so close to his that the clean scent of her hair filled his nostrils. Her smooth back pressed against his chest. Even though she seemed to still be asleep, she wiggled her hips a little to snuggle her rump closer against his groin. His cock began to swell, trapped as it was between the soft cheeks of her ass.

Arabella made a little noise of arousal in her throat. Awareness was stirring to life within her, thought Ransome. She knew what was going on, and she liked it. He put an arm around her and began to stroke her breasts. Her nipples hardened under his touch. Her chest rose and fell faster as her breathing increased.

"Do you want to . . . put it in my ass, Stephen?" she whispered sleepily.

He had to groan again before he was able to say, "Oh, God, yes. Please."

"You don't have to ask. Just get it nice and slick first."

The head of Ransome's cock already prodded against her tight opening. He pulled back slightly, enough so that he could reach between them. He spat on his fingers and worked the saliva into her anus, then spat again and rubbed it on his cock, which by now was as hard as an iron bar. Getting back into position, he pressed forward slowly and carefully. Even though he had never done this before, he knew instinctively that he shouldn't rush it.

The aperture eased open, and suddenly he felt himself sliding into her. Arabella breathed a heartfelt "Ahhhh . . ." but didn't seem to be suffering any discomfort. Ransome continued his slow but steady advance. He slipped his left arm underneath her so that he held her in both arms. His hands cupped her breasts.

The hair on his groin brushed her ass. He had buried himself inside her as far as he could go.

The heat and the tightness were incredible, as was the intimacy of this act. They were joined together as closely as possible. Ransome didn't even have to move. He just lay there as her interior muscles rippled and squeezed as if they were trying to milk him of all his vital juices. Arabella reached down with one hand. Her fingers moved between her legs and increased her arousal. Her chest began to heave. He held tightly to her breasts.

Finally she gasped. "Fuck me! Fuck me, Stephen! Come in my ass!"

Ransome had always prided himself on being a gentleman. He knew how to oblige a lady.

He managed only half a dozen or so slow, powerful strokes before his climax seized him. Luckily Arabella had worked herself into a frenzy by that time, so her culmination shuddered through her at the same time as he emptied himself into her bowels. It was as good as he had always hoped and dreamed it would be.

When it was over he lay there struggling to catch his breath. The experience had actually exceeded his expectations. He could die a happy man now.

Except that he didn't want to die. He wanted to live a long time, and spend the rest of that life making love to Arabella.

He would have to divorce Louisa, of course, and that would cause a scandal. He regretted that, but nothing could be done about it. He intended to marry Arabella, and he couldn't do that as long as he already had a wife.

And of course Arabella would give up her life as a prostitute. That went without saying.

The whole thing—the divorce, taking a scarlet woman as his new wife—might even jeopardize his military career, but Ransome was willing to take that chance. His career would mean nothing to him without Arabella, anyway.

She laughed then, and said, "You certainly know how to wake a girl up in the morning, Stephen."

"I . . . I love you, Arabella." There. He had said it.

By now he had slipped out of her, so she was able to turn in his arms and face him. She wore a surprisingly solemn expression on her face as she told him, "You shouldn't say that, Stephen."

"Why not? It's true."

"No, it's not. You're smitten with me, and we have a wonderful time together in bed, but that's not love." The little laugh she gave had a bitter edge to it. "You have a wife and family somewhere back East, I expect, even though we haven't talked about it. And I'm just . . . just a whore."

He reached up to stroke her cheek as he exclaimed, "Don't say that! It's not true. Well, I am . . . I am married, but . . . you're not . . . what you said."

"What would you call it? Men fuck me for money."

Ransome shook his head. "Not anymore. Never! You've put all that behind you. What you and I have between us is more pure than that. Innocent, almost." He realized how ludicrous that sounded, considering what they had just done, but he believed it anyway.

She smiled and cupped a hand against his cheek. "You're very sweet, Stephen, but you don't know what you're saying. You need to think about it. You need to realize that what's between us . . . well, it isn't what you believe it to be. And more than anything else, you need to continue with your assignment for General Crook. I know how much your duty means to you."

The general! Of course! He had to ride out today and search for more places where a fort could be located. That hadn't even entered his mind since he woke up.

A glance toward the window told him that the sun had fully risen. Bright sunlight slanted in around the curtains. But the hour was still relatively early. He had plenty of time to get back to the hotel, change into his uniform, and meet Dan Ryan at the livery stable. He would need to select some different troopers for their escort today, too, since he had dismissed Brundage, Hollis, and Lamont from that duty. If there was time, he might even try to grab a bite of breakfast and a cup of coffee at the hotel.

First things first, though, and that meant getting out of the Gem. He sat up and said, "We'll talk later. I mean it, Arabella. I'm not going to give you up, no matter what you say. Right now, though, I need to get dressed."

She swung her legs out of bed and stood up, stretching for a second like a healthy animal. A beautiful, gloriously nude, healthy animal at that. As she shrugged into a silk wrapper, she said, "There's a set of back stairs you can use, so you won't have to go down through the barroom. Not as much chance of somebody seeing you that way."

"I'm not ashamed of anyone knowing that I was with you," he insisted as he started pulling on his clothes.

"I know that. It never hurts to be discreet, though."

He supposed that was true. Within minutes he had finished dressing. Carrying the beaver hat, he followed her to the door. She opened it only a few inches and looked out.

"No one's in the hall," she told him. "This early, almost everyone is still sleeping. Mr. Swearengen may not be, though. I'm not sure he ever sleeps."

Ransome didn't care about Swearengen or anyone else. He put a hand on Arabella's shoulder as they stepped out into the corridor. She took him to a narrow door that opened onto an equally narrow set of stairs leading down.

"The door at the bottom opens into the alley behind the building," she said. "Good luck today, Stephen. You'll be back to see me tonight?"

"Of course I will. I wouldn't think of not seeing you." He bent to kiss her, a quick, urgent kiss, potent enough for him to feel it all through him.

"I'll be looking forward to it," she said when he straightened. "I like looking at those maps of yours . . . among other things."

He smiled and gave her a playful swat on the rump— something he *never* would have done to Louisa—and then went down the stairs, taking with him the beautiful memories of everything that had happened.

ARABELLA turned back toward her room, but before she reached the door, Al Swearengen emerged from his office and stalked toward her.

"Well?" he demanded.

"Well, what?" she shot back, not really in the mood right now for the man's crude banter.

"What happened with Ransome?"

"He spent the night with me, but he's on his way now to continue his scouting mission for General Crook. He promised to come back tonight and let me know everything that happens."

Swearengen nodded in evident satisfaction. "Good, good. You collect any money from him?"

"Just let me worry about that, Al."

He snorted. "Where money's concerned, I always worry. Puttin' you up here don't come cheap, you know."

Anger flared inside her. She tamped it down; the cool self-control she always cultivated meant a great deal to her, and she didn't want to lose her temper with Swearengen.

"I buy my own liquor and most of my own food," she said patiently. "The room itself is your main expense on my behalf, and it's not really costing you anything, now, is it?"

"I could stick some other whore in there."

"None of your other whores could ever get a man like Major Ransome in bed with them," she told him. "He'd be repulsed by them. He's your eyes and ears inside General Crook's headquarters, and if you want to have any influence on what Crook does, Ransome is your best bet. You're a gambler, aren't you, Al?"

He grunted. "Only when all the odds are on my side. I ain't so sure about this game. Too many wild cards floating around."

"You'll be glad you were patient when you have a steady stream of troopers flowing in and out of this place."

"We'll see," Swearengen said. "In the meantime, if you want to distract me from my worries, I can think of some mighty good ways to do it."

Arabella shook her head, well aware that Swearengen was leering at her nipples again as they poked against the silk of her wrapper. "That will never happen."

"Like I said . . . we'll see."

Swearengen turned and went back into his office. For a moment, as his back was turned, she wished that she had a gun so she could blast a bullet right through him. It would feel good to see him thrown forward by the impact, to stand there watching as he squirmed in agony and bled his life out on the floor. He didn't really deserve such a grisly fate, though, she supposed, because he hadn't really done anything except look at her and make crude, suggestive comments.

Unlike all the *other* men she had killed, starting with her father.

They had had it coming to them.

RANSOME checked his pocket watch and saw that the hour stood at a little before nine o'clock as he strode toward the livery stable. Dan Ryan would probably be waiting for him. But Ryan had kept him waiting a short time past the appointed hour the day before, so Ransome didn't feel too bad about making Ryan wait today.

Anyway, all such considerations paled next to the night he had spent with Arabella.

He tried not to think about what they had done together. He didn't need such a powerful distraction from his duties. It was enough to keep those fond memories in the back of his mind, where they were still strong enough to give him a warm glow from the top of his head to the soles of his boots. His blood seemed to sing in his veins. He felt more alive than he ever had before.

The sight that met his eyes when he came around the corner of the livery stable suddenly blunted his good mood. Dan Ryan waited there, as Ransome had anticipated, but he hadn't expected to see the three troopers standing with Ryan, holding the reins of their mounts.

Privates Brundage, Hollis, and Lamont . . . the three men he despised most in Deadwood.

"What's this?" Ransome demanded as he came to a stop facing them. "I thought I told you men that you were dismissed from the duty of escorting Mr. Ryan and myself."

"Well, sir—" Brundage began.

"I asked them to come along again," Ryan interrupted.

That surprised Ransome even more. He had thought from the way they all acted the day before that Ryan couldn't stand the three troopers, and that they felt the same way about him. Yet now Ryan was saying that it was his idea for them to act as escort once again.

"That's not your decision to make, Mr. Ryan," Ransome said, his voice stiff. "It's a military matter."

"Yes, sir, I know. But I thought . . . seein' as how they rode with us yesterday, and they already know the mission that we're on, it wouldn't hurt anything to have them come along again."

Ransome didn't like it, but he supposed that Ryan was right. The troopers hadn't caused any trouble the day before, and he knew them to be competent soldiers who could fight if they happened to run into any of the Sioux.

"Very well," he said with a frown. "But I expect you and your friends to be on your very best behavior, Private Brundage."

Brundage snapped a salute, as did the other two troopers. "Yes, sir, Major," he said. "Thanks for givin' us another chance."

"All right," Ransome muttered. "Mount up. We have more ground to cover today."

He wanted to find every possible location for a military post within half a day's ride of Deadwood. When it came time for the War Department to make its decision, General Crook would be armed with every bit of ammunition Ransome could find in favor of establishing a fort near here. Once that was done, then Ransome could start figuring out how he was going to get himself assigned to that fort, so that he could see Arabella all the time. . . .

The five men rode out of Deadwood. Numerous pairs of eyes watched them go.

Chapter Eighteen

W**HAT** the fuck is Dan up to?" Calamity Jane muttered. "I don't know," Cougar Jack said as he rode alongside her, "but if snakes like Brundage and his pards are mixed up in it, it can't be anything good."

Calamity gave an unladylike snort and said, "You got *that* right!"

Both of them had been mightily confused when Dan went off to the bar in the Gem with Brundage the night before. Their puzzlement had grown when, instead of just having a quick drink, Dan had stood at the bar talking to the weasel-like trooper for a long time. Dan hadn't looked particularly happy about it, but he had nodded from time to time as if agreeing with Brundage about something.

Even more confusing was Dan's attitude when he finally came back to the table to join them. "What the fuck was that all about?" Calamity had demanded.

"Just talking over old times," Dan had said.

"Old times with Brundage weren't so good," Cougar Jack had pointed out, but Dan just shrugged.

"He ain't such a bad sort now. Folks can change, I reckon."

Normal folks, maybe—although Calam wasn't completely convinced even of *that*—but not nobody low enough to steal guns from the army and sell 'em to the Injuns. Calamity just couldn't believe that for a second.

But Dan had been closemouthed about Brundage and his conversation with the man for the rest of the night, not saying anything more except that Brundage, Hollis, and Lamont were going to escort him and Major Ransome on their scouting mission again the next day. Calamity and Jack hadn't pressed him on it. This morning, though, Calamity had given the old scout a sharp nudge with her elbow, and when he woke up, she'd said, "I think we oughtta follow Dan today and make sure them varmints don't try nothin' funny."

They had been rolled up in a buffalo robe under Colorado Charley Utter's wagon at the time. Charley had started off to Cheyenne the day before with a few of his freight wagons, so they'd had some privacy the night before and Calamity had taken advantage of it. She'd also taken advantage of the fact that ol' Cougar Jack had a snootful of whiskey.

When she woke him up and told him her idea, he'd moaned and groaned a mite, then finally said, "Uh, last night . . . did we, uh . . ."

Calam gave him her biggest grin and said, "We sure as shit did, honey. Three times, in fact."

That was a bit of an exaggeration, since the third time hadn't been a charm for Jack, even though he'd tried mighty hard, bless his heart. The tryin' had been the only thing hard about him, though.

But he didn't have to know that, and anyway, he had put that aside and got around to thinking about the first thing she'd said.

"Yeah, Dan's actin' mighty funny," he'd said as he sat up and rubbed the big bald spot on top of his head. "Like Brundage put the hoodoo on him somehow. It wouldn't hurt anything to keep an eye on him."

So when Dan, Major Ransome, and the three troopers

rode out of Deadwood, Calamity and Jack had gotten their horses and trailed along behind, staying back far enough that they wouldn't be spotted easily, yet close enough they could reach the group in a hurry in case of trouble. For a couple of old hands like them, that wasn't much of a challenge.

They had been following the five riders all morning, and so far not a damned thing had happened except that Ransome had stopped from time to time to sketch maps and make notes. They'd reached the Belle Fourche and turned to follow the stream, circling northwestward at the edge of the Black Hills. Deadwood lay miles behind them by noon.

Calamity and Cougar Jack reined in on the lee side of a ridge and dismounted, climbing to the crest to stretch out on their bellies and watch as Dan, the major, and the three troopers stopped for a midday meal at the edge of a coulee. Jack frowned and said, "Did you, uh, happen to think to bring along any vittles, Calam?"

"Hell, no! It didn't occur to me that we'd be out this long. Reckon I knowed it, I just didn't think about it. How about you?"

Jack shook his head solemnly. "Afraid not, except for a couple o' pieces o' jerky in my saddlebags for emergencies. You reckon this qualifies?"

"Damn right it does. At least we won't starve." Calamity grinned. "'Specially since we can wash it down with the bottle o' who-hit-John I got in *my* saddlebags."

She slid down the slope a ways, then stood up and went to the scrubby bush where they had tied their mounts. A minute later she came back to the ridge with the bottle in one hand and the strips of jerky in the other. It didn't hardly qualify as a feast, but Calamity Jane had long since learned that folks had to make do with what they had. She had less'n most, but she didn't let that stop her from enjoying herself.

Trying not to loosen too many teeth on the jerky, she gnawed on it and took a swig from the bottle now and then as she and Jack passed it back and forth. They sat side by side on the slope with their knees drawn up in front of them. A lot of clouds floated in the sky, but when the sun shone through the gaps its heat warmed the bones, just like the whiskey warmed the belly.

After a while Jack said, "We ought to be watchin' Dan and them others."

"We'll hear their horses if they move out," Calamity said.

"Yeah, more'n likely." Jack hesitated, cleared his throat, and went on. "Calam, about what happened last night . . ."

"You don't have to 'pologize. You done just fine."

"I was gonna say, I don't really recollect all that much about it. I'd had quite a bit to drink, you know."

"Oh. Well, in that case . . . you said I was prettier'n a cactus rose and smelled better, too, and that I was the best fuck you ever had, o' course."

Jack took his hat off and scratched his head. "I said that, did I?"

Calamity let out a guffaw and dug an elbow in his ribs again, just like she had that morning. "Hell, no! Well, only the part about me bein' the best fuck you ever had, that is. I ain't lettin' you off the hook about that! But shit, I know I ain't pretty, and I don't smell all that good neither. Sometimes I wish it was different, but things is what they is." A serious expression came over her grimy face as her mood abruptly changed and she heaved a sigh. "If I'd been a mite prettier, though, Wild Bill might'a liked me better."

Jack patted her shoulder with a calloused hand. "I'm sure he liked you just fine, Calam."

She sniffled. "Him and me . . . we never did . . . I mean, I carried on like we did, but Bill . . . I reckon he just sorta felt sorry for me." The whiskey and the memories were getting to her again, as they often did if she let her guard down. "Aw, hell, Jack, I'm just a pathetic ol' fraud. No man's ever really gonna want me."

Jack scooted closer and put his arm around her shoulders. "Now, that ain't true at all," he told her. "You've had plenty o' men."

"I been fucked by 'em, yeah, but let's face it . . . most o' those fellas'd fuck a squaw or a toad if that was all they could get. Ain't a one of 'em really loved me."

"You'll find somebody—"

"What about you, Jack?" she asked in a plaintive voice. "You reckon you could ever love me?"

"I ain't the type to settle down," he replied hurriedly. "I'm too damn fiddle-footed. But if I was ever gonna put down roots—which I ain't—I'd be right proud if it was with a gal like you, Calam."

"Aw, that's sweet of you." She leaned up to give him a peck on his leathery cheek, then snuggled closer to him and rested her head on his shoulder. They sat together that way for a while, letting the warm sun play over them, until finally she said, "Jack . . . ?"

"Yeah, Calam?"

"You want to . . . ?"

"I reckon I just might."

That was how they came to be occupied with each other and not really paying attention to anything else when all hell broke loose on the other side of the ridge.

DAN had never been more torn about anything in his life, not even earlier in the summer when his friend Bellamy had been in such a big mess and Dan couldn't decide what to do to help him. What Brundage wanted of him went against everything he'd ever believed in, and not only that, it meant double-crossing Major Ransome. Dan didn't feel any particular fondness for Ransome, but he seemed to be a decent sort for an officer. Brundage's plan would make Ransome look like a fool at best; at worst it would cast suspicion on the major.

But Dan didn't have any choice if he wanted Brundage and the other two troopers to keep quiet about what had happened to Ezra Jessup. Brundage had made it clear that Hollis and Lamont knew everything he did about that night in Bismarck.

And it wasn't like Ransome would get hurt, at least not too badly. Dan might not like it, but he'd always had a pragmatic streak running through him that his life in the army had only strengthened. You did what you had to do.

In this case, that meant cooperating with Brundage, Hollis, and Lamont and helping them rob the safe in the Gem.

"Here's what you do," Brundage had told him the night before, when Dan had met with him and Hollis and Lamont after parting company with Calamity Jane and Cougar Jack. They stood in the dark in an abandoned hovel on the outskirts of Deadwood, not far from the cemetery where Wild Bill Hickok and Preacher Smith and the whore called Carla were buried. "You find a good lonely spot, and when we stop to eat, come up behind Major Ransome and clout him on the head. Make sure you knock him out and then tie him up real good, so he can't get loose. Then you fog it back to Deadwood and yell your head off about how the Sioux jumped us and captured me and Matt and Dewey, along with the major."

"What good's that going to do?" Dan had wanted to know, although he already had a sneaking suspicion about what Brundage's plan might turn out to be.

"The army and everybody in town will turn out to chase the redskins, and while they're doin' that, the three of us will circle around to Deadwood, go in the back door of the Gem, and bust that safe wide open. It's damned perfect, because then when they never find us, they'll just figure the Indians killed us."

"What about Major Ransome?"

"When you lead everybody back out there, go to wherever you left him and pretend that you didn't know he'd be there, that you just happened to find him. He won't know who knocked him cold, so when you say the Sioux must've tied him up and left him there, he won't be able to say that that ain't the way it happened."

"And the three of you . . . ?"

"We loot that safe, and you never see us again. Nobody in this neck of the woods ever does."

Lamont had chuckled then and said, "We'll be down south o' the Rio Grande, guzzlin' tequila and fuckin' little Mexican gals."

Brundage muttered a curse, and Dan knew he didn't like the way Lamont had tipped off their plans. But it didn't matter. Dan didn't want to know where they were going.

For one thing, he doubted if they would even make it out of Deadwood alive.

"It won't work," he said. "Too many people will stay in town instead of going chasin' off after some phantom Indians, no matter how well I tell the story."

"But there's been all that talk about how Deadwood's gonna organize a militia," Brundage objected. "Folks will turn out for that."

"Most of them, maybe. But not Al Swearengen, and not Dority and Burnes, his right-hand men. They won't leave the Gem unattended."

"Well, then, we'll deal with 'em," Brundage snapped, his voice hardening. "You leave Swearengen and his boys to us. You forget, Dan, we're experienced soldiers, real fightin' men, not some whiskey-soaked saloon rats."

And on further reflection, Dan had decided that maybe going along with Brundage's cockeyed plan was his best course of action, after all. Chances were the troopers would wind up dead, because they had no idea just how tough Al Swearengen and his men really were.

If that was the way it worked out, then Brundage and the others could never say anything to anybody about what happened to Ezra Jessup . . . unless, of course, they wanted to tell ol' Satan all about it, once they'd landed in Hell.

So even though he didn't like it, Dan had gone along with the plan, hoping that he wasn't making the worst mistake of his life.

He had kept an eye out all morning for a suitable place to put Brundage's scheme into action. Brundage was getting impatient, Dan could tell, but he couldn't do anything about that. The time and the place had to be right, or he wasn't going through with it.

When they stopped for lunch on the edge of a coulee that cut down out of the hills and appeared to run all the way to the Belle Fourche about half a mile to the north, Dan said to Ransome, "Not much point in trying to find a way across and going on in this direction, Major. The War Department wouldn't want to put a fort on the other side of this coulee from Deadwood."

"No, I suppose not," Ransome said as he rubbed at his clean-shaven chin and frowned in thought. "Unless, of course, it would be possible to build a bridge across it and connect the fort to the settlement that way."

Ransome had just played right into his hands, thought Dan. If the major hadn't suggested the possibility of a bridge, he would have. He gestured vaguely toward the coulee and said, "Let's walk over there and check it out, see how deep and rugged it is."

That put them with their backs to the three troopers. As they walked, Ransome said, "I'm beginning to think that we've located the best sites already, Mr. Ryan. We're getting pretty far from the settlement now, and I know General Crook wouldn't want the post to be established where the men couldn't reach Deadwood fairly easily."

"No, sir, probably not," Dan agreed. "So you reckon we ought to turn back after we eat?"

"I think we might as well." They reached the edge of the coulee. Ransome stopped and peered down into it, resting his fists on his hips as he did so. "I suppose it would be possible to build a bridge to span this," he went on, "but I'm not sure it would be a good idea."

Dan slipped his Colt out of its holster and wished Ransome would step back from the edge a little and stop leaning over like that. If Dan clouted him over the head now, the major might just topple into the coulee and break his fool neck. Maybe he could knock Ransome out and then grab the back of his shirt and pull him away from the brink. . . .

With no warning, a gun roared somewhere behind him, and as Dan heard the wind-rip of a bullet go past his head, one thought filled his brain.

Those bastards Brundage, Hollis, and Lamont had double-crossed him!

Chapter Nineteen

❦

OVER by the horses, the three troopers had been talking quietly among themselves while Ryan and Major Ransome walked toward the coulee.

"You reckon he's gonna do it here?" Lamont asked.

"He'd damned well better," Brundage snapped. "He won't ever get a better chance. And it works out just perfect for us, too."

"How do you figure?" Hollis asked.

"Think about it . . . Ryan wallops Ransome and knocks him out. He ties him up and rides back to Deadwood to lead everybody back to where the Indians are supposed to have jumped us. But what do they find when they get here?" Brundage grinned. "They find Ransome's body, dumped in that coulee with a .45 slug in the back of his head. How's that gonna look with the story that Ryan tells about bein' jumped by Injuns? Not too damned good, lemme tell you. Then when folks get back to town and find out that the Gem has been robbed, it'll look like Ryan killed the major just to distract everybody so his partners could rob the saloon."

Hollis frowned. "But they'll know that we were his partners," he pointed out. "Even if we don't leave any witnesses alive in the Gem, folks will figure it out easy enough when we disappear."

"But by then we'll be long gone," Brundage said with a shrug. "Look, you got your choice. We go along with the plan the way I laid it out to Ryan last night, in which case folks think the Sioux most likely killed us and we get away clean . . . but Ryan and Ransome both come through it alive, neither of 'em really much the worse for wear. *Or* we double-cross Ryan, kill Ransome once Ryan's gone, and make it look like he was in on the holdup, in which case he probably gets lynched."

"I like that idea the best," Lamont said. "Ransome's dead for sure, and Ryan prob'ly is. I sure like the thought o' him kickin' his life away at the end of a hangrope after tryin' to convince those folks he didn't have nothin' to do with the robbery. Hell, he'll be so scared he'll shit his britches."

"I like that, too," Hollis said, "but if we do it that way, we'll likely be fugitives for the rest of our lives."

"Which we're gonna spend in Mexico, where we don't have to worry about American law," Brundage said. He spread his hands. "Look, it's up to you boys. We've hashed it out two or three times now. You know the risks. Whatever you say, goes."

"I vote we kill Ransome," Lamont said without hesitation.

Hollis thought it over longer, but after a moment he nodded and said, "I vote we kill Ransome, too. Either way we wind up with the loot, and it's worth taking a chance to know that Ryan will get what's coming to him."

Brundage nodded. "Yeah, that's the way I feel about it, too. All we got to do is wait for Ryan to do his part and then ride off. As long as Ransome don't take too long about doing it, I want to wait until he comes to before we kill him." Again, Brundage smiled viciously. "I want that motherfucker to know who's pullin' the trigger when he gets his brains blown out."

Neither of the other two could argue with that sentiment.

They turned to watch and wait while Ryan and Major Ransome talked at the edge of the coulee.

"Ryan's got his hand on his gun," Lamont said after a moment, excitement in his voice. As they watched, Ryan drew the weapon. "He's gonna do it. . . ."

"Yeah," Brundage agreed. "Everything's workin' out just fine."

That was when a gun blasted somewhere nearby, followed instantly by shrill whoops of hate. The three troopers jerked around in shock as a swift rataplan of hoofbeats filled the air. A dozen or more painted, buckskin-clad figures mounted on sturdy ponies charged toward them from a couple of hundred yards away, seemingly having appeared out of thin air.

"It's a fuckin' Sioux war party!" Lamont howled as he threw his carbine to his shoulder and tried to draw a bead on one of the attacking riders.

Brundage uttered a heartfelt curse of his own. His carefully-worked-out plan was shot all to shit now.

All because the damn *real* Indians had shown up!

CALAMITY Jane and Cougar Jack left off with what they were doing and scrambled to the top of the ridge, grabbing their rifles and pulling up their buckskin trousers as they did so. Calamity was mighty pissed. Ol' Jack had been pumping away really good, putting his heart and soul into it and showing her a fine old time, when the shooting and the whooping and the yelling started. Calam had been so worked up, in fact, that it had taken a few seconds after the first shot for her to realize that a real ruckus had broken out on the other side of the ridge.

When they reached the crest, they looked over and saw that a bunch of Indians had jumped Dan, Major Ransome, and the three troopers. Dan and Ransome were banging away at the Sioux with their pistols while Brundage, Hollis, and Lamont ran toward the coulee, leading the horses. No cover was to be had along the deep, ragged slash in the earth—at least none that Calamity could see.

"What the hell are they doin'?" she asked as she jerked tight the piece of rawhide around her waist that served as a belt. "They can't retreat. Injuns got 'em pinned against that coulee."

"Well, they can't go forward either," Jack said. "Maybe there's a ledge or something we can't see from here."

That must've been the case. The troopers let go of the horses, leaving them for the Indians, and ran as fast as they could toward the coulee, carrying their carbines. When they reached the edge they dropped out of sight for a second, before reappearing to fire over the rim, back toward the Indians. Dan and Ransome hurried to join them, as the three enlisted men now provided the covering fire.

"That's it, by Godfrey!" Jack said. "They're standin' on a ledge just below the rim, firin' over it like it was a parapet on a stockade wall!"

Calamity knew he had to be right. Dan and his companions were relatively safe for the moment, because the rim of the ravine itself gave them good cover.

But they still had the coulee behind them and nowhere else to go. The Sioux stopped their charge and peeled off before they got too close, but as far as Calam could see, they still had the upper hand. They could wait out the five men trapped just below the rim.

"We gotta help 'em!" she said. "They'll run outta bullets sooner or later, and then those redskins'll have 'em trapped."

"I reckon you're right," Jack agreed with a grim expression on his leathery visage. "But you know that if we take cards in the game, that war party's liable to come up here after us."

Calamity grinned and said, "I don't think so. If we hit 'em right now, whilst Dan and them other fellas still have powder and shot, we'll have the red devils in a cross fire."

Cougar Jack grunted and eared back the hammer on his

Sharps. "Worth a try. See that big son of a bitch with the feathered headdress? He's got to be the chief. We'll see how much the others really want to fight with him dead."

That said, the old scout lowered his head and rested his grizzled cheek against the smooth wood of the weapon's stock as he peered over the sights. From this angle, he was able to rest the Sharps's barrel on the ground to steady it. He'd be firing downhill, though, which was always tricky, just like aiming uphill.

"Don't forget to correct up a mite," Calamity cautioned.

"I've shot this damn gun a time or two before, you know," Jack said testily. "You just get that Yellowboy o' yours ready to sing and dance."

Calamity picked up her Winchester and levered a round into the firing chamber. Jack kept aiming with the Sharps, and after a moment Calamity asked, "Are you gonna shoot him or wait for him to die o' old age and fall off his pony?"

"There are some things you can't rush, woman."

"Yeah, well, I wish you'd tell that to about ninety-nine percent o' the fellas I've fucked over the years."

Cougar Jack made a low, growling sound like his namesake, but he didn't take his eyes off what he was doing. Another couple of seconds ticked by, and then he stroked the trigger like a lover's caress. The Sharps erupted with a dull boom as a plume of gray smoke twisted from its muzzle.

Down below, eagle feathers flew and blood mist sprayed all over the neck of the war chief's pony as the heavy slug blew half the chief's head away.

The echoes of the shot had barely begun to roll over the hills when Calamity Jane's Winchester opened up. She sprayed the group of riders with bullets, working the rifle's loading lever as fast as she could. She didn't care about accuracy as much as she did about striking fear into the hearts of those savages and making them run. Even so, she saw a couple of the warriors topple off their ponies as her lead found them.

The Winchester held fifteen rounds. Calamity had cranked off eight of them when Cougar Jack's Sharps roared a second time. One of the Indians fairly flew off his mount as the shot tore a fist-sized hole through his back and chest. The scout began reloading the single-shot rifle again as Calamity finished emptying her repeater.

At the same time, renewed firing came from the coulee. After Dan and the soldiers had taken cover on the ledge, the Sioux had pulled back to regroup and figure out what to do next. Now the Indians unexpectedly found themselves in a deadly cross fire, and always practical when it came to fighting, they did the only reasonable thing they could.

They lit a shuck out of there, grabbing up their dead and wounded to take with them.

Calamity let out an exultant whoop. "Look at the fuckers go! Hell, they didn't even try to put up a fight against you an' me, Jack!"

"They got more sense than that," Jack said. "Let 'em go, and good riddance." He nodded toward the empty rifle in Calamity's hands. "You better get some fresh cartridges in there, just in case they decide to come back, though."

"They were whippin' them ponies hell-bent for leather," Calamity said. "They ain't comin' back." She took a handful of cartridges from a pouch at her waist and thumbed them through the Winchester's loading gate anyway. Being ready for trouble never cost anybody more than it was worth.

"Reckon we might as well ride down there and say howdy," Jack said as he closed the Sharps's breech after slipping a fresh round into it. "Unless they're blind, deaf, and dumb, Dan and those soldier boys know somebody was up here givin' 'em a helpin' hand. I don't know what we'll tell 'em about what we're doin' out here so far from Deadwood, though."

"Hell, they ain't got no reason to complain, since we saved their bacon," Calamity said with a grin, "but if they ask too many questions, just tell 'em you brought me out here to give me some good lovin'. Speakin' o' which . . ."

"Soon's we get another chance," Cougar Jack said. "You can count on it."

DAN had realized within a couple of heartbeats that the shot that had come so close to his head hadn't been fired by Brundage, Hollis, or Lamont. All he had to do was turn around and see the Sioux war party charging toward them and hear the bloodthirsty whoops that came from the hostiles.

The danger had driven all thoughts of Brundage's holdup plan from his mind. Instead, since Dan had already drawn his gun, he'd started firing toward the attackers, spacing his shots slowly and evenly so he wouldn't empty the Colt too quickly. Beside him, Major Ransome did the same. The range was a little long for handguns, but the main thing they wanted to do was give the three troopers some covering fire.

"This way!" Ransome shouted to them. "Over here!"

The men had started toward them, trying to bring the horses along, until Ransome shouted for them to let go of the mounts. That allowed them to run a little faster, but the Sioux were still gaining on them.

Dan had cast a glance over his shoulder, then paused in his firing to say, "Major, there's a ledge about five feet below the rim. It's not very wide, but it's big enough to hold all five of us."

Ransome had nodded his understanding of Dan's suggestion. Dan saw fear in the major's eyes, but Ransome had it under control. "We'll still be in a precarious position," he'd said, "but at least we'll have some cover."

Brundage, Hollis, and Lamont pounded up, red-faced and out of breath. Ransome waved them toward the coulee and called, "Drop down on that ledge, and then cover us!" The troopers obeyed, crawling carefully over the rim. The ledge was only about a yard wide, Dan recalled from his glance at it. If a man went over the edge too fast, he might miss it and fall all the way to the bottom of the coulee, which was a good seventy or eighty feet deep.

After that, the troopers had opened fire with their Springfields, giving Dan and Ransome the opportunity to climb down to the ledge and join them. The major had said that they would still be in a precarious position once they did that. Up shit creek was more like it, thought Dan. All the Sioux had to do was keep feinting at them until they had exhausted all their ammunition. Then they'd be easy pickings.

But a moment later somebody had opened fire on the Indians from the top of a nearby ridge with what sounded like a Sharps and a repeater, and several of the warriors had been hit, including the chief. "Keep firing!" Ransome had urged his companions. The arrival of reinforcements had changed the tactical situation, Dan told himself, thinking like a sergeant again. Now the Sioux were on the defensive because they were caught in a cross fire.

It came as no surprise to him when the Indians fled. They were smart fighters who liked the odds to be on their side. Even though they still had their enemies outnumbered, the Sioux were in a bad position where more of them were likely to be killed if they continued the battle. So they retreated at full speed.

By the time Dan, Ransome, and the three troopers had clambered over the rim of the coulee, two riders were moving slowly down from the ridge toward them. Ransome lifted a hand to shade his eyes against the noonday sun and asked, "Who are those people?"

A grin started to pluck at Dan's mouth when he thought he recognized the two figures on horseback. "Looks like Jack LeCarde and Calamity Jane, Major," he said.

"LeCarde?" Ransome repeated. "What's he doing out here?"

Dan had a pretty good idea. Jack and Calamity had been mighty suspicious of his behavior in the Gem the night before, after Brundage came over and made that comment about Jessup. The two of them had likely followed him out here today to see what was going on. A part of him felt that he ought to be a mite irritated with them for being such a pair of busybodies.

But a bigger part of him knew that their timely arrival had likely saved him and his companions from being killed by the Sioux, so he couldn't get too mad at them.

Besides, with his friends here he had a ready-made excuse for not going through with Brundage's plan after all. He couldn't very well knock out Ransome with Calamity and Cougar Jack as witnesses. That meant Brundage would have to abandon his robbery scheme, at least for now. A glance at the trooper's tight, angry face told Dan that Brundage had realized the same thing.

But Brundage and the others still knew what had happened to Ezra Jessup, Dan reminded himself. And they still wanted to get their hands on enough loot so they could desert from the army and make new starts for themselves somewhere else—Mexico, most likely.

So his dilemma had just been postponed, Dan thought with a sigh. It wasn't going away.

Not as long as Brundage, Hollis, and Lamont were still alive.

Chapter Twenty

THERE was nothing like almost being killed to crystallize a man's thinking, Ransome told himself as the group rode back toward Deadwood. As he'd crouched there on that ledge with the coulee gaping behind him, as he fired his pistol futilely toward those whooping, bloodthirsty savages, the thought that had been uppermost in his mind hadn't been fear for his own life or regret that he would never see his family again.

No, he had been afraid that he would die here and never again experience the joy of making love to Arabella.

Now that the danger was over and he was on his way back to Deadwood, his thoughts were still mostly of the beautiful blonde. He could hardly wait to see her again, to take her in his arms and feel the warmth of her body, to taste the honeyed sweetness of her mouth.

He couldn't completely forget about what had happened, though. As Dan Ryan rode beside him, Ransome said to the former sergeant, "I still don't understand where those Indians came from. I didn't see any cover around that coulee where they could have been hiding."

"Well, remember what we were sayin' earlier about how the hostiles can come out of nowhere?" Ryan shrugged. "I reckon what happened today was proof of that. I didn't see any sign of them either. Chances are there's another gully around there somewhere that runs into the coulee. It's probably shallower, but still deep enough to hide a man on horseback. They followed it until they were as close to us as they could get before coming out into the open. Leastways, that's what I *think* happened. Don't reckon we'll ever know for sure."

The filthy creature called Calamity Jane urged her horse up on Ransome's other side. If he hadn't known that she was female, he might not have guessed it. She said, "I seen a whole war party o' Pawnee vanish into thin air once. Looked like that anyway. Cavalry patrol I was packin' for rode all over that ground and never did figure out where them redskins got off to. Just goes to show you there ain't no sneakier critter on the face o' the earth than a Injun."

Ransome glanced back at the three troopers riding behind them. He wasn't sure he would agree with Calamity Jane's conclusion. It seemed to him that Brundage, Hollis, and Lamont were pretty sneaky, too.

The woman kept yammering about various things, most of them crude and borderline obscene, as they rode toward Deadwood. It was hard to believe, thought Ransome, that Calamity Jane and Arabella were actually members of the same sex.

That got him thinking about Arabella again, and he didn't pay any more attention to what Calamity was saying. In his eagerness to reach Deadwood and see Arabella, he rode out a short distance in front of the others. Not too far, though, because he didn't want a sudden attack by the hostiles to split him away from the rest of his party. No matter how distracted he was by his own emotions, he hadn't completely forgotten how to conduct himself in possibly unfriendly surroundings.

When they reached the settlement late that afternoon,

Ransome dismissed Brundage, Hollis, and Lamont and told the troopers to go back to the camp at the edge of town. "You won't be needin' us anymore, Major?" Brundage asked. "You don't plan on doin' any more scoutin'?"

"Not right now, Private," Ransome answered.

"Well, if you do, just let us know, sir. We'd be pleased to ride escort with you whenever you want."

The man's obsequious attitude didn't fool Ransome. He knew that the three troopers didn't like him. That was fine, because he didn't like them either. He wasn't sure what Brundage was up to by trying to be so cooperative, but he suspected that the goal couldn't be good, whatever it was.

He returned their salutes, gave them a curt nod, and sent them on their way. Along with Ryan, Calamity Jane, and the scout LeCarde, Ransome headed for Clarke's Livery. All four of them kept their mounts there.

"You need me to come with you while you explain your findings to General Crook, Major?" Ryan asked as they all swung down from their saddles.

Ransome shook his head. "No, thank you, Sergeant . . . I mean, Mr. Ryan. I have all the information the general will require." He turned to Calamity Jane and LeCarde. "Thanks to you two as well. Without your efforts on our behalf, I don't think Mr. Ryan and those troopers and I would have survived the day."

LeCarde rubbed his beard-stubbled jaw and said, "Well, it ain't the most pleasant thing in the world, helpin' out skunks like those three, but I reckon it was worth it to keep you and Dan from losin' your hair."

Ransome frowned. "What is it about Brundage, Hollis, and Lamont that rubs you the wrong way, if you don't mind my asking? I mean, I don't like them myself, but is that the way they affect everyone?"

"Only the ones who know what they did back at Fort Abraham Lincoln, while they were still sergeants in the Seventh Cavalry," Ryan said.

"And what might that be?"

The other three exchanged a glance, then Ryan nodded and said, "It's all part of the military record, so you could find out if you wanted to, whether I told you or not. They were mixed up in a scheme to steal some rifles from the quartermaster's depot there and sell them to the Indians."

Ransome knew that bad blood existed between Ryan and the troopers, and he had supposed that it stemmed from something Brundage and the others had done. But he hadn't expected anything quite that bad, so he exclaimed, "My God! And they're still in the army?"

"Well, you've got to remember that they didn't actually carry out their plan. They didn't even come close to getting away with it. And I heard that they might have testified against the civilians who were involved in it with them, so that those hombres wound up in jail, too. Brundage, Hollis, and Lamont were all busted back to buck privates, and they spent almost a year in the stockade at Fort Leavenworth. I guess the brass thought that was enough punishment. Colonel Custer didn't want 'em comin' back to the Seventh, though, so they transferred over to General Crook's command."

Ransome nodded. "I could tell that something had happened in the past to cause trouble between you."

"They blame me for their plan getting ruined and for them getting caught," Ryan said. "I found out about it, and I would have turned 'em in before I let them get away with it, but I didn't have to. Somebody else told what they were up to; not me. I never knew who, and I don't care, except that if I did know, I might could tell Brundage, Hollis, and Lamont and they wouldn't hate me so much." Ryan shrugged. "That is, if I actually gave a damn how they feel about me, which I don't."

"Well, I regret taking them along again today. It must have made you quite uncomfortable to have them around."

Ryan shook his head. "I was the one who asked you if they could ride escort with us again, remember, Major?

Brundage claims they've turned over a new leaf, and I've always figured that a fella deserves a second chance."

Calamity Jane snorted. "Anybody who'd try to sell guns to the Injuns don't deserve nothin' but a bullet in the head and an unmarked grave, if'n you ask me."

"Which nobody did," LeCarde pointed out.

"Yeah, well, that ain't neither here nor the other place," Calamity said.

"And this assignment is over," Ransome said. "Thank you again, Mr. Ryan." He shook hands with all three of them, even Calamity Jane. "My thanks to all of you. Now I have to go make my report to General Crook."

And as soon as he was finished with that, he added silently to himself, he would head for his room at the Grand Central, clean up a little, and then go to the Gem to see Arabella again.

Just the thought of being with her once more made his manhood start to harden and grow. He suppressed the reaction as best he could.

After all, he didn't want anything else standing at attention while he made his report to General Crook!

"**WELL**, that all worked out just fine," Lamont said with an edge of bitter sarcasm in his voice. "Ryan and Ransome are still alive, and we ain't a damned bit closer to gettin' our hands on all that loot in the safe."

Brundage snapped, "Don't even think about blamin' me for what happened. How in the hell was I supposed to know those fuckin' redskins would show up? Everything would've been fine if they hadn't."

"There's no point in letting it gnaw at your innards, either of you," Hollis said. "The question is, what do we do now? That plan of yours is out the window, Clyde, if we're through scoutin' with Major Ransome."

The troopers trudged wearily toward the camp at the edge of the settlement. Brundage had brooded all the way back to

Deadwood because he had already thought the same thing Lamont had put into words. They were right back where they had started.

"I'll come up with something else," he said. "This is just a temporary setback, I tell you."

Lamont grunted. "Who you tryin' to convince . . . us or you?"

With an effort, Brundage held his temper. "You just wait and see," he told Lamont. "We'll be rich men, and we won't never have to take any more orders from any fuckin' officers!"

"That sounds good, but remember, we don't know how long we're gonna be here," Hollis cautioned. "Crook could get orders for us to move out any day now. Hell, they could send us back out to look for Crazy Horse some more!"

That prospect was disheartening to all three men. They'd had enough Indian fighting to last them a lifetime. During the skirmish at the coulee today, Brundage had been convinced that he was going to die, without ever experiencing the luxury that rightfully should have been his somewhere along the way. He had lived a tough, mean life, without a break, only hard work and a bunch of bastards lording it over him like they were better than he was. He had come out of the riverfront slums of St. Louis determined to make something of himself, but life had thwarted him at every turn.

Not this time, he promised himself. This might be his last chance. And since he and his friends had been given a reprieve from death at the hands of those redskins, maybe that was a sign their luck had changed.

"Forget Ryan and forget Ransome," he said. "I'd rather have money than revenge. We're gonna bust that safe wide open and clean it out. There's no real law here in Deadwood to stop us."

Hollis gave him a dubious frown. "Just go in and rob it at gunpoint? Sounds to me like a good way to get ourselves killed. You said Swearengen's got a man with a shotgun watching the safe around the clock."

"Well, we'll still need a distraction of some sort. . . ." Brundage rubbed his jaw and frowned in thought. "Something that'll stir up the whole town, just like that phony business with the Sioux would have."

"Only thing besides Injuns that gets folks that worked up is fire," Lamont said.

Brundage stopped in his tracks and looked over at the burly Lamont for a second before breaking into a big grin. "Dewey," he said, "sometimes you're a fuckin' genius!"

"Huh?" Lamont looked confused. "I am?"

"Yeah. We'll start a fire." Brundage looked around, thinking hard. "Up at the Grand Central Hotel, maybe. General Crook and all the other officers are stayin' there, so when it starts to go up in flames, it'll draw plenty of attention."

"It'll burn the town to the ground, that's what it'll do," Hollis objected. "You know how fast a fire can spread in a settlement like this?"

"Sure," Brundage agreed. "That's why everybody will run up the street to fight it, even Swearengen and his boys. They'll know that if they don't put out the fire, it'll get the Gem, too. But the hotel's three blocks away, so we'll have plenty o' time to bust that safe open before the fire can ever get there, assumin' it spreads." He smacked his right fist into his left palm. "It's fuckin' brilliant! With the town on fire, nobody'll give a damn what's goin' on in the Gem, and they'll be too busy afterward to come find us!"

Hollis thought it over and then nodded slowly. "Maybe," he said. "It might work."

"It *will* work," Brundage declared.

Lamont's brow was still furrowed, though. "How you gonna get into the safe?" he asked. "That always has sorta bothered me."

"I got somethin' at camp that'll help us out with that. I

paid some old prospector for a couple of sticks o' dynamite. They'll blow the door right off, if we can't bust it open with a crowbar or somethin' like that. We'll try that first and only use the dynamite if nothin' else works."

"Even with the hotel on fire, people will notice a dynamite blast," Hollis said.

"That's why it's a last resort. I tell you, just have a little faith. We're gonna be rich . . . and we might get some of that revenge we wanted, too. Ransome is stayin' at the hotel. Maybe the fire will get him."

The prospect of Ransome dying in flames obviously appealed to Lamont and Hollis. Both men grew quiet and thoughtful, and Brundage knew they were imagining the situation. So was he, and it was damned nice.

"Matt, you'll start the fire," Brundage went on after a moment.

"Why me?"

"Because you're the best at slippin' in and out of places. While you're doin' that, Dewey and me will be at the Gem. We'll hang back when everybody runs out to see what the commotion's about. We'll get the drop on anybody who stays behind and then bust the safe open. While we're doin' that, you hotfoot it through the alleys back o' the Gem to join us. We'll all have our horses saddled and waitin' behind the place. We'll have the loot and be gone before people even know what happened."

"Well, all I can say is that I hope this plan works out better'n the last one," Lamont rumbled.

"It will," Brundage promised. "It's simple. Nothin' can go wrong."

Hollis said, "I've got one more question. When do we do this?"

"What's wrong with tonight?"

That took both of the other men by surprise. "That soon?" Hollis asked.

"Why not? Our luck's runnin' good right now. We got out o' that brush with the Indians alive and with our scalps in one piece, didn't we? By all rights we should'a died today." Brundage rubbed his hands together. "That's fate's way of tellin' us to make our move. By the time the sun comes up tomorrow mornin', fellas, we'll be a long way from Deadwood . . . and we'll be three rich motherfuckers!"

Chapter Twenty-one

RANSOME was on his way through the Grand Central Hotel's lobby, intending to go upstairs and knock on the door of General Crook's room, when he heard a familiar voice call, "Major Ransome! In here."

He turned and went through the arched entrance of the dining room. The place had been turned into an impromptu meeting room. Several tables had been pushed together and chairs arranged around them. General Crook stood in the front of the room while his staff officers and the commanders of the units that made up the column sat at ease at the tables.

"Join us, Major," Crook invited. "I was just sharing some news with your fellow officers, but that can wait a moment. What do you have to report?"

Ransome felt a bit uncomfortable with so many eyes on him, as all the other men in the room had turned to look at him. As he approached the front of the room, he held up the pages he had taken from his notebook and said, "I have some more maps here, sir, indicating possible sites for an army outpost if the War Department decides to locate one in this area. I believe that, combined with the exploration I conducted yesterday, this covers all of the most feasible sites between here and the Belle Fourche. And I also believe that locating such a fort in this vicinity is an excellent idea, although I know that will be for others to decide."

He stopped short of suggesting that he be assigned to such a fort, or even—if he dared to dream it—be given command of the outpost. He planned to bring that up the next time he and the general were alone, however.

"Very good, Major," Crook said as he held out his hand for the maps Ransome had drawn. He took them and went on. "Now have a seat, and I'll continue with this briefing."

Ransome found an empty chair. As he sat down he glanced around at his fellow officers, trying unsuccessfully to determine from their expressions whether the general's news was good or bad.

Crook set the maps aside and clasped his hands behind his back, striking a dramatic pose as he usually did, even when no reporters were around to witness it. "As I was saying," he resumed, "a supply train arrived from Camp Robinson today, so we no longer have to rely completely on the generosity of our civilian hosts here in Deadwood. We now have ample provisions not only for our men but for the mules and horses as well."

Ransome wasn't surprised that Crook mentioned the mules before he did the horses. Crook had a pronounced fondness for the sturdy beasts and usually chose one as a saddle mount rather than a horse.

"The officer in command of the wagons also brought new orders for me," Crook continued. "I'm to return with them to Camp Robinson, where I will prepare a report for Washington on the summer campaign against the Sioux."

At those words, the bottom seemed to drop out of Ransome's belly. If Crook was leaving Deadwood and traveling to Camp Robinson, down in Nebraska, he would probably take most, if not all, of his staff with him.

And that meant Ransome would no longer be able to visit Arabella at the Gem!

He swallowed the sick feeling that welled up in his throat. He was a soldier and would obey his superiors' orders, whatever they might be.

But for the fleetest of seconds, he wondered if his military career was really worth it. He had already decided that the possibility of a life with Arabella justified giving up his wife, and most likely his children. Could he give up the army as well?

He would have to think about that. For as far back as he could remember, the concept of duty had been drilled into him. First duty to God, instilled in him by his minister father. Then duty to the vows of matrimony he had sworn and duty to his family.

If he was prepared to cast all of that aside for the pleasures that he found with Arabella, why should he hesitate to abandon his duties as a soldier, too? The army would continue to function just fine without him. He could resign his commission and stay here in Deadwood, although he thought it more likely that he and Arabella would leave the mining town and seek a new start elsewhere. Too many men here knew about what she had done at the Gem. He could live with the idea that other men had fucked his wife, but he didn't want it thrown in his face all the time.

He tore his thoughts away from both the past and the future and forced himself to concentrate on the present. General Crook was saying, ". . . Most of the column will remain here for the time being, until I receive further orders. The past few months have been so arduous that the men still need rest, and so do the animals."

Ransome allowed himself to hope that perhaps he would be left in command of the troops that remained in Deadwood.

It wasn't a completely far-fetched notion. General Crook trusted him, he knew that.

But that hope was short-lived, as Crook immediately went on to appoint one of the colonels who commanded a cavalry brigade to take overall command of the column while he was gone. Ransome hadn't really expected anything else, even in that fleeting moment.

That concluded the briefing. Crook dismissed the officers and added with a smile that they should put the dining room's furnishings back the way they found them before they returned to their units. While that was going on, Crook caught Ransome's eye and beckoned him forward.

As he picked up the maps Ransome had given him earlier, the general said, "I just want to repeat, Major, that you've done fine work on this assignment. If the War Department *does* decide to locate a fort in this vicinity, it will be due in no small part to your efforts."

"Thank you, sir," Ransome said, wondering if he ought to ask Crook whether or not he would be going along to Camp Robinson.

Before he had a chance to do so, Crook asked a question of his own. "Did you encounter any problems in your scouting today?"

The general was bound to hear about that skirmish with the Sioux, because the troopers would talk about it and word would spread through the enlisted men, who were always avidly interested in the details of an Indian fight. From there the officers would hear of it, and eventually the news would reach Crook.

"Actually, sir, we were attacked by approximately a dozen hostiles. Sioux, from the look of them, although I didn't recognize any of the individual Indians."

Crook's eyebrows rose. "Indeed! Were there any casualties?"

"Not in our party. Several of the hostiles were killed or wounded. It was a near thing, though, and we probably wouldn't have escaped unscathed if not for the timely arrival of some reinforcements."

"What reinforcements?"

"The scout, Jack LeCarde, and a local civilian named Martha Cannary."

"You mean Calamity Jane?"

"I believe that's the name she's best known by, yes, sir," Ransome said.

The general laughed. "So Cougar Jack and Calamity Jane saved your bacon. Well, I'm glad to hear that no one on our side was hurt." He grew serious again. "I'll expect a full report on the incident before I leave for Camp Robinson tomorrow."

"I'll have it for you first thing in the morning, sir," Ransome promised.

"Very good." Crook reached for his cork sun hat, which he had placed on one of the tables. "I'll bid you good evening, then, Major."

"Good evening to you, too, sir."

A mixture of emotions went through Ransome. First and foremost, relief that now he could go to his room, clean up, and then head for the Gem. But worry was mixed in with the relief, because Crook hadn't said anything about whether or not Ransome would be going to Camp Robinson with him, and Ransome had been distracted by telling the general about the fight with the Sioux and hadn't gotten around to broaching the other subject.

In a situation as uncertain as this, bold action was required, Ransome decided as he bounded up the stairs to the hotel's second floor. Regardless of whether or not he remained in Deadwood, Arabella needed to make a clean break with her past if they, were going to have any chance of a life together.

Tonight, he told himself, he would ask her to marry him. If he had to go to Camp Robinson, then she would go with him. Not as an officer's wife—not yet, because there was still the matter of freeing himself from Louisa—but he wouldn't leave her here to continue her sordid existence. He couldn't.

And so, tonight everything had to change.

"**NOTHIN'** like an Injun fight to get the juices flowin', ain't that right?" Calamity Jane asked as she picked up a glass of whiskey.

"If those varmints'd had their way, our juices would'a been flowin', all right," Cougar Jack agreed. "Mostly our blood, outta where our scalps used to be."

Dan sat back, leaning against the wall behind him as he took a sip from the mug of beer in his hand. He liked the solid feel of the wall, even though, unlike Wild Bill Hickok, he wasn't particularly worried about somebody coming up from behind and shooting him.

He supposed that he thought about Wild Bill because he and Calamity and Cougar Jack were in the No. 10 Saloon, sitting only a few feet from where the Prince of Pistoleers had been murdered. A card game went on at that table tonight, just as it had on the afternoon of Hickok's death.

Calamity looked over at him and said, "You're as quiet as a bump on a fuckin' log tonight, Dan. Somethin' wrong?"

Dan shook his head. "Not really. I guess that almost gettin' killed makes a man stop and reflect on the life he's led."

"Oh, hell, don't go gettin' all mired down in that sort o' muck." Calamity threw back her drink, then licked her lips. "The past is dead an' gone, and it don't do a damned bit o' good to brood about it. Anyway, you ain't got all that much to worry about. You been a straight arrow all your life, from what I know of you."

Dan shook his head. "You don't know me all that well, Calam. I've done plenty of things I ain't proud of."

"Shit, I'm the queen o' doin' things I ain't proud of! Ain't no rule says you got to be proud o' your life, though. You just got to live it the best way you can, doin' what you have to, to get by."

Cougar Jack set his own beer down and stared at her for a second before he said, "Good Lord, Calamity, that's a mighty profound sentiment. I didn't know you was such a deep thinker."

She grinned. "I ain't deep, I'm thick."

"What's that mean?"

"Fuck if I know. That I'm already a mite drunk and hankerin' to get a lot drunker?"

Jack waved a hand. "Well, let's get to it, then." He waved at Carl Mann behind the bar. "Hey, Carl, reckon we could get some more whiskey over here?"

"Comin' up, Cougar Jack," the bartender replied.

Dan drank the rest of his beer and then said, "That's enough for me. I've got some things I need to do."

Calamity frowned at him. "What could be more important than celebratin' the fact that all three of us still got our hair? We could'a died out there today, you know."

"I know," Dan said. He scraped back his chair. "That's why I've got to go take care of some unfinished business."

"Ooohh, that *does* sound important," Calamity mocked him. "When you get finished with that business o' yours, come on back an' join us. Me an' ol' Jack got some business of our own to finish, but we'll get around to that later, won't we, honey?"

The scout just smiled serenely as Calamity leered at him, his weathered face already turning placid from the amount of booze he had put away.

"We'll be here at the Number Ten for a while," Calamity went on, "and then we'll prob'ly go over to the Gem for a spell. You'll find us one place or t'other, happen you come lookin' for us, Dan."

"I'll remember that," he said as he got to his feet. He thumbed his hat back, nodded to the two of them, and headed for the door.

The early evening air had more than a hint of a chill in

it, reminding Dan that this was late September in Dakota Territory. Winter wasn't that far off, and he suspected it would be a ring-tailed howler. It usually was, this far north. He wondered what it would be like to spend those months in a warmer climate, say, Texas or Arizona or California. He had never been to California before. Folks said there were places there where it was always warm, and where you could hear the sound of the ocean rolling in to the shore all day and all night. Here the air would be cold and dank all winter, and instead of the quiet, endless song of the ocean you'd hear tinny piano music and raucous laughter, the curses of men and the screams of women, the all-too-frequent gunshots from the dark alleys, and the roar of blasting powder from the haunted slopes of the hills.

He wanted to leave. Gold wasn't worth it. He had left the army to find a new life here in Deadwood, but it wasn't any better than the old life. Backbreaking work, squalid conditions, loneliness . . . Maybe that was all he deserved, he thought as he trudged through the night, his steps taking him toward the Grand Central Hotel without him having to think about his destination. He had killed that crazy little enlisted man Jessup, after all. That was the worst thing he had ever done, but it still made him a murderer. That thought had filled his mind as he crouched on the ledge that afternoon, firing toward the charging Sioux. He'd been fully convinced that he was going to die there, and he would die with that boy's blood on his hands, unforgiven and unredeemed.

He stopped, leaned against the railing along the edge of the boardwalk, and covered his face with both hands. "I'm sorry," he said aloud, his voice muffled by his calloused palms. "I'm sorry for all the bad things I've done. Forgive me, Lord, please forgive me."

He wished Preacher Smith were still alive. The preacher could have guided him through this dark night of the soul and maybe helped him find redemption. He wasn't sure he could do it alone.

Death paraded before him as he stumbled on. Carla and old Ulysses Egan, both of them killed by those claim-jumping Galloway brothers . . . Fletch Parkhurst, shot down by Bellamy Bridges, as much by accident as anything else . . . The preacher, killed by an unknown gunman, almost certainly *not* Indians, but still just as dead either way . . . Even Wild Bill Hickok, whose death still hung over the entire community a month and a half later. Deadwood might be known for a lot of things, but always chief among them would be Hickok's murder. *Ace and eights. Dead man's hand.* People already threw those expressions around as if they had been saying them all their lives. What happened in the No. 10 that day had already passed into legend, and the legend was one of blood and death.

Hell, it was even in the town's name.

In the midst of so much death, how could anyone hope for life? With the weight of a man's evil on his shoulders—whether that evil had been intentional or not—how could he hope to throw off the burden and truly live again? The paths of righteousness were just too damn narrow. Folks were bound to stray from them and wander off into the darkness and never find their way back, so that they spent the rest of their days crying in the wilderness, always seeking a light they could never find. How could they keep going? Why didn't folks just fall down on their knees and throw their hands in the air and give up? That meant dying, but hell . . . they were all gonna die anyway, sooner or later. Why postpone doom, why turn away from the last dark trail that led into eternal nothing? Just cross the divide and get it over with. . . .

"Dan."

While those torturous thoughts had filled his brain, instinct had kept his stumbling steps pointed toward the Grand Central. Without even being aware of it, he had turned and gone down the dark passage next to the hotel, coming out in the alley that ran behind it. And now as he heard her voice and lifted his head to gaze toward it, he saw her standing there in the open kitchen doorway, silhouetted by the lamplight behind her, an unlikely vision with an empty wicker basket in one hand and the potato peelings she had just thrown out scattered across the alley outside the door.

"Lou," Dan said brokenly, grasping on to the last hope he held. "Lou, I want you to marry me. I want you to be my wife."

Chapter Twenty-two

ARABELLA set her hairbrush down and turned away from the mirror on her dressing table when the knock sounded on the door. "Who's there?" she called.

"It's me, Al."

Swearengen's raspy tones, soaked in whiskey and smoke, made her reach for the collar of her wrapper and pull it tighter at her throat. She'd been about to get dressed in expectation of Ransome's arrival later in the evening.

"What do you want, Al?" she asked as she stood up. She didn't make a move to open the door. The thought of Swearengen being in her room made her skin crawl.

"I got something for you."

Arabella had no idea what Swearengen might have for her. She couldn't imagine wanting anything the man might decide to give her. Hoping that he would just forget about it, she said, "You'll have to come back later."

"Just open the damned door, Arabella."

The sharp edge to his voice made her frown, and for a moment she was more determined than ever to keep him out. But then she thought better of being stubborn. They still had to work together to accomplish what they wanted, after all. She could at least be civil to him.

She went to the door, turned the key in the lock—she never left the door unlocked, even when she was in the room—and opened it. Swearengen stood there, a swath of colorful fabric in his hands. As he thrust it toward her, she saw that he held a dress. A dress of dark golden silk that surprised Arabella with its beauty.

"Here," he said. "I thought you might like this."

The gesture took her even more by surprise. She hadn't known him very long, but he'd certainly never struck her as being a generous man. Quite the contrary, in fact. He thought only of what was good for him and his business.

Maybe this fell into that category, she thought, as her natural suspicion cropped up. Maybe he thought he could buy his way into her favor.

"What is it?" she asked without taking the gown from him.

"It's a dress. You can see that."

"No, I mean, why are you giving it to me?"

Swearengen shrugged. "There's a new ladies' shop just opened up. First one in Deadwood. I saw this and thought you might like it."

"You were moved to buy a present for me?"

"Yeah, that's right. Is that so hard to understand?"

Arabella hesitated, then finally reached for the dress. She took it from him and held it up to study it with a critical eye. She found herself admiring its clean lines and the delicate touches of lace at the waist, sleeves, and neck.

"It's very nice," she admitted.

"You'll accept it, then, and wear it?"

"I suppose so." She knew what he was waiting for. "Thank you, Al."

"You're welcome. Put it on."

She held the dress in front of her, keeping it between the two of them as if it were a shield. "Now?"

"Yeah. I'd like to see it on you. Please."

The word sounded odd coming from his mouth, and Arabella would have been willing to wager that he didn't say it very often. She still didn't like the idea of inviting him into her room, but she supposed it wouldn't hurt anything. She wasn't exactly afraid of him, just . . . wary.

"All right," she said. "Come in."

He stepped into the room and closed the door behind him while she unfolded a dressing screen in front of the wardrobe. Carrying the dress, she moved behind the screen. A glance around the edge of it showed Swearengen standing on the other side of the room, his hands thrust in his pockets. He didn't look directly at the screen as he rocked forward and backward a little on the balls of his feet and cleared his throat.

He was trying to act like a gentleman, she realized. Clearly, he wasn't comfortable in the role, but at least he was making the effort.

Arabella shrugged out of the wrapper, put on her undergarments, and then slipped into the gown. Evidently he had a good eye for such things, as unlikely as that was.

On the other hand, she thought, a significant portion of his business had to do with women. Whores, to be sure, but still women. Unlike a lot of men on the frontier who might go months at a time without ever seeing a female, Al Swearengen spent most of his days and nights around women. He had to have learned a little about them.

She stepped out from behind the screen. The gown was cut low enough, and tight enough, so that the upper third of her breasts showed over the top of it. Swearengen's eyes went there first, but she couldn't hold that against him. Ninety-nine out of a hundred men would have looked at the exact same place when they first saw her in this dress.

"What do you think?" she asked.

Swearengen lifted his gaze to meet hers, and she had to give him credit for that, too. "It's mighty lovely," he said, "and so are you, Arabella."

"Thank you." She turned, just fast enough to make the skirt swirl out a little and give him the full effect, and as she came around to face him again she saw the appreciation in his eyes. "I'm impressed, Al."

"How's that?"

"You've been in here a good five minutes and haven't made a single crude comment yet."

"Yeah, well, some women like for a fella to be on his best behavior around them. They don't want to hear 'fuckin' this' and 'fuckin' that' coming out of his mouth all the time." He caught his breath. "I didn't mean to—"

"That's all right," she told him. "I know what you meant."

He came closer but didn't crowd her. "Look, Arabella, you and me, we got off on the wrong foot. I know I ain't what you'd call a gentleman. Not even close. But I've been running a saloon for a long time, and let's face it . . . when you wallow in the mud with pigs, some of the mud sticks to you."

"I understand," she said, more touched than she had thought she would be by his words.

"Fact of the matter is, I don't think I've ever known a lady like you before," he went on. "Dority and the others got it right. You deserve to be called Lady Arabella."

"That's very kind of you."

"Not a bit. I'm just tellin' the truth," Swearengen said.

Unsure what moved her to do it, and confident that Major Ransome wouldn't arrive at the Gem for a while yet, she said, "Al, are you still interested in who I am and where I come from?"

Now he was the one taken by surprise. "Well, yeah," he admitted. "But that's your business and none of mine."

"Unless I choose to share it with you." She turned toward the bedside table and the crystal decanter that rested upon it. "I still have some excellent brandy that I might be persuaded to share with you as well."

He smiled, and the expression relieved the harsh lines of his face somewhat. "I'd like that," he said.

It had taken the last of their money to buy the bottle, but Brundage, Hollis, and Lamont were downstairs in the Gem, sharing a drink and studying the layout from the table where they sat.

Brundage nodded toward the shotgun guard who sat on the high stool and said, "Dewey, after a while you amble down to that end of the bar. I want you close to that hombre when the trouble starts." He kept his voice pitched low enough so that only the other two troopers could hear.

Lamont scowled. "Why? So's I can get my head blowed off that much quicker?"

"No, because you're the only one of us big enough and strong enough to knock that stool over before the bastard can use his scattergun. Once he's down, I plan to be right there to bend my Schofield over his head." Brundage touched the butt of the revolver tucked behind his belt and under his shirt. Enlisted men weren't issued handguns; only officers carried them. But Brundage had stolen this one a long time ago and tried to keep it close to him when he thought he might need it, like tonight.

He went on. "After I clout the son of a bitch, you grab the shotgun and cover the rest of the room. I'll deal with the bartender, if he's still here, and see about gettin' the safe open."

Hollis said, "And meanwhile I'll be headin' for the back of the building where the horses are."

Brundage nodded. "That's right. You come in that way, just be sure to call out to us so that we don't accidentally shoot you."

"I think I can remember that," Hollis said with a faint smile.

"When are we gonna do this?" Lamont asked.

Brundage considered and then said, "Let's give it another half hour. There'll be that much more money in the safe by then. When that time's up, Matt, you'll mosey down toward the Grand Central. You got that tin o' coal oil from the mess wagon?"

Hollis nodded. They had stolen the coal oil from the wagon when they left the camp earlier on their way to the Gem.

"All right," Brundage said with a grin. "Don't forget . . . it won't be much longer now before we're rich men, and the army can kiss our asses good-bye."

"**DAN** Ryan, are you drunk?" Lucretia Marchbanks asked as her eyebrows arched over her dark, angry eyes.

"Not a bit," he told her. "I've had a beer since I got back to town a while ago, that's all."

"Then you gone plumb crazy. Showin' up here at the back door o' my kitchen like this, askin' me to marry you when you know good and well I can't—"

"Why not?" he interrupted.

"Why not?" she echoed in astonishment. "Because in case you ain't noticed, I'm a nigger woman and you're a white man!"

"You're a woman and I'm a man. Seems to me that's all that's required. The colors don't matter."

Lou snorted. "The hell they don't. Where you been the last fifteen years? Remember that war you white folks fought?"

"To make people like you free," Dan said. "Free to marry whoever you want."

Slowly, Lou shook her head. "You believe that? You really believe that?"

"Of course I do."

"Then you *are* crazy. That war was fought 'cause rich men on both sides wanted to get richer, just like all the other wars ever been fought. Colored folks may not be slaves no more, but that don't mean we're free. Not by a long shot."

Dan moved closer to her and raised a hand, reaching out to her. "Come with me," he urged.

"Go with you where?"

"Away from here. Away from Deadwood."

"I'm leavin' Deadwood. Already told you that. I'm gonna cook for the Father De Smet mine."

He shook his head. "No, I mean away from Dakota Territory. We'll go someplace warm, before winter gets here. California, maybe. I think I'd like to see the ocean."

For a moment she didn't say anything. When she did speak, her voice held a wistful note. "I wouldn't mind that myself, I truly wouldn't."

"Then come with me!"

"I can't."

"Because you're afraid of what people would say?"

A humorless laugh came from her. "I learned a long time ago not to be hurt by what people *say*. I'm more worried about what they'd *do*. You and me both liable to wind up lynched, we go an' try to set up housekeepin' together. You know that, Dan. You know it."

"It shouldn't be—"

"Shouldn't don't mean nothin' in this world. All that means anything is what *is*."

His shoulders slumped in defeat. "I can't talk you into coming with me?"

"No." Her voice softened again. "I'm sorry, Dan. I really am." She paused and reached back into the kitchen to set the basket aside, then wiped her hands on her apron. "Tell you what I'll do, though. You come on in here and I'll pour you a cup o' coffee and give you a piece o' buttermilk pie, the same pie that General Crook and his officers got with their dinner tonight. I got a little left."

All the tortured soul-searching he had done earlier was

hungry work, he realized. It might not be what he really wanted, but Lou's buttermilk pie *was* mighty good.

"That sounds nice," he said. "Thank you."

She smiled at him. "Come on in, then. This kitchen ain't California, and you can't see the ocean from here, but for right now, maybe, it ain't too bad."

"Not too bad at all," Dan agreed as he climbed the wooden steps and followed her into the waiting warmth.

DRESSED in his suit again, Ransome clattered down the stairs to the Grand Central's lobby and was about to cross it when someone called from behind him, "Major Ransome, a moment please."

Ransome suppressed the urge to groan in impatience and turned to recognize the speaker as Captain Bourke, General Crook's adjutant.

"What is it, Captain? Does the general want to see me?"

"Not exactly." Bourke held out several pieces of paper. "He doesn't understand some of the notations on these maps you made and asked me to go over them with you."

"Now?" Ransome couldn't believe it. He was on his way to see Arabella, to make love to her again, and Bourke wanted to talk about *maps*?

"The general is leaving tomorrow for Camp Robinson, remember?" Bourke reminded him. "He wants to be sure that he's clear on all the details before he presents the findings from your scouting mission to the War Department."

Ransome took a deep breath. He had undertaken that mission—the mission that had almost gotten him killed earlier today, he noted to himself—so that the case for establishing a fort in the vicinity of Deadwood would be as strong as possible. Surely he could take a few minutes now to be certain of that.

"All right, Captain," he said as he gestured toward a

table and a couple of armchairs on the other side of the lobby. "Let's go sit down, and I'll clarify anything that the general is unsure about."

After all, he told himself, Arabella wasn't going anywhere. She would be waiting for him at the Gem whenever he got there.

Chapter Twenty-three

❧❧

THE brandy loosened her tongue. She had known that it would, and normally she would be on her guard against such a thing. But Al really did seem like he was trying to change. He was actually charming, and he didn't say or do anything improper as they sat and drank and talked.

"I'm from New York," she told him.

"Really? I figured you might be from England or some place like that, even though you don't really talk like a Limey."

Arabella shook her head. "No, I'm an American, through and through, even though I've spent a considerable amount of time on the Continent. Europe, you know."

Swearengen nodded.

"My father was a banker. A very rich and powerful man. I was raised in *very* comfortable surroundings. My mother was sickly, and there were no children other than me, so I got whatever I wanted."

"Must've been a mite lonely," he said with surprising insight. "A kid living in a big, stuffy old house with no other kids around."

Arabella leaned forward. "Exactly! It *was* lonely, even though I had the finest of everything. But it wasn't a terrible life, by any means. Not until I turned fourteen."

"What happened then?"

She smiled and said, "My father noticed that I had grown breasts and turned into a woman."

Swearengen's face darkened, and his fingers tightened on the brandy snifter he held. "Why, the despicable old goat!" he exclaimed. "I haven't drawn the line at many things in my life, God knows, but—"

Arabella lifted a hand to stop his angry words. "Please, Al, don't get the wrong idea. I wasn't trapped in some lurid novel. My father didn't have any interest of *that* sort in me. But he was canny enough to know that other men would, and he immediately started thinking of who he could marry me off to in order to make his financial empire even stronger."

"Oh." Swearengen subsided. "Well, that's not so—"

"It's not?" Arabella's voice was sharper now. "Not so bad, you were going to say? To be looked on as a commodity to be traded by my own father? I think I would have almost preferred the other!"

"Like it or not, women have always been bargaining chips. Those kings over in Europe did it all the time, didn't they? They'd marry some royal gal from another country rather than going to war with her father and things like that?"

"That's true enough," Arabella admitted. "But that doesn't make it right."

Swearengen sipped his brandy. "Did you do it? Did you marry the fella your father wanted you to?"

"Eventually, yes. He plotted and schemed for several years before he decided exactly who he wanted to sell me to. Because that's what it amounted to, you know. He sold me to a man twenty-five years older than me who had made a fortune in the shipping industry . . . a fortune that ended up in my father's bank."

"So you *were* married?"

"Yes, to a man who treated me horribly and came to hate me because he couldn't satisfy me. He beat me. I went back to my father's house—my mother was already dead by then—and told him that I couldn't go on with it, that I had to leave my husband. He told me that was out of the question, that it didn't matter whether I was happy or not. A lot of money was at stake. That was all that was important to him."

"What did you do?"

She had never told anyone else what had happened next, and she wasn't sure why the words came out of her mouth now, but they did.

"I knew there was a loaded gun in his desk. He kept it for protection, because he always had a great deal of money in the house." She laughed. "For a man who owned a bank, he didn't really trust the institution. I got the gun when he wasn't looking, came up behind him, and shot him."

She said it so matter-of-factly that for a second he didn't seem to comprehend what she had just told him. Then his eyes widened and he said, "You gunned down your own pa?"

"He had it coming," Arabella said, "and as he lay there dying I asked him if his money was still so important. I asked him if he would have traded it all for another minute of life." She laughed. "I think he would have, but of course . . ." She spread her hands to demonstrate the futility of the idea.

Swearengen didn't say anything for a long moment. Then he asked, "What did you do after that?"

"Well, I was already a murderess, wasn't I? I went back to my husband's house and killed him, too. I had to use a knife instead of a gun, though, so that it would be quiet. He had servants in the house, unlike my father, who was thrifty and employed only a cook and a housekeeper who came during the day."

"You murdered your father *and* your husband the same night?"

She nodded. "Yes, and then I used some of the money I

had taken from my father's house to buy a ticket to England. I booked passage on one of my husband's ships, in fact. I thought it fitting. Of course, the authorities discovered the murders, found out that I was on the ship, and cabled ahead to Liverpool to have the police there arrest me when the ship docked. But I was expecting that and had already made arrangements with one of the ship's officers to leave the ship disguised as one of the maids who worked on it. The British police never even caught a glimpse of me."

"You paid off the ship's officer?"

"Well, he wasn't that interested in *money.*" She smiled. "I suppose you could say that was actually the beginning of my real career, although my father prostituted me as effectively as any whoremonger." Her smile widened. "Like you, Al."

"I don't mind what you call me. I know what I am."

"Oh, I meant no offense. I've discovered over the years that a whoremonger usually has as much integrity, if not more, than a banker."

Swearengen grunted. "Yeah, I reckon that's true. So you made your way around Europe after that, I imagine, livin' off of rich men?"

"That's right. I even married a few of them. They left me some tidy sums when they passed away."

"Fucked 'em to— I mean, they were older, I reckon, and uh, couldn't stand the strain of . . ."

"Sometimes. Other times I had to help them along, if you know what I mean. I became quite adept at the use of poisons."

His eyes widened again as he glanced down at the brandy in his snifter. Arabella couldn't help but laugh.

"Don't worry, Al. If you remember, I poured out of the same decanter for both of us."

"Yeah, but you could've slipped something in my glass."

"I didn't. You have my word on that. We're getting along so well now—which I'll admit surprises me a little— that I wouldn't want to harm you."

He looked like he wasn't sure whether he believed her, but he said, "How'd you wind up going from Europe to Dakota Territory? That's a mighty big trip."

"I got homesick eventually," she said with a shrug. "And when I got back to the States, I trusted the wrong man . . . A mistake I seldom make, I assure you. He caught the gold fever and came out here determined to make a fortune. Unfortunately, he caught another kind of fever, the kind that killed him and left me to make my way alone. I had a buggy, my clothes, a few pretty things, enough money to buy a few more pretty things. All I needed was a place to set up—"

"And I furnished that," Swearengen finished for her.

"That's right." She set her empty glass aside. "Now you know the story of my life, Al. Were you surprised by it?"

"Damn right. I knew you were a cool customer, but I didn't take you for . . ."

"A murderess? A girl does what she has to in order to survive."

"Yeah, I reckon." Swearengen put his glass on the table, too, and then rested his hands on his knees in preparation for standing. "Thanks for the brandy and the talk. Guess I'd better leave you alone now."

She got to her feet as he did and moved to place herself between him and the door. "You didn't come here for a drink or the story of my life," she accused.

"Oh?" He regarded her solemnly, standing close to her now. "Then why *did* I come here?"

"To convince me that you had changed, to charm me . . . and then to fuck me."

"You think so?"

"I know so. And now that you've accomplished the first two of those goals . . . you're not going to leave without even attempting the third, are you?"

Their eyes locked in bold stares for a long moment, then a growl rasped in Swearengen's throat and he stepped even closer to her. His hand came up under her chin and grasped her jaw, holding her head steady as he brought his mouth down hard on hers. She responded instantly, clutching at him with both hands.

It would still be a little while . . . long enough . . . before Ransome showed up, she thought. And if he got here too soon . . .

Well, then, the stupid, stiff-necked son of a bitch could just wait.

MATT Hollis whistled a little tune between his teeth as he moved along the alley that would take him to the rear of the Grand Central Hotel. He intended to start the fire back there. It might not be discovered for a few minutes, which would give it time to catch hold good. If somebody came along and put out the fire right after it started, then it wouldn't cause a big enough commotion to empty out the Gem.

Normally he kept his emotions on a tight rein. Brundage and Lamont were different. They couldn't help but let people know how they felt. Brundage thought he was slick, but he really wasn't. Still, he was Hollis's partner, and sometimes he did come up with good plans. Like the one tonight. Hollis thought it stood a good chance of working, which was why his characteristic reserve had slipped a little, resulting in that merry whistle.

He wanted to be a rich man. Money solved everything. Warm sun, good liquor, willing gals . . . all those things came with having plenty of money.

Dinero, he told himself. That's what they called it down south of the border. He'd have to learn how to talk that Mex lingo. But the effort would be worth it so he could tell those little gals what he wanted them to do to him.

He reached the back of the hotel, slipped a hand inside his shirt, and took out the tin of coal oil he had hidden there earlier. He had a gun in there, too—a pocket pistol that he had won in a poker game. Still whistling, he unscrewed the cap on the tin and began to pour the reeking coal oil along the base of the wall.

INSIDE the Gem, Brundage and Lamont left the table where they had been sitting and wandered, seemingly aimlessly, toward the bar. They wound up at the end next to the high stool where Johnny Burnes sat with a shotgun across his knees. The two troopers had to elbow their way into that spot, wedging aside a couple of men in the boots and big hats of cowboys. One of them turned toward Brundage and Lamont with a flash of anger on his face.

"Hey! You fellas can't just shove your way in like that!" The young man's hand dropped toward the butt of the gun holstered on his hip.

A ruckus that would draw attention to them was the last thing Brundage wanted right now, so he put a contrite expression on his face and said, "Sorry, amigo. I didn't mean to bump up against you like that. I'd buy you a drink to make it up to you, but I'm afraid I'm flat busted right now."

The other cowboy put a hand on his friend's arm and said, "Take it easy, Sam. The soldier boy didn't mean any harm." He chuckled and thumbed his hat back. "Tell you what, just to show there ain't no hard feelin's, *I'll* buy you fellas a beer. We're pretty flush right now. Just drove a herd up from Texas to Kansas and decided to come on up here to Deadwood. We've heard a heap about the place, and so far it's livin' up to the yarns. How about it?"

Brundage didn't want to insult the Texan by refusing the offer of a drink, so he nodded and said, "That's mighty kind of you, mister. We'd be much obliged."

"Glad to do it." The cowboy signaled to Dan Dority to bring them four beers. "By the way, my handle's Joel, and this here is Sam."

"I'm Clyde, this's Dewey," Brundage said, inclining his head toward Lamont.

"You with Crook's cavalry?" Joel asked.

"That's right."

"Well, I'm mighty glad you boys are around to make the redskins behave, but I don't reckon I could ever be a soldier myself. I just can't abide rules and shit like that."

"You get used to it," Brundage said, although he and his friends never had. That was one reason they were about to leave the army far behind them.

The four men stood there drinking their beers, and even the somewhat truculent Sam grew more friendly. He was originally from Indiana, he told the troopers, but he had been down in Texas for a while and had met Joel in San Antonio. They had been riding together ever since.

Brundage didn't care about any of that, but he listened politely anyway, not wanting any trouble to break out before somebody ran in and yelled that the Grand Central Hotel was on fire. That would empty the place out in a hurry, if all went as planned.

"We thought we might try our hand at minin'," Joel said, "or maybe freightin' if the prospectin' don't work out. Whatever ain't too hard and'll make us the most money, ain't that right, Sam?" He dug an elbow in his friend's ribs as he laughed.

"That's right," Sam answered. "I don't even care overmuch if whatever we wind up doin' is legal."

Joel laughed again. "Now, don't say that. You'll give these soldier boys the wrong idea about us. Why, we're law-abidin' hombres, ain't we?"

Sam just grunted.

Brundage wished they'd both shut up. He didn't know what was taking Hollis so long. Hell should have broken loose by now. Worry started to gnaw at Brundage's brain.

"Lookee there," Lamont said quietly a moment later.

Brundage turned his head and saw Major Ransome heading up the stairs to the second floor. He felt a twinge of disappointment. He'd hoped that Ransome would burn to death in the hotel fire, but it looked like that wasn't destined to happen.

You couldn't have everything, Brundage told himself. The loot in the safe would just have to be enough.

That is if Hollis ever got around to starting that fuckin' fire!

IMPATIENCE chafed at Ransome like a burr under the saddle. He wanted to see Arabella again, to hold her and make love to her, and that damned Captain Bourke had kept him occupied at the hotel for much longer than Ransome had intended.

But he was here now, he told himself, and as he reached the second-floor landing he paused and drew a deep breath. Within mere moments, he would be with Arabella again. He walked along the hall, the carpet runner muffling his steps, and paused in front of her door. He lifted his hand to knock.

And stopped as he heard the voices coming from the other side of the thin panel.

Chapter Twenty-four

❧

Naked and breathless, Arabella sprawled onto her side next to Swearengen. She had been riding him with his cock buried deep inside her as his hands roughly squeezed her breasts. She didn't mind the mauling. In fact, she rather enjoyed it. For a man who was mostly concerned with his own pleasure—as all of them were—Swearengen was a decent lover. She hadn't climaxed, of course, but she had reached a higher peak than usual.

"Damn, you *are* good," he said, pausing to catch his breath before he added, "for a fuckin' whore."

"Don't fall back into your old ways, Al," she told him. "I much prefer the new you."

He moved so swiftly that it took her by surprise. His hand cupped her chin again, but more roughly than when he'd kissed her. In fact, his grip was painfully tight as he loomed over and said between clenched teeth, "Well, that's just too fuckin' bad, because this is the only *real* Al Swearengen, you little cunt."

Arabella's heart began to hammer in her chest. The bastard had fooled her—and she had believed him! That *never* happened. She had never been so taken in by a man in her entire life.

But then again, perhaps she had never met a man quite as evil as Al Swearengen before.

"Listen to me," Swearengen hissed at her. "I'm tired o' you prissin' around here actin' like you make the rules. From now on, you fuck who I tell you to fuck, when I tell you to fuck 'em, and you fuckin' well charge what I tell you to charge. You got that?"

He squeezed her jaw harder, bringing a gasp of pain from her. But she managed to nod, so he let off a little on the pressure.

"As for that story you told me about killin' all those men . . . you didn't really expect me to believe that, did you? That's just a whore story. You've all got 'em. You tell men a pack o' lies to make 'em feel sorry for you, so you can get more money out of 'em. Well, that don't work with me. I know better than to believe anything that comes out of a whore's mouth about her past. Only time they tell the truth is when you force it out of 'em."

She wanted to shake her head, to assure him that everything she had said was true, but she couldn't move. He had her pinned to the bed.

"Now, there's one more thing," Swearengen said. "I get to fuck you whenever and however I want. I come in here and tell you to suck my cock, you suck my cock. I tell you to roll over and stick your ass in the air so I can fuck it, you roll over and stick your ass in the air. Now say it."

He let go of her, but her jaw still ached. To keep him from hurting her even more, she said, "S-say what?"

"Tell me what I can do to you, anytime I want."

She knew what he wanted to hear, and why. He wanted to revel in the power he had over her.

Well, let him revel . . . for now. But when she got the chance, she would show him just what a terrible mistake he had made.

What a fatal mistake.

She took a deep breath and said in a loud, clear voice,

"You can fuck me, Al. You can fuck me anytime you want to, any way you want to."

Swearengen jerked his head in a nod of agreement. "Damn right, I can."

Then he rolled out of bed, stood up, and reached for his clothes. Arabella turned on her side, buried her face in the pillow, and tried not to shake from the anger and humiliation and, yes, fear that filled her. She didn't doubt that Swearengen was capable of killing her if she didn't cooperate with him.

She heard an odd, choked sound from out in the corridor, but she couldn't identify it. It didn't matter anyway. She just lay there trembling and waiting for Swearengen to go away.

RANSOME turned away from the door, a sob welling up in his throat. He managed to catch most of the sound before it escaped, but a little got out. Numb, not even knowing what he was doing, he stumbled down the hall toward the door to the rear stairs that Arabella had shown him the night before.

How could she? he asked himself. How could she betray him like that?

Because she's a whore, a voice answered inside his clamoring head. *You knew that. You knew she fucked other men. How can you be surprised now?*

But things had changed. He'd been about to ask her to marry him. Everything was different now. At least it should have been . . .

It *would* have been, if Arabella hadn't shown her true colors. Ransome jerked the narrow door open and stepped through it, stopping on the top step to turn around and peer through the inch-wide opening he left as he pulled the door almost closed behind him. A wide, staring eye fastened on the door of Arabella's room, and after a moment it opened. Al Swearengen, the Gem's proprietor, stepped out into the corridor with a satisfied leer on his ugly face. He closed the door and went back along the hall, away from the hidden spot where Ransome watched.

He had been ready to leave his wife and children, thought Ransome. Ready to abandon his family and turn his back on his duty as an officer in the United States Army. He would have betrayed everything that he had ever held dear. . . .

Just so he could keep fucking a filthy, treacherous slut like Arabella.

Thank God he had seen the error of his ways in time, before he ruined his life. He wished he had never met the whore. What he needed to do now was go down these stairs, slink back through the night to the hotel, and pretend that none of this had ever happened. He would leave tomorrow and go to Camp Robinson with General Crook.

And if the War Department *did* decide to locate a fort near Deadwood, he would move heaven and earth *not* to be assigned to it.

He actually went down a couple of steps before he stopped himself. He couldn't leave things unfinished between him and Arabella. She had to know that he had discovered the truth about her. He would pay her one last visit, he decided. He would tell her how disgusted he was with her . . . and with himself. Then that would be the end of it. He would never see her again, and he could go back to his old life, if not with a clear conscience—after the things he had done, it would never be clear again, he feared—but at least with a sense of resolution.

He opened the door and stepped out into the hall once again, then started toward Arabella's room with a determined expression etched on his face.

DAN stopped with a forkful of pie halfway to his face and sniffed. "What's that?" he asked.

"Don't you go tellin' me there's anything wrong with the way that pie smells," Lou warned him. " 'Specially after you done ate two pieces of it already."

"There's nothing wrong with the pie," Dan told her as he set the fork back on his plate and stood up. "I smell something else . . . Coal oil, maybe?"

Lou sniffed, too, and then nodded. "So do I. Where in the world's that comin' from?"

Dan glanced at a small window in the kitchen's rear wall. The pane had been raised a few inches, since the kitchen was always the hottest room in a place and needed fresh air, even on a cool night like this.

"It's outside," Dan said. He started for the door and reached for his gun at the same time. Nobody would be splashing coal oil around unless they were up to no good. The Colt cleared leather in his right hand just as his left grasped the doorknob and twisted it. He jerked the door open and stepped out onto the top step.

The sharp smell of the coal oil was even stronger out here. He turned toward where it seemed to be coming from and heard a muffled curse. His gun came up as he spotted an indistinct figure in the shadows at the rear of the hotel.

Then he heard a familiar voice exclaim, "Ryan!" and the figure stepped forward into the light that spilled from the kitchen door. Dan just had time to recognize Matt Hollis before the gun in Hollis's hand stabbed toward him and cracked wickedly, flame spouting from its muzzle.

A sharp pain pierced Dan's body and made him stagger back a step, but he managed to jerk the trigger of his Colt. The revolver roared and bucked in his hand. Instinct made him ear back the hammer and fire again. His vision had gone blurry, but he could still make out the shape of Hollis's body as the renegade trooper doubled over, obviously gutshot. Hollis dropped to his knees and struggled to lift his pistol for another shot, but he couldn't manage to pull the trigger until he was pitching forward. The gun's barrel was almost touching the ground when the muzzle flash flared from it again.

And suddenly Hollis began to scream and flail despite being shot, as flames erupted all around him and along the base of the wall.

That horrible sight etched itself on Dan's brain just before he slumped to the floor and utter darkness wiped out the garish light of the blaze.

RANSOME jerked open the door of Arabella's room without knocking. She stood beside the bed, her face white with strain as she knotted the belt of the red silk wrapper around her waist. Once her beauty and the fact that she was obviously nude under the wrapper would have taken Ransome's breath away and driven every thought from his brain except for his overwhelming need to make love to her.

Now the sight of her sickened him.

"Stephen!" she said. "What are you—?"

"What am I doing here?" he broke in. His voice shook so that he could barely get the words out. "I was supposed to come see you tonight, remember? We were supposed to be together. I'm sorry I nearly interrupted you with your *lover*!"

She gasped. "What are you— You mean *Swearengen*?" She started to shake her head. "You're mistaken, Stephen. You've got it all wrong—"

He overrode her protest. "How could I make a mistake? I heard what you told him!" He stalked toward her, his anger and the great hurt inside him causing his hands to shake as he raised them toward her. "I heard you tell Swearengen that he could fuck you anytime he wanted to!"

Her face suddenly hardened, as if she were too tired to argue with him. "That's what I do, isn't it?" she said. "I fuck men for a living. Why the hell do you think I was fucking you?"

Ransome blinked. It felt like she had just punched him between the eyes. "Because I love you and you love me," he said simply.

Arabella laughed. "Neither of us ever said anything about love. You're a fool, Stephen. What did you think, that you were going to leave your wife for me and that we would live happily ever after?" She collapsed onto the edge of the bed. "That's just a fucking fairy tale. I never loved you and you never loved me and I'm in no mood for this right now. Just get the hell out."

"I did love you," Ransome whispered. "I did."

"Then you're the biggest fool on the face of the earth to even believe in such a thing," she told him. "Get out."

He raised his trembling hands and covered his face with them. Another sob wracked his body, and he didn't try to hold this one back.

"Oh, Lord," Arabella said, rolling her eyes.

But the next instant they widened in shock and terror as Ransome lunged at her, fastened both hands around her neck, and bore her over backward onto the bed.

BRUNDAGE and Lamont had just exchanged the latest in a long line of worried glances when they heard the shots from somewhere down the street. The Grand Central Hotel was in that direction, and Brundage suddenly had the horrible feeling that something had gone wrong. Hollis hadn't been able to carry out his part of the plan, and now they were all screwed.

But then, less than a minute later, one of the locals galloped into the Gem and yelled, "Fire! The Grand Central's on fire!"

Brundage looked at Lamont and gave him a curt nod. Whatever happened, whether Hollis was able to join them or was already dead, they had come too far to turn back. They would go ahead with the rest of the plan.

Just as Brundage expected, nearly everybody in the saloon stampeded out through the batwings, including the two young cowboys, Sam and Joel. That left the two troopers alone at the end of the bar. The bartender hadn't run out with the others, though, and neither had the shotgunner on the stool. He looked like he wanted to follow the crowd, though, and called to the Gem's owner, who had just reached the bottom of the stairs, "Should I go help fight the fire, too, Al?"

Swearengen pointed a finger at him and snapped, "Stay right where you are, Johnny."

There was no point in waiting any longer. Brundage said, "Go!" to Lamont, and reached under his shirt for his Schofield. Like a runaway bull, Lamont let out a roar and charged the stool. He crashed into it before the guard could swing the shotgun in his direction. The man let out a startled yell as the stool went over and crashed to the floor. The shotgun slithered out of his hands.

Brundage jerked his revolver free and pivoted toward the bartender. He pulled the hammer back and pointed the barrel right in the bearded man's face. "Don't move or I'll blow your fuckin' brains out!" he shouted. "Dewey, you got the scattergun?"

Lamont had scooped up the double-barreled weapon and now tracked it from side to side, covering Swearengen and the handful of other men left in the Gem. "Got it!" he told Brundage.

A grin creased Brundage's face. Keeping the gun in his hand pointed at the bartender, he looked at Swearengen and said, "All right, mister. Open that safe, because we're about to clean it out!"

Chapter Twenty-five

RANSOME recoiled in horror from the thing that lay on the bed beside him. Arabella's eyes bulged from their sockets now as they began to glaze over in death. Her tongue protruded from her mouth, and her face, no longer lovely, had frozen in agonized lines and acquired a bluish tinge. Her wrapper had come open during the brief struggle, revealing one bare breast, but Ransome couldn't stand to look at it. He tore his eyes away from her entirely and gazed instead at the hands he lifted in front of his face.

The hands that had choked the life out of her, crushing her windpipe and killing her in a matter of moments. Her thrashing underneath him had quickly turned to death spasms.

An image of poor Spotted Dog toppling from his pony, back there on the banks of the Rosebud, flashed through Ransome's mind. He was a murderer twice over now. Before, he had been able to rationalize what he had done in battle as a terrible mistake. It was, of course, but that didn't change the fact that in the heat of the moment he had taken that young scout's life.

The same thing had happened here. Hate and rage had filled him, and he had killed Arabella with wanton, brutal swiftness.

Murderer. Murderer.

Suddenly he twisted toward her and grabbed her by the shoulders, shaking her uncontrollably. "Don't be dead!" he cried. "I didn't mean it! Oh, God, I didn't mean it! Please don't be dead!"

But her head just lolled back and forth limply, and her eyes remained as glassy as before.

Some things you just couldn't take back, no matter how much you wanted to.

That realization hit Ransome like a sledgehammer. He let go of her again and reeled to his feet. Unable to look at her anymore, he turned toward the door and stumbled in that direction. He had to get out, away from that accusing stare. He had to escape, otherwise they would know who had killed her. They would come for him and hang him, or put him up before a firing squad. That wouldn't be fair. He shouldn't die just because he had killed a . . . a whore. He was an officer in the army. His life meant more.

He jerked the door open but had to grab hold of it to steady himself as sickness hit him, almost knocking him to his knees. Some sort of commotion came from downstairs, but he didn't pay any attention to it.

The sickness came from deep inside, Ransome realized, as he gulped down air and tried to keep from passing out. It came from his very soul, which was as tainted and black as any evil soul could be. He seemed to see and hear his father standing in the pulpit, pounding on it and bellowing out the Lord's word, warning sinners that they would burn for all eternity in the pits of perdition.

And that was exactly what he deserved, thought Ransome. No turning back now. He was going to Hell.

But he wouldn't go alone, he thought as he dropped his hand to the army revolver he wore under his coat.

There was still one more sinner who needed to have the Lord's vengeance visited upon him.

"**PUT** those guns down, you idiots!" Swearengen shouted at Brundage and Lamont. "I'm not openin' any safe!"

Brundage jabbed the Schofield's barrel toward the bartender. "Do it!" he ordered. "Do it or I'll kill him!"

"Al . . ." the man said, his face washed out by fear.

Swearengen just shook his head.

The stubborn bastard. . . . Brundage reached inside his shirt with his other hand and yanked out the sticks of dynamite. "I'll blow it open, then!"

For the first time, Swearengen looked genuinely shaken. "Damn it, you'll blow us all to kingdom come! Be careful with that fuckin' stuff!"

"Then open it," Brundage said through clenched teeth. Nothing was going to stop him from becoming a rich man. Nothing.

A voice came from the batwings. "Drop it, Brundage."

The trooper's head jerked around. Dan Ryan, of all people—fuckin' *Dan Ryan*—stood there with blood on his shirt and a gun in his hand.

When Brundage turned to look at Ryan, his gun drifted away from the bartender. The man suddenly lunged across the hardwood, grabbed Brundage's wrist, and started trying to wrestle the weapon away. He shouted, "I got this sumbitch, Al!"

Brundage dropped the dynamite and slammed his left fist into the bartender's face. "Kill 'em!" he shrieked at Lamont as he fought with the bartender. "Kill 'em all!"

STRUGGLING to hang on to consciousness, Dan shifted his aim as Lamont lifted the shotgun. In the close quarters of the Gem, the buckshot would cut Swearengen to ribbons if the burly trooper fired both barrels. Dan's Colt barked first, though, as he squeezed off a shot that whipped past Brundage and tore into Lamont's side. Lamont staggered as the bullet plowed deep into his body. He grunted in pain and tried to keep the shotgun raised, but the barrels drooped toward the floor just as his finger jerked convulsively on one of the triggers. A deafening boom filled the room as the right-hand barrel discharged. The load of buckshot blew a ragged hole in the planks of the floor.

Lamont stayed on his feet and tried mightily to swing the scattergun toward Dan, who took a deep breath and fired again. This time the slug hit Lamont in the throat, just under the jutting beard, and threw him backward as blood spurted from the wound. He crashed to the floor on his back, gurgling hideously as a crimson fountain rose from his ruined throat.

Brundage finally succeeded in knocking Dan Dority loose from him. He stumbled away from the bar, looking around wildly, as if he couldn't figure out what was going on. He saw his old enemy, though, and recognized him. Screeching, "Ryan, you fuckin' bastard!" he brought the Schofield up.

Dan's Colt roared for a third and final time. The bullet knocked Brundage back against the bar as it slammed into his chest. He tried to stay upright, but he began sliding down the front of the bar. He ended up in a sitting position, blood bubbling from his mouth.

"Swearengen!"

Now what? Dan thought wearily. He looked up and saw Major Stephen Ransome stumbling down the stairs, gun in hand. The revolver crashed a couple of times as Ransome fired at Al Swearengen and shouted, "You filthy beast!"

Swearengen hadn't survived a rough-and-tumble life by being slow to react, though. He dived to the floor as Ransome's bullets went over his head. His hands found the shotgun Lamont had dropped, and as he tilted the barrels up, smoke and flame and noise erupted from the left-hand one. Ransome had almost reached the bottom of the stairs when the charge slammed into him and knocked him backward. He slumped on the stairs with a gaping hole in his midsection.

With a wound like that, he had only seconds of life left. He spent them saying, "Arabella . . . Arabella . . ." and then a couple of other strangled words that Dan would have sworn were "Spotted Dog."

But that didn't make any sense, and Dan was too tired and weak to try to figure it out.

He went over to Brundage instead, keeping his gun trained on the fallen trooper. Lamont was dead—the huge pool of blood around his head made that obvious—but Brundage was still alive. He still held the Schofield loosely in his right hand, although he no longer had the strength to lift it. Dan kicked the revolver away from him anyway, just to be sure Brundage wouldn't try anything.

Instead, though, Brundage just tipped his head back against the bar and looked up at Dan. "I'm dyin'," he rasped. "You've killed me, you son of a bitch."

"You didn't give me much choice," Dan said. "You never did."

Brundage's pain-wracked face twisted in a grin. "I ain't . . . dead yet," he said. "I'll live long enough . . . to tell about . . . Jessup."

"Go ahead," Dan told him. "To tell you the truth, I just don't give a damn anymore."

Incredibly, Brundage started to laugh. "You damn fool! You . . . you never . . . killed Jessup! I did! You . . . knocked him out . . . but I . . . broke his neck and . . . cleaned out his pockets . . . Figured I'd make you think . . . you did it . . . Keep you from tellin' anybody . . . about our plan to . . . steal those rifles . . . Should'a worked out . . . that way . . . How'd you . . . know about . . . what we were doin' down here?"

"Hollis told me before he died," Dan said, "after I pulled him out of the fire he accidentally set off while he was lying in a pool of coal oil." Dan touched the bloodstain on his shirt. "He got a shot off, grazed me pretty good, made me pass out for a minute. If he hadn't, I might've been able to get him out of the fire sooner."

Not that it would have mattered, Dan thought. Not with

two bullets in Hollis's belly already. But he didn't say anything about that.

Brundage laughed again, a harsh, ugly sound. "I should'a knowed . . . it wouldn't work out like I planned . . . Never had a bit o' luck . . . in my whole life . . . Not one fuckin' . . . bit . . ."

The last word came out accompanied by a long sigh, and Brundage's head fell forward to rest with his chin on his chest. His chest stopped rising and falling as death claimed him.

Shreds of gray smoke hung in the air, and the sharp scent of burned powder filled the Gem. Dan was so tired he wanted to sit down beside Brundage's body and go to sleep, but he straightened as more men came into the saloon with a rush of footsteps. A strong hand gripped his arm to steady him. He looked over into the leathery face of Cougar Jack LeCarde. Calamity Jane flanked him on the other side. General Crook strode toward him, followed by several officers.

"Mr. Ryan!" Crook said. "That colored woman at the hotel said you came down here to foil a robbery being carried out by some of my enlisted men. Is that true?"

Dan holstered his gun and waved toward the corpses scattered around the room. "No offense, General, but see for yourself."

Crook's eyes widened with outrage. "What I see is the body of one of my officers! What happened to Major Ransome?"

Al Swearengen stepped up and said, "I shot him, General, because the crazy son of a bitch was trying to shoot me. There are half a dozen men here who'll swear to that, I reckon, including Ryan there."

Dan nodded. He didn't like Swearengen, but the saloonkeeper hadn't had any choice but to defend himself when Ransome came down the stairs blazing away like a madman. Dan had seen the look on Ransome's face. Whatever the reason for it, the major *had* been crazy.

"That's the way it happened, General," he told Crook.

"Well . . . we'll get to the bottom of this, I promise," Crook said. He added gruffly, "In the meantime, we seem to owe you a debt of thanks. Due to your quick action in discovering that fire, we were able to extinguish it with no loss of life and minimal damage to the hotel. You've done an excellent night's work, Ryan. I see that you're injured. If you'd like, I'll have my chief surgeon attend to that for you."

"General, I—"

Later on, Dan couldn't even remember what he'd been about to say. All he knew was that he had pushed himself, body and soul, as far as he could go that night. With a groan, he swayed backward.

Cougar Jack and Calamity Jane were there to catch him, although he didn't remember *that* either.

HE woke up in a nice soft bed, an unknown number of hours later, and when he opened his eyes the first thing he saw was a messy pile of dirty clothes on a chair next to the bed. When his vision cleared a little, he saw that it wasn't a pile of clothes at all, but rather Calamity Jane, head down and snoring. Dan turned his head and saw Cougar Jack in another chair at the foot of the bed, also dozing. He recognized the room by the short walls that didn't go all the way to the ceiling. He was in one of the rooms on the second floor of the Grand Central Hotel.

A cool hand rested on his forehead for a second. "You just rest, Dan," a voice murmured. "You just rest."

He turned his head the rest of the way in that direction, though, and saw Lou Marchbanks leaning over him, a worried expression on her handsome face. "Lou," he whispered.

"You lost too much blood," she told him, "but you're gonna be all right. You're gonna be just fine."

"I will be," he said, "if you come to California with me."

She got a stern look on her face. "You are the stubbornest man! It ain't fair, you tryin' to take advantage of me worryin' about you this way. You know I can't go nowhere with you, not the way you want. But look around you, Dan Ryan. Look at Calam and ol' Cougar Jack. You may not have ever'thing you want in life, but you got good friends. Ain't that enough?"

No, he thought silently. It wasn't enough. It never would be.

But she was right about Cougar Jack and Calamity.

And it was a start. He clung to that thought as he slipped back into sleep.

It might not be happiness . . . but it was a start.

Epilogue

＊

NEWLY enrolled as a civilian scout, Dan Ryan left Deadwood a week later with the cavalry, which was under orders to meet with the Indians who had come in peacefully to the agencies in Nebraska and collect their arms. After that, the prospect of a winter campaign against the hostiles loomed. Dan figured he would be fully recuperated from his wound by then, and he and Cougar Jack would spend the winter months looking for Crazy Horse. It wouldn't be warm, and there sure as hell wouldn't be an ocean, but he would still get around to that one of these days, Dan promised himself.

Calamity Jane wanted to come along as a packer, but General Crook himself turned down the request, stating that they had enough such employees. From the sigh of relief Cougar Jack heaved when he heard the news, Dan wondered if the old scout might have influenced the general's decision in some way. "That gal's already just about wore me to a frazzle," Jack declared, "and I ain't as young as I used to be!"

The minor fire at the Grand Central Hotel was quickly

forgotten, as was the attempted robbery and the deadly shootout at the Gem Theater. The official report glossed over the circumstances of Major Stephen Ransome's death and had him trying to stop the robbery. Dan never said otherwise, at least not for the record. Bad enough that the man was dead. No need for his family back East to know that his death might have been connected to a prostitute who'd been found strangled in one of the rooms of the Gem's notorious second floor. Dan didn't know that for a fact himself, although it seemed likely. The only one who might know the truth was Al Swearengen.

And as usual, Swearengen wasn't talking.

The other momentous event in Deadwood in that month of September 1876 was the arrival on the twenty-fifth of the first regularly scheduled stagecoach, with an old plainsman named Dave Dickey handling the reins. One more sign that civilization was coming to Deadwood, and there wasn't a damned thing anybody could do to stop it.

Cold winds had begun to whistle down out of the north, a harbinger of the approaching winter, as the two happy-go-lucky cowboys, Joel and Sam, sat on the porch of the Grand Central one day, smoking. They had taken a room at the hotel, but their money had started to run low and they had to think of something to do.

"Reckon we ought to get us a claim and start lookin' for gold?" Sam asked.

Joel shook his head. "It's already too damned cold for prospectin'. We'll have to come up with something else to make some dinero."

While they were sitting there pondering on that, two men rode up the street, reining their mounts to a halt in front of the Grand Central. "This the best hotel in town?" one of them asked. He was a tall, stern-looking man with a drooping mustache. The same description fit the other man, and in fact a strong family resemblance existed between them. They were brothers, most likely.

"Yeah, I'd say it's the best," Joel answered the question. "We're stayin' here anyway, leastways for now."

"Come to look for gold, have you?"

"Yes, sir." Joel didn't elaborate on what he and Sam had been discussing a few minutes earlier. "How about you?"

The two newcomers swung down from their saddles and looped the reins around the hitch rack in front of the hotel. "Gambling's more our line," the first man said as he came up the steps to the porch. "Though I've been known to wear a peace officer's badge on occasion. My name's Wyatt Earp." He pointed with a thumb at the other man. "My brother Morgan."

Joel grinned and nodded his head. "Pleased to make your acquaintance, boys. I'm Joel Collins, late of San Antonio, Texas, and this here is my pard, Sam Bass."

Sam nodded and said, "Howdy." The Earp brothers returned the nods and went on into the hotel, carrying their rifles. Their coats swung back a little, revealing holstered Colts.

The two cowboys looked at each other, and Joel said in a low voice, "Peace officers, eh? We want to steer clear o' those two fellas."

"Damn right," Sam said. "Let's go down to the Gem and get a drink."

"Sounds good." They stood up, crossed the street, and ambled in that direction, and as they walked, Joel went on, "You know, I've been thinkin' about those stagecoaches that have started runnin' between here and Cheyenne. I may just have an idea how we can make us some money. . . ."

Author's Note

~~~

LIKE the other books in this series, *The Troopers* is a mixture of fact and fiction. A large force of soldiers under the command of General George Crook engaged the Sioux led by Crazy Horse and Sitting Bull in a battle along Rosebud Creek a little more than a week before those same chiefs would encounter Custer and the Seventh Cavalry on the bluffs overlooking the Little Bighorn River. Crook's pursuit of the Indians eventually led him to Deadwood, as it does in this novel. The rest of the story is largely fictional, although considering the amount of vice and violence that went on there, similar events must have taken place.

As for that meeting between Wyatt and Morgan Earp and Sam Bass . . . well, history doesn't record it, but Bass arrived in Deadwood with his friend Joel Collins in the late fall of '76, and according to Wyatt Earp's own words, he and his brother Morgan left Kansas and headed for the Black Hills on September 9, 1876, arriving there several weeks later. There's no way of knowing if they ever exchanged nods and howdies with each other . . . but they could have.

Special thanks to Kim Lionetti, Sandy Harding, Carolyn

Morrisroe, and Samantha Mandor for their roles in making this series possible. Thanks as well to all the historians for providing such a rich canvas on which to paint these word pictures. As always, any errors, minor liberties with the facts, usages of dramatic license, and outright lies are the responsibility of the author, and he begs your forgiveness.

Mike Jameson
Azle, Texas

MIKE JAMESON

Tales from
DEADWOOD

The first in a new series of fictionalized tales, based on real-life characters, that show Deadwood as it really was— and might have been.

Deadwood is the infamous and lawless cesspool where a man is as likely to strike it rich as he is to lose everything. Now, the legendary Wild Bill Hickok— who has lost his eyesight—and Calamity Jane are coming to start their own trouble.

penguin.com

MIKE JAMESON

Tales from DEADWOOD:
The Gamblers

*Imagine a town with no law,
and you have Deadwood.
Second in the new series of fictionalized
tales based on real-life characters.*

The famous Wild Bill Hickok has come to
Deadwood to stake his claim—and some
of the town's gamblers worry that the
legendary lawman will clean up Deadwood.
For help, they call on the Gem Theater's
ruthless owner, Al Swearengen—who knows
a stone-cold shootist who can end Hickok's
wild days permanently.

penguin.com

M108T0907

M258G0208